CODE SONG: THE SIGNAL

Joshua S. Duchan

The Chronicles of Will Driver
Book One

Thank you to my family for their patience, valuable feedback, and encouragement.

TABLE OF CONTENTS

PART ONE

BACKSTORY

1

Barents Sea

"Steady as she goes," remarked Commander Jim Harper calmly as he stood before the large, flat-screen monitor on the forward bulkhead of the USS Royal Oak's control room. His arms were crossed in front of his chest, his right hand rubbing the stubble on his chin. It had been a long night.

The Royal Oak was a Virginia-class nuclear attack submarine, modified for intelligence missions like the one she was currently on. Harper, the captain (or "skipper" in the silent service), was on his fourth deployment on the boat. His closely cropped brown hair matched his eyes, which could be kind or piercing, depending on the situation. By now, the crew was accustomed to his quiet, understated demeanor. He was a thinker. He often rubbed his chin or ran his fingertips over the facial hair surrounding his mouth. He gathered information and recommendations, considered options, and made decisions. Input was welcome until the decision was made. After that, the crew knew the discussion was closed.

On the screen, Harper could see what the high-powered lenses on top of his submarine's photonics mast saw: the ocean surface, about sixty feet above his head, lit by moonlight. The cold shoreline. Russia. The "Great Bear" had been restless as of late, making missions like this one more dangerous, and more important, than ever. To say the crew needed to stay on their toes was an understatement.

"Conn, radio," the speaker above Harper's right ear chirped.

Without taking his eyes off the screen, Harper reached up with his right hand and pressed a button next to the intercom speaker, activating the microphone. "Radio, conn. Go ahead."

"Sir," Lieutenant Sadow Katashi, the boat's chief radio officer, continued. "I'm receiving a new transmission, which I'm sending on to the SigInt suite. But it's kind of…" The voice trailed off for a moment as Katashi considered how to describe what the signal intelligence team aboard the boat had heard. "Musical."

The crewmen manning the planes, the large fins on the outside of the submarine that helped guide it down and up through the ocean's depths, looked up over their shoulders at the skipper. It was their mission to intercept Russian communications, of course. But it wasn't every day that those signals were described using that particular adjective.

A moment passed before Harper responded. "COB, get Mr. Worth up here, would you?" he said, looking at Randy West, the Chief of the Boat, the senior enlisted crewman on board. Harper's voice sounded perfectly calm, unfazed by the strange report. That was the Harper charm: always cool and quiet. Well, almost always. "Wake him if you have to."

West nodded. Approaching fifty years old, he was older than anyone else on board. And of the entire crew, he was the one who'd served on Royal Oak the longest (even longer than Harper). But that wasn't why he had the crew's respect.

They knew the COB would have their backs, no matter what, as long as they did their job and didn't bring any shame to the boat. They also knew that, if they failed in either of those tasks, the COB would have them over a barrel so fast they'd wish they'd never joined up to begin with.

The COB moved purposefully toward the rear bulkhead, ducking to get through the opening into the passageway beyond. There, the cabins belonging to the skipper and the executive officer ("XO"), Robert Worth, were located.

"Understood, radio," Harper spoke into the mic. "Can SigInt make anything of it?"

"Well, sir," Katashi's voice responded, "they tell me it's more, well, upbeat." The statement ended like a question.

"Of all the places to crank up the stereo, the Russians choose the Arctic?" Worth asked as he entered the control room, followed by Mr. West.

Harper looked over his shoulder at his XO, momentarily feeling a little sorry for him. He'd only had about half an hour of sleep. Of course, when the commanding officer needed you, it didn't matter how little sleep you got—and both the skipper and the XO knew that. "Cranky, Mr. Worth?" His eyes flashed a smile, even if his mouth didn't.

"I wonder why," Worth replied sarcastically. "I take it SigInt's got something interesting for a change?"

"Mmm," Harper responded.

"And the only thing they can tell us is that it's 'upbeat'?"

"Mmm-hmm."

"We've come all this way in a multi-billion-dollar metal tube, pushed along through the frozen depths of the Arctic Circle, with the most advanced electronics-sweeping technology in the world and the most highly trained analysts and the best they can come up with is 'upbeat'?"

"Indeed, Mr. Worth," Harper said, staring once again at the screen showing the video feed from the photonics mast. "I don't see anyone out there dancing, though."

"Maybe it's not dancing music, sir," Worth responded with a raised eyebrow. "We're sure we're out here alone?"

Harper reached up and pushed another button on the console above. "Sonar, conn. Report all contacts."

Another voice, that of Chief Petty Officer Greg Findlay, the boat's sonar officer, came back through the speaker seconds later. "Conn, sonar. I've got tracks on four contacts, all surface vessels, sir. Three commercial shipping. Sounds like two heading for Murmansk and another coming out. And an icebreaker. If there's a Russian warship out there, sir, it's too quiet to hear right now."

"Thank you, Mr. Findlay," Harper replied, moving his eyes to Worth.

"Aye, sir," Findlay responded. It was his job to operate the boat's sensitive listening equipment, discerning the sounds careening through the ocean waters and classifying them with the help of a powerful computer.

Worth took a deep breath and ran his left hand through his greasy hair. It was a slightly lighter shade of brown than Harper's. And Worth kept himself more closely shaved. A pair of glasses rounded out his face, which was about a decade younger than that of his skipper and mentor. "I think it's time, Jim."

Harper nodded and reached up again. "Radio, conn. We're going to back off and call home. As far as this transmission goes, log it and bag it. We'll send it back during our next check-in. Along with the others."

"Conn, radio. Yes, sir. Logging this one as 'Disco Three.' Compressing all Disco intercepts for burst transmission via satellite to base at your command."

"Very well," Harper said. Looking back to Worth, he addressed everyone in the compartment. "One strange transmission is an anomaly. Two is suspicious. Three, well, three makes a pattern. I don't know what we're dealing with here, but I'm sure some people smarter than I will want to hear these songs.

"Lower the masts, set your depth for 150 feet, course three-one-zero, ten knots, ten degrees down on the planes."

The various men in the control room started repeating their captain's orders, a redundant practice that helped to ensure they were clear and understood. Soon there was a flurry of activity as the boat turned, sped up, and the deck tilted gently forward.

"Rob," Harper said quietly to his XO, "you'd better get back to sleep while you still can. In a few hours, we'll send all this musical stuff back home and they may have new orders for us."

"Yes, sir. Thanks." Worth responded, heading back toward his cabin.

"Mr. Hargraves," Harper turned to the boat's navigation officer, "you have the conn."

The navigator, Lieutenant (junior grade) Curt Hargraves, nodded as Harper too made his way aft toward his stateroom. It was his first tour on the Royal Oak, and he didn't want to disappoint, no matter how tired he was.

It had been a long night.

2

Election Day

THE FIRST SALVOS in the latest iteration of the Cold War were launched on Election Day. Millions of Americans woke up to text messages directing them to "new" polling locations, coming over the national network of emergency alerts usually reserved for kidnappings and missing persons. Because the messages came from a known source, they were more believable than the sort of junk messages many were used to ignoring.

As a result, hundreds of thousands showed up at the wrong places to vote, causing confusion and clogging a system already strained after years of attacks on poll workers—mostly through the media, but occasionally verbal or physical—had decimated their ranks. Hundreds of thousands more went where they were told, only to find it wasn't a poll at all. Others voted at their respective polling places but then received messages saying that they owed back taxes so their votes wouldn't count.

No matter who won, a significant number of voters never

got to vote. They never got the chance to have their say, so the presidency was severely challenged even before it began. But that was hardly the end of it.

A RED, CIRCULAR light began blinking rapidly on the panel in front of Nancy Dash, a Second Lieutenant in the United States Air Force and a ballistics analyst stationed at the North American Aerospace Defense Command, known as NORAD, in Colorado Springs, Colorado. It *had* to be a glitch. Maybe she'd missed an email about computer maintenance or upgrades or something? (And why would they schedule that sort of thing on Election Day, when national security was especially fraught?) Regardless, protocol dictated she check it out. The label beneath the light read "SEWSS," one of the many acronyms sprinkled across the US government, especially its military. Her eyes widened and then narrowed as they scanned the five capital letters, and she flicked her head to the right without thinking, throwing some pesky strands of straight blonde hair away from her face.

"Major," she said, gently pushing a button on the desktop with her right thumb and speaking into the headset she wore, "I've got a master alarm on the SEWSS network."

Major Peter Berry, Dash's commanding officer in the control room, responded immediately. "Put it up."

With a few buttons on her computer keyboard, Dash had her station take control of the large screen on the wall at the front of the room. The image quickly changed from an overhead view of the world, with lines outlining the continents, to a closer view of Eastern Asia. Several white dots appeared in the area corresponding to the upper part of the Korean Peninsula.

Above the screen, the large numbers on the three clocks read "0900," "1000," and "1200," indicating 9:00 AM on the

West Coast, 10:00 at NORAD, and noon, Eastern Time. Beneath the map appeared the words, *Sentinel Early Warning Satellite System*. SEWSS.

Berry's gravelly voice took on a new sense of urgency as he moved toward the center of the room, positioning himself directly in front of the screen and on the third of five concentric levels that rose up from the front wall, each lined with desks, computer stations, and other equipment. "Confirmation! I want confirmation!" His shouts grabbed the attention of everyone in the control room. Officers who weren't already looking up at the screen stopped what they were doing and did so, immediately recognizing what they were seeing.

The response came almost immediately from a male officer on the opposite side of the room from Dash. "Vampire! Vampire! Vampire! Keyhole Alpha-227 detects multiple ICBM launches in the vicinity of Chonjin, DPRK!" *Vampire* was the codeword for an incoming missile attack, in this case originating in the Democratic People's Republic of Korea, also known as North Korea.

"Comms, sir! Flash traffic on emergency channel!" Shouted yet another voice, this one from the top row, somewhere behind Dash. "Wakkani MWOP confirms launch. Repeat: Wakkani confirms launch visually!" Personnel at the Missile Warning Observation Post just outside the northern Japanese city had seen it with their own eyes.

"Alright, people, we've got a live one," Berry announced. "Activate the Civilian Alert System! Comms, alert Washington, we have—ballistics, how many birds have we got?"

"Reading six, repeat, six incoming ICBMs on ascending vector. Initial target analysis indicates probable West Coast impacts in," Dash paused as she finished the rough calculations, "nineteen minutes." Her voice trembled. This all seemed like a drill until they heard from Wakkani. Visual confirmation cannot be denied. It wasn't a drill.

"You heard it, Comms," Berry resumed. "Inform Washington: six birds, nineteen minutes." A siren was already sounding in the building. "I want air defense units scrambled out of SOCCs McChord and Elmendorf," he continued, ordering planes to take off from the Sector Operations Control Centers at McChord Air Force Base just outside Tacoma, Washington, and Joint Base Elmendorf-Richardson in Anchorage, Alaska. Finally, he ordered, "Set Defense Condition. Standby SBIRS!" as another airman readied the US Space Force's Space-Based Infrared System, a network of satellites that could detect and, in theory, neutralize enemy ballistic ordinance.

OF COURSE, IT wasn't the first time the North Koreans had launched missiles. They'd managed to scare the populations of Guam and American Samoa, as well as Hawaii, in the late 2010s. But never before had their weapons appeared to have the clear capability to target the American mainland. This was a significant escalation, and with the Election-Day confusion spreading across the country, the timing couldn't have been worse.

Sirens blared and the National Guard was activated in cities up and down the West Coast, from Seattle to San Diego, further fueling scenes of mass confusion. Americans hadn't practiced for enemy bombing in generations. For many, the closest they'd come were stories their parents or grandparents had told of hiding beneath wooden desks in grade school. And although some older buildings still bore faded "Fallout Shelter" signs, they hadn't served that purpose in decades.

Where were people supposed to go? Should they head out

to vote (and if so, where?), go to a shelter, or just stay home and await a mushroom cloud? There would barely be time for the panic to set in before it was all over.

THE SIX NORTH Korean ICBMs reached the apex of their parabolic trajectory, separated from their first- and second-stage rockets, and were preparing to descend back toward the planet below. Now was the moment they were most vulnerable. They were moving at the slowest rate of speed since launch. There wouldn't have been a better time to take them out.

Seven minutes to impact.

"SBIRS intercept from STSS-ATRR 205 has failed, sir," Dash reported. "I'm showing a massive current overload fault in the LCPS. 205 indicates the laser emitter is permanently damaged, sir."

The Space Tracking and Surveillance System-Advanced Technology Risk Reduction satellite had attempted to strike the North Korean missiles and destroy—or at least disable—them with an advanced laser system. At the time of the satellite's construction in June 2008, STSS-ATRR 205 was designated a demonstration platform. Its purpose was to test and show the effectiveness of detection and coordination systems in orbit and on the ground. It was never meant to be an operational, battlefield weapon.

With this in mind, United Launch Systems, the aerospace contractor tasked with building the satellite, had used consumer-grade copper wiring in the primary and secondary laser heat exchangers, which helped to keep the already-astronomical cost of the unit just a little bit lower. As the laser system prepared the fire, the amount of current pushed through the off-the-shelf, eight-gauge conductors was more than they could handle and generated more heat than they were able to dissipate into the cold emptiness of space in the time allotted. After forty seconds of heavy load, the copper began to melt, causing a fault that the Laser Circuitry Protection System sensed and responded to in the manner in which it was programmed: by shutting down the entire laser system. As a weapon, STSS-ATRR 205 was dead.

"Damnit!" Berry shouted, a bead of sweat running down his right temple. "In English, Dash!"

"It's fried, sir. Probably the internal wiring. It was originally a demo model, proof of concept. But Congress axed funding for the battlefield model so it's all we've got."

Berry's face turned an even deeper shade of red.

With four minutes left before impact, the missiles reentered the Earth's atmosphere and descended rapidly toward land, picking up speed.

"Can we use Patriots?" Berry asked aloud, cutting through the control room's tense silence.

Dash shook her head. "I'm sorry, sir. The Patriot missile system wasn't designed for this sort of intercept. They could actually trigger the nuclear warhead in the atmosphere, which could, arguably, be worse than a ground impact depending on the altitude."

Berry nodded in understanding. He didn't think the Patriots would work; he already knew what Dash was telling him. But the situation was now desperate. No, "desperate" didn't adequately express just how hopeless things looked. Millions were about to die, and the United States military could not protect them. Berry felt a deep sense of sorrow, as if he had, personally, failed.

A voice rang out from across the room. "Sir, possible aspect change on incoming ordinance!"

"What?!" Berry shouted, spinning around toward the excited airman.

"Yes! Yes! I'm reading new headings on five—no, all six!—

13

inbound ICBMs!"

Dash looked up from her computations. "Confirmed, sir! New target identified as...an empty sector of the Pacific. Off San Francisco."

Berry spun back around to face Dash. "Empty ocean?" He didn't believe it.

Dash replied with a smile. "Yes, sir, I can confirm—"

Another voice cut in. "I concur, sir! Missiles no longer targeting American territory. Their course has been adjusted!"

Dash continued, "—I just," she swallowed. "I can't tell you *why*."

Berry breathed a sigh of relief. "Lieutenant," he said in a much quieter and calmer tone, "at this moment I don't give two shits about the why. Don't know, don't care. Maybe it's just our lucky day, or maybe someone's God is smiling down on us. Doesn't matter. Millions of lives were just spared."

With an even wider smile, Dash responded, "Yes, sir."

RUSSIAN HACKERS BEHIND ELECTION DAY CHAOS

By Leigh Kierfer, Washington Advocate

A group of computer hackers, supported by the government of the Russian Federation, is responsible for the phony messages millions of Americans received on Election Day causing mass chaos across the country last week. An investigation, involving multiple anonymous sources in Moscow, St. Petersburg, and Washington, D.C., has found compelling evidence of a vast international effort to disrupt election processes in all states and territories.

Directed by the Kremlin, the Russian hacker

organization known to Western intelligence agencies as The Red Cabal carried out a multi-pronged effort to wreak havoc in this country. Text messages misdirected American voters, sending them to locations at which there were no polls. Other messages falsely warned of votes that would not be counted. Additionally, voter rolls in multiple states were infiltrated, altered, and in some cases, erased.

Within the past few days, American officials said on background, the Central Intelligence Agency has narrowed down the location of The Red Cabal to the Novgorod Oblast, an area roughly halfway between Moscow and St. Petersburg. The area has seen concerted investment in information technology infrastructure in the past twenty years, largely funded by the Kremlin using funds raised through weapons sales to North Korea, Venezuela, and other countries.

"We've seen Russian interference in American elections since at least 2016," one American intelligence official commented anonymously. "But the scale has only increased in recent years, and we've never before experienced this level of interference."

Multiple sources described the Russian efforts as a "plot" and as an "attack" on American institutions and Americans' faith in the democratic system. "It was intended as an attack," a mid-level official in the Russian government remarked.

"Believe it or not, an attack based on misinformation and data manipulation is actually rather restrained," cautioned Andrea Tong, a professor of international relations at the University of America in Washington. "Not a single person was hurt or killed. But the Russians shined a pretty harsh light on the fragility of our election systems. And those systems are among the most fundamental to the way our country works, to our very way of life."

Indeed, it could have been worse. The Pentagon has identified North Korea as the source of multiple intercontinental ballistic missiles launched at the West Coast on Election Day. Although none reached their targets, the attack indicated a real and dangerous threat to national security that surprised many analysts. "I wouldn't say we were caught with our pants down," one American official said on the condition of anonymity. "But pretty darn close to it. We didn't know the North Koreans could shoot that far. Now I'm worried."

Members of Congress are expressing worry too. Hearings are scheduled for next month to question Pentagon and intelligence officials on the apparent failure to anticipate and adequately defend against the hacking and missile threats. The Secretary of Defense is scheduled to appear, along with top military brass.

The President struck a more confident tone. "Our country has faced many threats, many challenges in its history. We rose to meet each and every one. I am confident that this time will be no different," he remarked on the White House lawn. He then declined to respond to questions, instead boarding the Marine One helicopter bound for Camp David, where he is scheduled to hold closed-door meetings with party leaders to discuss the next round of elections.

"Sir," Dash said to Berry, again flinging stray hairs away from her face. "I think you'd better take a look at this." She tapped the end of a pen against her lips as she reread her calculations from the computer screen in front of her.

Berry walked across the carpeted floor and up a few steps inside the NORAD control room. His square jaw was set. The excitement of the Election Day attack had died down. Now, two weeks later, they were in a state of intense focus, analyzing all the data they could gather to find out what exactly happened, and when—as well as why they couldn't anticipate it.

"Look at this tracking data from Sentinel satellite J-104. We've got six North Korean ICBMs incoming, right? They are on a perfect course for the West Coast—I mean *perfect*. Like, there are few militaries in the world that can calculate trajectories and make real-time adjustments like that." She took a breath and reminded herself to slow down. She sometimes spoke too quickly when she was excited by a discovery, and right now, she was speaking at the velocity of a descending ICBM on atmospheric re-entry. That is, really fast. "And then, at this point—" she placed her finger on the computer monitor at her station, "—there's a sudden and pretty dramatic change in the trajectory. It's like someone waited until the very last second to pull these birds off course and send them into the Pacific."

Berry grunted, indicating he was thinking about what Dash was telling him and examining the positioning, heading, and speed figures closely.

"Like some kind of sick game of chicken," Dash added. "Sir." It was, perhaps, a dramatic way to describe the movement of the missiles. But it wasn't inaccurate.

"I don't know about you, lieutenant, but I prefer not to play chicken with twenty-megaton nuclear warheads." Berry glanced at her out of the corner of his eye, then looked back at the screen for a moment. Finally, he turned to face her. "You said there aren't a lot of folks who could pull off this sort of thing, right?"

"Yes, sir."

"Then who did it?"

"Sir, I can't really speculate. That's a little outside my—"

"Indulge me, lieutenant."

Dash took another breath. Berry wasn't known for his supportive and encouraging comments. This was going to be a leap, a big one. Hopefully she wouldn't regret it. "If you're asking me, sir, my gut feeling is that there's no way in hell the North Koreans are this good. It may be their missile, and it may have been launched from their country. But unless they made some genius advancements in ballistic mechanics in a very short time, I think they had help." She took one more breath before finishing. "And I think it was the Russians, sir. They've shared technology and expertise before, and I think they did it again."

Another moment passed. Berry's nostrils flared and his eyes narrowed as he thought about what Dash was suggesting. Then he started nodding, slowly at first. "Given the timing, with all the other bullshit going on with those fake text messages, it would seem to fit. I mean, we knew Moscow and Pyongyang were close. I just didn't think they were *this* close." He straightened his back and cleared his throat. "I've got to run this up the flagpole. Good work, Dash."

She smiled. Berry didn't hand out compliments often. "Thank you, sir."

3

MALAISE

WILLIAM DRIVER SAT uncomfortably on the plastic chair at the foot of the folding table that served as a conference table. It was an apt metaphor for the entire state of affairs at the University of Philadelphia, where they had everything they needed but it just wasn't quite what they would have wanted. Every year was another budget cut—they called them "reductions" and "realignments" in the corporatespeak that passed for administrative language these days—so they couldn't expect their folding tables and plastic seating to be replaced with anything nicer in the foreseeable future.

The classrooms were a similar story: good enough. The audio/visual systems were serviceable but not fancy. Most of the time, when Will plugged in his laptop to display some slides on the screen while teaching a class, it worked—but sometimes it didn't. He'd quickly learned to improvise. Likewise, the sound system was fine in the three classrooms controlled by the Music Department, but not in the general-purpose classrooms where some of his "music appreciation" courses were held. Those were aimed at the general student population, not at music majors, who couldn't earn degree credit for such basic course content. Once, he was even scheduled to teach in a classroom with no speakers at all. He resorted to singing a semester's worth of music, which was especially challenging when discussing pieces that didn't use any voices.

Still, he reminded himself, he should be grateful. He *had* a job. A full-time job, with benefits, in the field of his choice! Some of his old friends from graduate school hadn't been so lucky. Even now, over a decade after they finished their doctoral degrees, some were still on the adjunct circuit, working multiple part-time jobs at multiple institutions just to make ends meet. A few had left academia altogether. Most were bitter, exasperated by the years of study whose completion seemed unrewarded. Some were outright jealous.

As Jackie Fletcher, the department chair, droned on about something or other, Will thought through his career, indeed, his life. Four years of college, six years of graduate school, a one-year post-doc position, a two-year position that was cut down to one (again, budget "reductions"), a few years of part-time work, and then the golden ticket: the tenure-track job. It was even a position specifically focusing on ethnomusicology, his chosen subfield of the broader field of music studies, which centered on understanding music in its cultural context, usually gathering "data" through direct interactions with people in a particular "music culture." It was exactly what he'd trained and studied for.

He had been thrilled to move to the City of Brotherly Love with his wife of just over a year and their newborn daughter. Frankly, they would have moved almost anywhere for a tenure-track job, since it carried the promise of lifelong employment. That is, if he could survive the dreaded tenure review in his sixth year.

As it turned out, Philadelphia was more than they ever hoped for. There were arts and culture, the lifeblood of someone in his line of work. And a genuine international airport, which had been useful for his two summer trips back to Lesosibirsk, the Siberian town where he'd done his fieldwork years before. "Music, Politics, and Resistance Among the Ket of the Central Krasnoyarsk Siberian Lowlands," his doctoral dissertation, cemented his reputation as an expert on the little-known ethnic minority that lived on the permafrost along the Yenisei River in what was, today, the Russian Federation. In fact, he was the *only* expert on the subject, something his graduate-school advisor had promised him would make him special and sought-after.

So why did he feel so lost? With a pair of articles published in selective academic journals and his monograph completed in his third year at UP, he'd easily passed the mandatory review and was promoted to Associate Professor with Tenure. In a world that was famously (and truthfully) described as "publish or perish," he had decidedly not perished. By some accounts, he'd thrived. His colleagues patted him on the back. His friends bought him a beer. His parents gifted him a nice watch. In their own ways, they were all nice sentiments from people who'd seen him through the academic ringer.

That was two years ago.

He'd been warned about the "post-tenure malaise," a general feeling of a lack of direction following the intense sprint toward tenure. He thought that a new take on his research, focusing more on the language and folklore of the Ket people, rather than their troubled past interactions with more mainstream Russians, would keep him focused and motivated. Those two summers back in Lesosibirsk, expanding his ethnography, provided him with plenty of material to work with. But the malaise hit him nonetheless.

Hard.

He no longer felt the existential need to research and publish. What was the difference if it took three, six, or eight years to finish his next book? Did he really need to polish an embarrassing combination of elevator pitch and groveling to woo the acquisitions editor of a top university press when a second-tier publisher would be thrilled to print a few hundred copies—and might even forgo the lengthy and arduous process of peer review? Either way, the book would eventually appear on the shelves of a small handful of academic music libraries (plus the bookcase in his parents' basement), where it would promptly begin to collect dust. No, there was no difference at all. He still had a job, he just needed to show incremental progress on his annual productivity reports so nobody could accuse him of being a "deadbeat professor."

He didn't care to put quite as much effort into his teaching as he used to, either. Sure, at first it was exciting, preparing new seminars and supervising thesis projects for the graduate students in his department. But now, each year's students seemed more and more entitled and less and less prepared. They wanted to be spoon-fed the right answers. They didn't understand—or *want* to understand—that, in ethnomusicology, a "right answer" rarely even exists. The undergraduates chorused "will this be on the exam?" while the graduate students, whose education was interrupted by the COVID pandemic from which they never really caught up, were constantly looking for shortcuts to "help" with their research and writing. And putting together a new syllabus required a lot more time and effort than simply reusing one from a year earlier. Maybe he'd swap out one or two reading assignments that didn't spark much in the way of student engagement, or redesign one of the smaller writing assignments. But that was it. The path of least resistance.

These days, his time was filled with service on various committees. An advisory committee for the institution's Arts & Humanities Center. The curriculum committee for his department. The faculty council for the college his department was part of. A university-wide awards and scholarships committee. A search committee for a new full-time lecturer in music theory. An endless parade of meetings during which everyone wanted to talk but nobody actually said anything consequential.

What was the point?

To Frank Woodley, the modest, two-bedroom house outside Providence, Rhode Island, was cozy and familiar. So, he didn't mind visiting when he wasn't at sea. It was where he grew up; his parents still lived there. Many of his friends from high school still lived in town. And it was an easy drive from Groton, where his boat was home-ported.

What he didn't appreciate, however, was the way his parents didn't give him any space. The way they doted on him, tried—and often failed—to anticipate his every need. It was all too much. He was twenty-one years old now, not a toddler. He didn't need constant supervision! He knew it came from a place of love, and perhaps also a little fear. After all, any visit could be his last; his was a dangerous line of work.

As they finally closed their bedroom door, Frank plopped himself down on the couch and turned on the TV, grateful for some time to himself. He had always been a political junkie, so naturally he turned on the news.

"In the wake of the Election Day attack, and following a brief period of terse diplomatic exchanges, Russia and its allies have reacted to the NATO deployments over the past few weeks with troop buildups of their own," the anchor was saying. "The Russian Army has reinforced key positions. After the war of the early 2020s in Ukraine ended in a stalemate, Russia occupied the eastern third of the country, plus the Crimean Peninsula. Just west of Kharkiv, it built a large military base, on which about twenty thousand soldiers and support personnel were stationed. Now, the base appears to have been expanded to accommodate thousands of additional soldiers and dozens more tanks, armored personnel carriers, and artillery."

The screen showed a mix of top-down satellite images and archival footage of Russian military parades. Frank shook his head. Most viewers probably wouldn't be able to tell that most of what they were seeing on the broadcast was ten or fifteen years old. But he could tell. And Army stuff wasn't even his area of expertise.

"Outside St. Petersburg," the anchor went on, "old Soviet-era fortifications have been repaired and hardened, enabling the western division of the Russian Army to gather and train within arm's reach of Northern Europe and Scandinavia. And in Vladivostok, a sizable naval presence has been augmented with troops comprising the Army's eastern division. From the fortifications there, on the western edge of the Japan Basin, they could easily assist their nearby North Korean allies while simultaneously threatening Japan, the large number of American military personnel stationed there, and the islands of the Western Pacific.

"Meanwhile, on the Korean Peninsula, North Korean troops have begun to mass along the edge of the demilitarized zone, using the city of Kaesong, near the western coast and about thirty-five miles from Seoul, as their base of operations. American satellite imagery, obtained from a Pentagon source, shows several large camps containing barracks and support facilities, plus about three dozen tanks, armored personnel carriers, and artillery.

"All in all, an impressive and menacing force."

"Well, shit," Frank muttered to himself. "At least it's just land forces so far—"

"On the high seas," the anchor continued, "navies from around the world are on alert. Increased American patrols around Taiwan are bound to irk the Chinese, who have attempted to restrict access to parts of the disputed South China Sea…"

"Pff," Frank threw his hands up in the air in mock disbelief. "Here it comes…"

"…And the North Korean Army Navy has been harassing shipping in and out of the South Korean port cities of Incheon, on the west coast, and Busan, in the east. But the largest naval response has come from the Russians, whose Northern and Pacific Fleets, operating in the Arctic and Atlantic out of Murmansk, and in the Pacific out of Vladivostok, seem to have fanned out across the world's oceans."

Frank was paying close attention now. Leaning forward, elbows on his knees, he ran his hand around his face as he thought. With the world's only true blue-water navy aside from the American fleet, the Russians would probably harass and intimidate military and merchant ships in equal measure. To some, it may seem like a surprising turnaround for a navy that suffered greatly following the collapse of the Soviet Union. Then, the country's political and economic future was unclear, and ships sat in port, rusting away for lack of funds for maintenance and repair.

But Frank knew otherwise. He had studied Russian naval history as one of his elective courses in submarine school, so he had some knowledge in this area. The Russian Navy's more aggressive approach was merely an incremental step. It had experienced a renaissance as oil prices rose in the 2010s and 2020s, with renewed funds for the overhaul and maintenance of its surface and submarine fleets, as well as for the design and construction of newer classes of vessels.

With these improvements came new confidence, and, with that, a renewed sense of swagger and entitlement—a growing attitude that Russia not only *could* control the world's waterways but *should* do so.

All of which is to say, they were well positioned and well prepared to threaten American and NATO forces.

Feeling his cell phone vibrate next to him on the couch, Frank looked down at the screen to see the notification. Had it just been a sports score or an email from a high school buddy, he would have ignored it. But it wasn't.

Instead, it was a message from Randy West, his friend and boss, the COB on his boat. "To all crew," the text message read, "liberty curtailed. Report to Naval Submarine Base New London no later than 24 hours from now to prepare for deployment."

Well, thought Petty Officer Woodley, at least he wouldn't have to worry about overstaying his welcome.

"I AM CATEGORICALLY against any effort to undermine the artistic excellence of our programs," said one of Will's colleagues. The middle-aged man's blazer had the requisite elbow patches, and his tie was loosened and askew. The paragon of professorial.

Will quickly reached to his throat, feeling for his own tie, only to recall that he hadn't worn one that day. Or, really, any day since getting tenure. Catching Jackie's eyes turn toward him, he scratched his throat as if an itch was the reason for his sudden movements. He also said a silent prayer, wishing the faculty meeting a speedy end.

"Of course, Roger," another colleague said, placatingly. "We all want to protect the quality of our programs. But if we don't do something we won't have any programs to protect."

A third colleague chimed in, leaning forward over the table. "I'll tell you where the problem truly lies," she said, stabbing at the air with her pen, "it's in the Dean's Office. The bean counters over there don't understand what it is we do down here—and they don't *want* to understand."

Roger nodded. "When was the last time this dean came to one of our meetings, huh?"

"Or approved a grant for my newest recording of Babbitt's piano works, scored for string quartet?" One of the full-time, but not tenure-track, faculty added bitterly.

"Or even sent a damn email to congratulate me on a publication," the pen-wielding professor said. "It took *years* to perfect that article on the second draft of Shostakovich's third piano sonata—you know, the one he totally rejected and nobody's ever heard? Will, *you* know what I mean, don't you?"

Awkward silence.

"Nobody wants to hear a rescoring of Babbitt's piano works, Marty," Roger said quietly.

The silence continued.

"Will?"

He snapped to attention, suddenly realizing that all eyes around the so-called conference table were on him. Shit. These people were still here, like a family you can't escape. And the meeting was still going on. "Uh, yes, of course," he stammered. "What is it you were saying, Linda?"

She placed the pen on the table in front of her, sighing loudly. "Will, we all know you're good at navigating these sorts of campus politics. We *need* you right now. Can you stay in our reality for just a few moments please?" Linda forced a smile. Poorly.

"Of course," Will said, feeling his cheeks flush. "I'll see if I can get a read on the situation at the next council meeting, okay?"

Linda nodded slowly, and the others around the table

seemed mollified, at least for the moment. Roger sat back, the plastic seat of his chair squeaking. Will breathed a sigh of relief. At least he'd kicked that can down the road a bit. In truth, he wasn't even sure he'd be attending the next council meeting—or if the dean's glamorous travel schedule would allow him to be there either. Where was he this week, Dubai? Rio? How much university business could he possibly be conducting in Vanuatu?

Sensing that at least one item was resolved, Jackie feigned bringing down a gavel. "I think we're done here. Our next faculty meeting will be four weeks from today. Same time, same place. Before then, please don't forget to email me your annual productivity reports."

Her last words were barely audible as Will, Linda, Roger, and the rest of the department faculty slid their chairs back from the table, packed their belongings, and headed for the door.

4

MOVES AND COUNTERMOVES

AMERICAN MILITARY CONTINUES GLOBAL DEPLOYMENT

By Bridget Peposki, Washington Advocate

Following the troubling events of Election Day, the United States military continues to deploy and position troops, ships, aircraft, tanks, and other equipment around the globe. While declining to offer specific numbers, the Pentagon has confirmed the marked increase in the number of military personnel stationed in South Korea, Germany, and Japan. Likewise, massive construction projects have been observed on American bases in Europe and the Middle East. Observers in the South China Sea report American naval patrols have tripled in the vicinity of the island of Taiwan, likely an effort to deter China from contemplating an invasion or annexation of the disputed territory at a time when the White House and Pentagon are focused on Russia and

North Korea.

The American military presence in Germany, a fixture since the end of World War II, has become more significant as the White House seeks to, in the National Security Advisor's words, "contain the Russian threat." Ramstein Air Base, a sprawling facility between the German towns of Miesenbach and Landstuhl, has seen its runways extended and its hangers filled with new aircraft and equipment.

The Navy's footprint in Japan is similarly expanding. The base in Yokosuka, home of the Seventh Fleet, has added piers and pier-side facilities to support the additional ships and submarines now assigned to the region. "We work all day and all night," Haruto Asakai, a local contractor and electrician, said of the recent uptick in activity.

Meanwhile, the largest expansion appears to be in South Korea, which already hosts almost 30,000 American personnel, primarily from the Army. New barracks and weapons depots, along with logistical and administrative buildings, have appeared in Camp Humphreys almost overnight. By some estimates, the facility, about forty miles south of Seoul and already the largest American overseas base, now accommodates nearly 60,000 American soldiers and military contractors.

"The United States mission in the Republic of Korea remains unchanged since it began in 1948," Army Spokesman Jared Klinghoff said in a written statement. "We are here at the request of the Korean government to support and assist in the protection of the democratic republic, as well as American citizens and interests on and near the Korean Peninsula."

Finally, observers have confirmed a marked

increase in American naval activity in the vicinity of Taiwan, whose technology and manufacturing industries have been vital to the United States and its allies. Beijing has long considered the island to be part of China and routinely denounces the independent Taiwanese government as renegade. The recent buildup puts two of the world's largest navies in close proximity, particularly in the narrow Taiwan Strait. Some analysts fear the powder keg is ready to explode.

"I can imagine a situation where, eventually, something happens," says Robert Vennig of the Brakefield Institute for International Naval Study. "It can be small yet still be catastrophic. All it takes is one ship getting a little too close to another and, boom, you've got an international incident. It's not a huge leap to go from one incident to a shooting war across the Strait. And with everything going on with Russia and North Korea, now's not a good time for a tussle with Beijing."

ALEXANDER BURKE HAD always been his mother's son. Not just because his father left before his first birthday. Cigarette dangling from her mouth, she had encouraged him to play soccer in elementary and middle school. So, he did—and he was pretty good at it. Then, cigarette in hand, she encouraged him to play football in high school. So, he did—and it turned out he was pretty good at that, too.

But she knew that college was not in the cards for Alex. First, there was just no way, on a single mother's hourly wage, that they'd be able to pay for it. And second, with Alex's learning disability, she wasn't sure he'd get in, to say nothing of getting out with a degree in hand.

So, when a recruiter for the Navy came to Alex's high

school during the fall of his senior year, something clicked for the eighteen-year-old wide receiver. He saw an opportunity to make something of himself, to achieve the kind of financial stability that had long eluded his mother. That afternoon, when he got home after football practice, he told his mother all about it.

Clutching a fading photo of her own father from his time in the service, and with tears in her eyes, she encouraged him to do it. So, he did.

In the beginning, life as an enlisted sailor wasn't nearly as glamorous as the recruiter had made it out to be. He wasn't immediately good at it. Rather, it was downright hard, even harder than some of his most difficult football practices. But like a well-planned offensive play, Alex could see his path forward, through and around obstacles and challenges. Indeed, his physicality was an asset to the Navy in a way it had never been to his teachers. He felt like he'd found his place.

When he graduated from Boot Camp, his mother had been so proud. She may have had to lug a canister of oxygen behind her, but she somehow got herself from their home in St. Louis to the Great Lakes Naval Training Center, north of Chicago, to witness Alex's accomplishment. Her smile was so big, it even made Alex grin.

"You know what this is," she said to him after the ceremony, over dinner at a nearby bar and grill. Alex nodded as she coughed and held out the cap from a Navy dress uniform. "It's…" she began to explain, but had to stop and cough again.

"I know, Mama," he said, gently placing his hand on her frail shoulder. He was afraid to give her a loving squeeze; she might crumble in his hands.

But she was determined to say what she came to say, a determination that wasn't lost on her son. Coughing again, she tried to resume. "It belonged to your grandfather," she said. The patriotic country music blasted from behind the bar as another table, also celebrating a Seaman's graduation, made a raucous toast. But she stayed focused on her task. Only six more words to go: "He would have been so proud."

"I know, Mama," he replied. It was the only thing he could think to say, even though he felt so much more.

Alex wished with all his heart that she'd held on a little longer so he could share the good news with her a few weeks later: he'd be joining the silent service. His new friends had warned him that it would be a career of constant learning, practice, study, and testing, a thought that sowed seeds of doubt in the back of his mind. But people would help him along the way, they'd assured him. The Navy wanted him to succeed. And it would all start with the basics: after six months of training in faraway Connecticut, he'd set sail on a submarine.

5

A New Signal

The Chairman of the Joint Chiefs of Staff looked around the polished walnut conference table in his large office on the top floor of the Pentagon. He'd called the special meeting of the top brass in all the military branches, plus the Secretary of Defense, so that they could put their heads together and coordinate their responses to the latest global and tactical developments.

"Like game pieces in a global chess match," he said, his deep voice echoing around the room, "Washington, Moscow, London, Paris, Pyongyang, Seoul, and Beijing are moving their troops, weapons, aircraft, and ships around the oceans and continents. Make a move, counter, make the next move. Nobody wants a real shooting war, especially since North Korea has brandished its new nuclear, or nuclear-capable, weapons in this conflict's opening act. But nobody wants to appear weak, either. Especially with nationalist, nativist, and protectionist sentiments on the rise, worldwide, since at least the mid-2010s."

The generals, admirals, and other senior officers seated around the table nodded and offered words of agreement. Their aides and staffs, seated around the room's perimeter, did the same.

The Chairman stood and began to pace around the table, continuing his speech with urgency. "As brigades and divisions, task forces and strike groups navigate the treacherous landscape and waters of this new Cold War, *communication* is more important than ever. Missed cues, crossed wires—whatever you choose to call it—could be embarrassing at best and deadly at worst. You can be sure, ladies and gentlemen, that all sides will use their networks and satellites at full capacity, sending and receiving orders and reports. And listening for the enemy's.

"I want to know, first and foremost, what our capabilities are, in terms of both communication with and within our own forces, and in terms of intercepting and understanding our adversary's messaging."

The Chief of Space Operations, from the Space Force, was the first to offer a report. He mentioned satellites for intelligence gathering, but then began talking about space-based platforms for offensive and defensive weapons and operations. The Secretary of Defense asked a pointed question about how well those offensive and defensive platforms worked on Election Day. That prompted the CSO to bring his remarks to an unceremoniously quick conclusion.

When it came time for the Chief of Naval Operations to make a report, he focused more squarely on communications and intelligence, determined not to dig himself the same kind of hole—or fall into it.

"One of our best means for intercepting enemy communications, sir, is our pair of spy submarines," the CNO began. "The USS Tucson, SSN-772, is based out of Pearl Harbor, and the USS Royal Oak, SSN-812, is based out of

Groton. Tuscon is a modified Los Angeles class attack sub; Royal Oak is a modified Virginia, our newest class of attack boats. Both maintain their offensive capabilities, including torpedoes and cruise missiles, but sacrifice some weapon storage and berthing space for intelligence-gathering and analysis equipment. Since the conflict began, both boats have been at sea almost continuously."

"Tell me about their missions so far," requested the Chairman.

The CNO nodded. "Sir, the Tucson's missions in the Pacific have been routine. They've observed Russian and North Korean naval units, and intercepted and deciphered their communications. The information her crew has gathered is crucial to our efforts to cover the Pacific.

"The Royal Oak, however, made the first big intelligence discovery of this conflict. I'm told it sounds like pop music being broadcast from near the Russian submarine base at Polyarnyy, just north of the city of Murmansk, at the far-western end of Russia's Arctic northern coastline. In addition to being an unusual sound, it's carried on frequencies well outside the range typically used by domestic radio. In other words, no Russian civilian radio receiver is even capable of tuning in and playing these songs."

The Commandant of the Marines spoke up. "So, if everyday Russians aren't listening to these songs, who are they broadcast for, and why?"

"We've been asking ourselves the same questions," the CNO replied with a nod to his colleague. "Over the past three months, the Royal Oak has intercepted three of these strange Russian signals. At the same time, her crew recorded a significant *decrease* in the number of messages transmitted on the Russian Northern Fleet's usual channels. Few in Office of Naval Intelligence think this is a coincidence. Instead, it has become increasingly clear that we're dealing with a new form of Russian code."

This revelation prompted overlapping discussions of concern throughout the room. Lesser officers might have panicked, but the men and women gathered for this meeting were exceptionally skilled at remaining calm under fire.

The Chairman soon brought the meeting back to order. "To understand it, we have to break it. What do we know about these...songs? What have you been able to determine so far?"

"Well, sir," the CNO replied, "the songs appear, on the surface, to be harmless pop tunes. Any teenager could recognize the sounds. Hell, they could probably even learn to sing along. Of course, there are plenty of Russian-language experts in our intelligence community, and those of our allies, but what use is a lyrical translation if all it says is 'her beautiful eyes,' or 'the sexy way he moves'?"

For a moment, the room was filled with laughter.

"Adding to the frustration," the CNO continued, prompting the laughter to disappear, "all the language experts we've consulted have been stumped by a few words in each song. They clearly aren't in Russian, but no one can tell us where they come from, which language. Moreover, analysts from the ONI, the CIA, and even the DIA have complained about 'wrong notes' in the music, parts of the melody or background instruments that 'just don't sound right.' The more people we ask to listen to our three samples, the more we hear about these 'wrong notes.' And that, sir, is where we stand."

The Chairman had stopped pacing several minutes ago, enthralled by the CNO's report. A new Russian code could be a dangerous thing, and the possibility had his complete attention.

"This much is clear," the Chairman said from the head of the table. "We don't fully understand what we're dealing with. We can't confidently translate the lyrics, and we can't account for the problems in the musical accompaniment—much less describe or analyze them. Unknowns are the coin of the realm in intelligence work, but this many makes me nervous. If we can't break this code, we'll have no idea what we're really dealing with. I'm looking for ideas."

The questions, comments, and suggestions came in fast.

"Maybe the Brits know something we don't?"

"Has anyone reached out to Mossad?"

"Maybe it's a ruse? A red herring? You know, make us spin our wheels?"

Sitting back down, the Chairman glanced sideways, toward the large windows that looked down upon the center of the Pentagon. Then, when he spoke, the rest of the room went quiet. "Maybe we're going about this the wrong way." He turned back to face the CNO. "You've been focusing on the language—and I would have done the same—but it's getting us nowhere. Is there another angle?"

"Sir," came a voice from the back of the room. Heads turned, and suddenly all eyes focused on a portly middle-aged naval officer who stood, holding reading glasses in his right hand. He looked to the CNO, who nodded, granting permission to continue.

"Sir," the officer said again as he cleared his throat and straightened his back. The three stars on the shoulders of his uniform caught the afternoon sun as it shone through the windows. "I'd like to suggest another angle: the music. My office is currently trying to locate an expert in non-Western music. We need someone well versed in the artistic traditions of Russia and the various groups of people within it. Someone who can speak to the significance of music in those people's cultures. We don't normally have someone like that on staff in our intelligence agencies and offices. But I believe that, when we find the right person, they'll be able to make a real breakthrough in our understanding of this new code. We just need to find that person, sir.

"We need...well, we need an ethnomusicologist."

PART TWO

RECRUITMENT

6

Home Front

After pulling his decade-old, green Subaru Forester slowly into the left side of the attached two-car garage, Will put the transmission in park, turned the ignition off, and let out a slow sigh. It was good to be home, wasn't it? He looked toward the closed door that led into the modest two-story colonial-style house. It was about five o'clock in the afternoon on a Tuesday.

"We're going to have to eat fast," Ashley Driver, Will's wife, said to him as he stepped through the door into the kitchen. Her tone was stern; he could tell right away that she was annoyed.

She had straight brown hair, worn just long enough to cover her shoulders. Her glasses, a gentle oval shape, nicely framed her eyes. She was a physician's assistant at a local medical clinic. Clearly, she had come home directly from work but hadn't yet had a chance to change, as she still wore a rather nice, yellow blouse and dark gray slacks. For a moment, Will looked down at his own clothing: a wrinkled blue Oxford shirt that was mostly tucked into a pair of fading blue jeans, with a tweed blazer over the top. Frumpy. Professorial. Could he be any more stereotypical?

Looking down at his watch as he crossed the room to put down his briefcase at the small desk in the corner of the adjoining living room, Will nodded. "Of course," he replied, trying to tread lightly and not make the situation worse.

Ashely and Will had been married for almost fifteen years now, and they had two children. Margaret, whom they lovingly called Marz, was thirteen going on, well, any age that didn't require any sort of parental approval. She was a voracious reader who also excelled at math and athletics but enjoyed music and drama. (Although her talent didn't always match her enthusiasm.) They could track her moods by the average number of syllables she spoke. The lower the number, the less pleasant the conversation was likely to be. She had inherited her mother's hair and eyes. And temper.

In contrast, Jacob Driver, Ashley and Will's ten-year-old son, was nearly always a pleasure. Unlike his seventh-grade sister, Jake was usually personable and extroverted. But his learning challenges were a sore spot that would reliably sour his mood, even if, at times, it was necessary to discuss them. Reading was a particularly sore subject, although both Ashley and Will were hopeful that the worst was behind them now. It would have pained Will to see his son struggle in any subject, but for the hurdle to be reading, an activity around which his professional life centered, was especially difficult. Outside of school, Jake especially loved soccer. He hoped to join the local travel team after their next round of try-outs in two months, and then the middle-school team after that.

If Jake's dream of playing on the travel team came true, then the Driver family's complicated schedule would only grow more complex. As it was, Ashley was slated to take Marz to a rehearsal for the middle-school play that evening, while Will would bring Jake to soccer practice. (As a music professor, one might think Will would prefer the rehearsal, but there was a limit to how much of that he could handle.) Tomorrow it was voice lessons for Marz and the reading tutor for Jake. Sometimes Will felt reduced to being merely a chauffeur.

The microwave beeped. "Could you grab the peas, Will?" Ashley asked without turning around to look at him or the appliance. "Margaret!" she yelled in two syllables toward the stairway to the second-floor bedrooms. "Come scarf down dinner before rehearsal!"

"One minute, Mom!" Marz's voice, carrying the same annoyed timbre, came back. "Just give me a freakin' minute! Gosh!"

They could hear her eyes rolling from the kitchen.

"Hi Dad," Jake said, coming in from another room, dressed in his soccer jersey, complete with shin guards. "When do we leave for practice?"

Will tussled his son's hair. "After we eat something." He reached for the peas. The hot bowl surprised him. "Ow!" He shook his hands, then grasped the bowl more carefully. "How was school?"

"Eh," Jake replied. "The usual."

"What did you do?"

"Stuff. You know."

"Ah, yeah, I know," Will said, nodding as he placed the peas on a wooden trivet on the small, round table nearby. "I remember doing *stuff* when I was your age."

"Not funny, Dad," Marz intoned as she briskly walked across the kitchen toward the table. She spat out each word as if it tasted like burned food. How could she be annoyed with him already? He'd just walked in the door and hadn't even spoken to her yet.

They all sat at the table, quickly filling their plates with food.

"Did you pick up the dry cleaning?" Ashley asked Will as she scooped mashed potatoes.

"Oh. Damn. I forgot," Will replied. It wasn't the first time.

"Damn it, Will. I need my black slacks for that meeting tomorrow!"

Now at least she had a reason to be mad at him.

"I'm sorry," he responded, trying to diffuse some of the tension. "It just…slipped my mind, okay?"

"It's not okay. I asked you to do one favor for me today. On a day when you, what, read a few student papers and sat in on one faculty meeting?"

"Look, dear, it's not like I—"

She interrupted him. "Do you want to know how many patients I saw today? Our new corporate overlords are increasing our targets. Again. I just can't do it. It's not good medicine. At some point, something's got to give. Somebody's going to get hurt."

Will put down his fork, a bite of meatloaf still on it. "Take a breath, Ashley. We're on your side here."

"Well, sometimes it doesn't feel like that."

"Is it possible for you two to take your bickering somewhere else?" Marz asked, using the same tone as when she entered the room a few minutes earlier. "It's giving me a headache."

Jake pointed at his older sister with his fork. "Are you sure it's not your boyfriend causing the headache?" He teased.

Will's eyebrows shot up and he looked askance at his daughter. Ashley reached over and pushed Jake's arm down.

"I can't believe you!" Marz shouted across the table. "You promised!"

Jake smiled. "It's just a text message," he said, mimicking his sister's voice. "That's what you told me, right?"

"Yeah, right before you promised to keep it secret! Traitor!" She stood now, hands on her hips. "Gah!" She let

46

out a half sigh, half scream, and executed a full 180-degree turn, storming away from the table and nearly knocking over her chair in the process.

"Not cool, buddy," Will said quietly to Jake.

"But you should know about this guy, shouldn't you?" Will couldn't tell if Jake was genuinely confused or faking it. "I mean, if she's going to marry him—"

"Nobody marries their middle-school boyfriend," Ashley said. "Will, you deal with this one." She gestured toward Jake. "I'll get that one. We have to leave now anyway." She got up from the table and carried her plate to the counter next to the kitchen sink before turning back.

"Oh, and Will," she said, "The light switch in the family room is acting up again. It would be really great if you could fix that tonight—this time without forgetting, okay?" Without waiting for a response, she continued on after Marz.

"Okay..." Will responded to his wife as she left the room. Then he turned to Jake. "Yeah, I want to know about the boyfriend, but you also shouldn't break a promise. Loyalty is important." Jake nodded. "In the Ket community, there's this saying—"

Jake interrupted his father, whining. "Dad. I don't want to hear about your Russian music people again!"

"First of all, they're not Russian, they just live in Russia. They are what one might call a 'First Nations' group..." Will's voice trailed off as Jake cleared his place setting from the table and walked away. "We have ten minutes before it's time to leave. I'm going to see if I can fix that wiring before I forget."

He cleared the rest of the dishes from the table and piled them in the sink. He would have washed them and loaded the dishwasher, but he had only nine more minutes to become an ace electrician. So, he opened one of the drawers nearby and pulled out a screwdriver and a pair of pliers.

"XO, COB, WARDROOM in ten minutes, please," Harper said. Worth and West nodded and watched the skipper leave the conn and several other crewmen shuffled in, out, and through the compartment. They'd arrived back in their home port, the submarine base in Groton, Connecticut, two days earlier. Immediately after securing the boat to the pier, the crew of the USS Royal Oak began cleaning and making initial preparations for their next round of provisioning. That way, the boat would be ready to depart quickly if the need arose. The process typically took two or three hours, after which most of the crew were allowed to leave the sub and head up the pier to the base.

This wasn't going to be a lengthy shore leave, Harper had informed everyone just before their arrival. Just long enough to resupply, rotate a few men on and off the boat for various reassignments, and make any necessary minor repairs. Everyone would get at least one night, maybe two, in the barracks, where they'd have a real bed with a real mattress, a significant upgrade from the berths onboard. For some, the part they were looking forward to most would be a lengthy hot shower.

After ten minutes, Worth and West met Harper in the wardroom. He'd already poured coffee for his fellow officers. They thanked him and sat at the table, which wasn't particularly large but seemed sizable when there were only three men gathered around it instead of the usual eight or nine. Harper slid a piece of paper across the table to each of his men, and each read it carefully while the skipper sipped from his mug.

"A visitor, huh?" Worth said, the first one to speak. "It doesn't say who, though."

The COB scratched his chin. "Do you know, skipper?"

Harper shook his head. "I'm not sure the base commodore

knows yet, either. Heck, the CNO may not even know. They're all probably waiting on the ONI for that information. And the ONI is probably still trying to find the right person for the job."

"Who's in charge of this navy, anyhow?" West asked with a smirk. "The Chief of Naval Operations or the Office of Naval Intelligence?"

Harper chuckled and shrugged. "Beats me, sometimes."

"Well, taking on additional personnel isn't anything new for this boat. Intelligence work is like that sometimes. That's why the boat was modified, why we have the extra space and extra berths," Worth said as he leaned against the back of the bench seat.

"True, but what irks me about this," West replied, gesturing to the paper he'd replaced on the table in front of him, "is that these orders don't specify whether the 'visitor' is even from the Navy. I'm a little concerned we're going to get a civilian, which adds all kinds of wrinkles to our day-to-day operations. Do you remember last time, skipper?"

Harper nodded. "I do. And I think it was a mistake to try to keep that CIA spook in his cabin for the entire transit. If our roles were reversed, I wouldn't want to be, essentially, imprisoned in a tiny closet three hundred feet underwater, either. I don't blame him for complaining like he did." He looked around to see West and Worth both nodding before he continued. "I even told the CNO that I thought it was a mistake. I put it in our after-action report."

"Do you think he listened to you, sir?" the COB asked.

"Well, I don't see any mention of any requirement to keep our visitor confined this time around," Worth answered, picking up the paper to read it again.

"Look, bottom line is, we don't know who we're getting and we don't know when," Harper said. "All we know is that it'll be someone the ONI wants us to work with, and it'll be sooner, not later. Maybe two or three days, a week at most. Whenever he gets here, let's have him meet with you first, XO. Talk with him. Get a feel for his attitude. If you think he's going to be a problem, getting in the way and such, then you order him to his quarters. You'll have my support. But if not, if he seems harmless, let's see if this time we can be a little more gracious. Maybe it will encourage some goodwill. Maybe it'll be better for everyone."

"Aye, sir," the COB replied.

"Understood, sir," the XO said.

"Now, I want the two of you to get off this rust bucket, have a shower and a real meal, and I'll see you back onboard for our regular daily briefing at oh-eight-hundred tomorrow." Then Harper smiled and added, "That's an order."

AS AN ACADEMIC, Will had spent more time over the course of his life reading and writing than learning to work with his hands. But he had some fond childhood memories of assisting his father with repairs around the house. In retrospect, he was mostly just passing tools to his dad and putting others back in the toolbox. Still, he did pick up a thing or two. (One of those things was to keep a screwdriver and a pair of pliers in the house so he wouldn't need to go and get the toolbox for small jobs like this one.) Hopefully it would help now.

Stepping into the family room, he flipped the light switch. The overhead fixture turned on for a second, then flickered, then went dark. A moment later it repeated the process. Clearly, something was amiss. He took off the faceplate from the switch and, using the screwdriver, removed the screws from the switch assembly. Pulling it out a few inches, he could see the wires attached. A second set of wires entered the junction box from the side, while a third set exited the box, going up. All of that made sense to Will.

What made less sense was the way all the wires were connected in the junction box itself. There was a layer of black electrical tape wrapped tightly around some paper, beneath which were the wires themselves. "They couldn't just use the twist-on connectors, huh?" Will muttered.

"What'd you say, Dad? Time to go?" Jake called from his bedroom upstairs.

"No, just talking to myself. Five minutes," Will shouted back as he walked over to the electrical panel near the door to the garage. He had spent a long Sunday afternoon several years ago carefully labeling each circuit breaker, so now it was easy to just reach in and disable the power going to the family room lights. Truth be told, he should have done that before even removing the faceplate from the switch.

Just then, he had a flashback. He was standing next to his father, who was trying to repair an electrical connection in his childhood home. Will couldn't have been more than seven or eight years old, but the memory was so strong it filled the senses: he could feel the steel shaft of the screwdriver he was holding for his father as he waited for him to ask for it. He could see the green wallpaper his mother had loved so much, despite the way its color was fading unevenly. He could smell the aromas of her cooking, wafting in from the kitchen. And he could hear his father's voice.

"William," he said, using a tone Will recognized as both his father's way of teaching him a lesson and the same way he, himself, sounded when he was lecturing to his students. "Because this is an older home, the way they connected the wires in here isn't as elegant as you might find in a newer building. You see that paper in there? William?"

Will could feel himself gasp, just like he did many years ago, when the memory was made. "Um, yes, Dad. I'm trying to. Can I see?"

His father stepped aside so Will could peer into the dark junction box. There he saw the way several wires were wound together with carefully placed layers of paper to make sure the right wires touched—and the wrong ones didn't.

"The key here, son, is the insulation. The *insulation*. Without it, there's going to be a heck of a spark and you're not going to want to be anywhere nearby when that happens." Will could see his father looking straight at him over the top of the glasses that rested on the tip of his nose. "The whole thing is rather delicate, you see. You don't want to jostle it while you push it back into the wall, or the paper might slide around and reveal bare wires and you wouldn't even know it until there's a fire."

Smiling and shaking his head, Will knew exactly what to do with the faulty wiring in his house's family room. He quickly went out to the garage, grabbed a couple of plastic twist-on connectors, and ran back to the family room. He was just making the final connection when Jake came bounding down the stairs, aiming for the garage door.

There, Jake picked up a small black duffel bag and slung it over his shoulder. "Are you coming, Dad?"

"Yeah, I'm coming," Will replied, screwing in the switch assembly. "Let me just put this faceplate back on so your mother doesn't yell at me for not finishing the job."

"Dad," Jake whined again. "I don't want to be late again!"

Will exhaled slowly, once more conjuring the image of his father from his memory. Before walking over to join his son, he whispered, "Thanks, Dad."

7

SEMINAR

LATE THE FOLLOWING afternoon, Will looked around the table, the same one he and his colleagues had sat at the day before. His eyes met those of some of the young graduate students sitting on those uncomfortable plastic chairs; other students averted his gaze like it was poisonous. The room filled with an awkward silence as his question hung in the air. It was supposed to prompt a discussion—this was a seminar, after all—but seemed to have the opposite effect.

"Come on, everyone," he pleaded. "What are the major differences between Saussurean and Peircian semiotics?"

"They're both just theories, right?" one student, a bespectacled, blond, twenty-something replied after a pause. His voice carried a hint of annoyance. Will figured he probably came from one of the more affluent Philadelphia suburbs. He just exuded entitlement.

A redhead in her thirties, sporting a less refined look that suggested mixed-neighborhood urban living, leaned forward to respond. Her plastic chair squeaked. (Was that where Roger sat yesterday?) "Sure, but one is an American theory and the other is French. That's a difference."

"True," Will said, grateful that the conversation had begun, though there was a long way to go. Had the students even read the articles he'd assigned for this week's class? "But those are just labels, right? Calling one 'French' and the other 'American' doesn't actually tell us what sets them apart, substantively. So, what sets them apart?"

A student at the far end of the table, wearing a Ramones t-shirt, spoke up. "Well, I'm not sure about this, but Saussure's theory or model or whatever is, like, about language, right?"

"Yes," Will confirmed. "He was a linguist, among other things."

The blond asked: "Then why make us read about him in a music class? How is that even relevant?"

"Ah, that's an important question," Will said, gesturing to the twenty-something. "It might help if we had some idea about what Saussure actually said." Inside, Will was having a hard time restraining himself. This stuff should have been easy; it's like the students weren't even trying. He was tempted to just stand up and lecture at them for the next hour about the application of semiotic theory to music and cultural analysis, but he knew that wasn't the point of a seminar. In fact, it would probably make matters worse as the students—already barely engaged with the material—would surely tune him out.

"Alright. Yes, Saussure was concerned with language," the redhead said. "He proposed a two-part model of meaning. I mean, that's what this whole semiotics thing is really about, right? Meaning?"

"Go on," Will encouraged her, smiling.

"Okay. So, Saussure is basically saying that there's the thing we actually say and then there's this whole *other* thing connected to it. And the second thing, the *other* thing, is the meaning of the first."

"Right," Ramones t-shirt said with just a slight hint of enthusiasm. "He called one of them the 'signified' and one of them the 'signifier.' But which was which? The first thing or the second?"

The twenty-something shook his head. "This is getting pretty confusing."

A fourth student, who'd been occupied with the doodling in her notebook until now, picked up her head. "See? This is why I don't do theory."

Will ignored that comment. "You're on the right track," he said to the Ramones t-shirt. "The thing we actually say is the signifier, and what it means is the signified. Now, before we talk about what that has to do with music, we need to clarify Charles Peirce's version."

The twenty-something put up his hands in surrender. "That one was even worse than the French one. Weren't there, like, *three* parts? I just don't understand. You've got the thing and the thing's meaning. What's the third part? Where does that come in?"

"It's all just theory…" the doodler sang quietly.

Will ignored her again, but it was getting harder to tune out her snarky comments. "Yes, Peircian semiotics is a tripartite system. That's true. But Peirce didn't make it three parts just to be confusing—"

"Coulda fooled me," the doodler said under her breath.

That was it. "You know what?" Will asked rhetorically. "You call all of this 'just theory,' and that's true. But it's more than that. Theory is how you make sense of the world. Even people who claim they don't have a theory or use a theory," his voice forceful and passionate now, "they've still got one and they still use one. They just don't realize it. And you know what that's called? Ideology. And *that* can be dangerous."

He didn't realize how loud his voice had become, or how quickly he'd slipped into lecture mode. The students sat back, stunned.

"Come *on*, guys," Will pleaded more quietly, "this is life-changing stuff if you just give it a chance."

After another pause, the redhead spoke up. "Alright, I'll try. Am I right to assume, then, that in music it's not about spoken language as much as about, well, musical language?"

"Yeah," Will said, a hint of a smile returning to his face. At least one of them was starting to get it. "But what's 'musical language'?" he asked. That would surely ruffle their feathers again.

"Seriously?" The doodler asked using the same exasperated tone as Marz. "I thought you were cooler than that, Professor Driver."

Will chuckled. "Fooled you." A muted round of laughter circled the table. "But seriously. In language, whether you're using Peirce's system or Saussure's, the thing we actually say isn't the whole story and isn't even permanently connected to any kind of meaning. How can we adapt that idea to music? When we speak, we use words. Some cultures and languages use prosody too. What do we use when we make music?"

"Melody."

"Chords."

"Harmony."

"Timbre."

Will nodded. "All good suggestions." As his father used to say, now things were really cookin'.

"So, are you saying that those things are, well, the 'thing' we've been talking about in semiotics?" The twenty-something blond asked, his brow furrowed.

"Indeed, I am," Will responded. Was it possible that these kids were starting to get it? Had he actually begun to make an impact on them? It only took eight weeks or so. But maybe this semester's seminar wouldn't be so bad after all. "And what about, to borrow Saussure, the signified?"

"That would be...I guess, what those musical things *mean*," answered the redhead.

"Yeah," Will said. "Let's get concrete about this. Can anyone think of an example of music meaning something in a semiotic sort of way?"

"Well, in an undergrad music history course," the blond offered, "we learned this whole story about a Beethoven symphony where the melody was supposed to be all triumphant and stuff."

Will nodded.

"And wouldn't Wagner's Leitmotiv be a kind of semiotic thing? I mean, the whole point was that a bit of music would mean something, and that changes in the music were, like, a signal that something in the meaning had changed," the redhead said. "Right?"

"Yes," Will responded. "And you could use semiotics to interpret meaning in lots of different genres, including not only a symphony and an opera, but also popular music, folk musics from around the world, and so on. The key, of course, is the word *interpret*. After all, if meaning is as arbitrary as Saussure and Peirce thought it was, then you can only *argue* for a particular signifier's signified. You can support that argument with evidence, hopefully, but there's no right or wrong answer. You can never be a hundred percent sure."

Most of the students nodded slowly. They were really thinking about it, and Will could just about see the gears turning as they wrestled with several of the concepts they'd touched on: the arbitrariness of meaning, the idea that meaning is made and not prescribed by nature, and the notion that meaning-making is interpretive. The room was quiet for a moment.

"Okay," the doodler said, finally breaking the silence. "But will this stuff be, like, on a test or something?"

8

APPROACH

WILL PICKED UP his jacket and empty travel coffee mug from his office before heading down the stairs along the back side of Franklin Hall and out to his car in the nearby parking lot. As he stepped outside, he looked up at the sky. It was dusk; the sun was just beginning to set over the Schuylkill River separating Center City from West Philadelphia.

Taking a deep breath, he hurried away from the building, fishing around in his pocket for his car keys. That's why he didn't notice the two men at first.

"Professor Driver?"

The voice surprised Will, startling him. He looked up quickly, seeing two figures about ten feet in front of him. Both wore black suits. Both had closely cropped hair and an athletic physique. Will stopped short.

"Professor Driver?" the one on the right repeated.

"Yes…" Will answered slowly.

"Dr. Driver, we'd appreciate a few minutes of your time." They both stepped closer and, in unison, pulled black leather wallets out of their pockets, opened them, and revealed large gold badges. "We're from the Office of Naval Intelligence and we're here on a matter of national security."

This must be a joke. Some kind of prank. Will flipped through a mental Rolodex of possible colleagues or college friends who could have arranged for this charade. Was it Roger? Certainly, this wasn't Jackie's style, and she didn't know Will well enough to pull a practical joke on him anyway. Besides, this was pretty elaborate. They even had badges!

"Dr. Driver? Professor?"

Will's gaze shot up again, looking over the alleged officers closely. "Who put you up to this, huh?" he asked, trying to smile. "Was it Roger? I could kill him!"

It suddenly occurred to Will that, at this very moment, there could be a camera recording his every word and move. Narrowing his eyes, he began to look around. There weren't a lot of places for a cameraman to hide. He supposed it was possible to stand behind one of the cars in the lot, but at this hour there weren't many of those left. Most of the faculty and all the academic staff had gone home an hour or so earlier. There were a few trees on the grassy embankment that separated the lot from the road, but none were particularly large, and it wasn't likely that a grown adult could hide behind one.

"Dr. Driver, I assure you, there's no need for threats."

At that moment, Will thought he could see a little bulge on the speaker's hip. A sidearm? Or just an old-style, belt-mounted cell phone holster? He instinctively raised his arms in front of him, palms out. "What did you say your name is again?"

"My name is agent Richard Harris, and this is my partner, agent Nathan Fisher. We're with the Office of Naval Intelligence. We have a matter we'd like to discuss with you."

Flicking his eyes from Harris to Fisher and back, Will was struck by their serious demeanor. "Alright, I'll hear you out. Let's go into my office."

HARRIS TAPPED THE screen of his phone to stop the recording from playing. It had been incomplete but certainly intriguing. On first listen, Will thought it sounded a lot like a run-of-the-mill Russian pop song, but it certainly did have some odd features to it.

"So, you're telling me the Russians are broadcasting pop songs like this into the Atlantic?" Will was a bit incredulous.

"Mostly the Barents Sea, but yes," Harris replied, sitting across from Will and watching him over the stacks of paper that covered his desk.

"And you're telling me that the best analysts in these United States of America have only been able to determine that there's something strange about the lyrics and the background music?"

"That's correct, Dr. Driver," Fisher said with a nod.

Will chuckled. "Well, if that's not a commentary on our society's current disdain for the humanities, I don't—"

"With your expertise," Harris began, "on Russian music and culture—"

"Not Russian. Ket." Will held up an index finger as he corrected the officer. "They're a distinct ethnic group."

"Ket music and culture," Harris repeated slowly, "our agency believes you to be uniquely equipped to assist in our understanding of these songs."

There was a moment of quiet as Will thought. Finally, he sighed and said, "Okay, I'll bite. *Why* is the Office of Naval Intelligence so interested in Russian pop songs?"

"Because..." Fisher began, speaking up for the first time. He looked toward his partner, who nodded, and then back across the desk to Will. "We suspect that the songs are not actually songs at all. We believe they are Russian military codes."

THE CAR PULLED into the parking lot of a nondescript strip mall somewhere in Chester, Pennsylvania, just south of Philadelphia. From the back seat of the Ford Explorer, Will hadn't followed the street signs too closely, especially once Fisher had taken the car onto Interstate 95. Now, he could see a nail parlor, a liquor store, and an insurance broker's office. At this time in the evening, about eight o'clock, the liquor store was still open but contained few customers. The nail parlor was closed and dark, as was the insurance office. The sun was well on its way below the horizon, illuminating the wisps of clouds that hovered above.

"We're here," Fisher announced.

"Here?" Will asked, confused. It certainly didn't look like a government facility. For one thing, where were the waving flags?

"It's not always like the movies," Harris said, craning his neck from the front passenger seat to look at Will. "But looks can be deceiving."

They exited the car and Will followed the two agents as they approached the insurance office. Harris produced a key from his pocket and unlocked the door. He held it open while Fisher led Will into a foyer with a couple of battered chairs and a small table with magazines and insurance brochures. Most of the lights were off, except one bank of tacky fluorescents on the far side of the room. The place smelled musty.

Once inside, Harris closed and locked the door behind them. Then he moved to the opposite wall and held a rectangular plastic keycard in front of a device that looked like a thermostat.

With a beep and a click, a section of the wall the size of a doorway slid back and to the side, out of the way. Beyond it, Will could see a large, well-lit space with several cubicles and what looked like additional doors leading to other rooms deeper inside. Eyes wide, Will followed the two agents through the doorway, which promptly slid back into place, hiding the inner office.

"Hey Fisher," a woman said as she looked up from her laptop computer, sitting on the reception desk on the right, just past the secret door. "Working late tonight?" She smiled at the agent.

"That'll depend on this guy," Fisher responded, pointing a thumb over his shoulder toward Will.

Harris cleared his throat. "This is Professor Will Driver of the University of Philadelphia. He's going to assist with the pop song project. He'll need the paperwork first, though."

The woman reached for the top paper in a stack on the side of the desk and held it out.

"Thanks, Robin," Harris said, taking it and handing it to Will. He then grabbed a pen from a nearby cup and passed it over. Looking right at Will now, he said in a rather monotone voice: "This is a standard non-disclosure agreement with additional criminal penalties commensurate with the sensitive nature of the material you'll be working with."

Will nodded and spoke slowly. "Okay…" He didn't really understand anything the agent had just said to him. Maybe it was the late hour. Or maybe the fact that he'd just been admitted to a secret office with two agents from one of the country's intelligence agencies? (This wasn't like the movies —it was somehow better!) The look on his face must have told Harris all he needed to know.

"It means, Dr. Driver, that you can't tell anyone about who we are, what you see here, or what we do here. Not even your family. This material may be so sensitive that agents of foreign governments would attempt to bribe, blackmail, kidnap, extort, or even kill to get it. Your friends and loved ones will be safer if they don't know anything about this. So do not speak of it to anyone. Not to your wife. Not your kids. Not your parents. Not even your goldfish." Harris eyed him intensely.

Now Will understood. And he could feel the tension increasing as Harris kept watch on him, waiting for him to sign the form.

Will decided to try to bring the tension level back down. "Not my cockatoo?" he asked with a smirk. He'd come this far. Did they really think he would turn back now?

"*Especially* not your cockatoo," Harris responded without breaking character—although Will could swear, he saw just a hint of a smile on the agent's face.

9

First Analysis

Agent Harris showed Will to a small conference room, where a laptop computer sat on the tabletop. Will couldn't help but admire the polished wood of the table and leather of the chairs. A flagpole, complete with an American flag, stood in one corner of the room. Elsewhere, fake plants sufficed as ambiance.

"The computer is air-gapped," Harris said matter-of-factly.

Will met him with a confused look.

"Right. That means it is not connected to any computer network, so it can't be compromised. Hacked," the agent explained.

"Ah, of course," Will replied with a nod. He moved toward the table and leaned over the top of one of the chairs, looking at the computer's screen. He could see a media player was visible.

"The song we played for you back in your office is all cued up," Harris added with a gesture toward the computer.

"Thanks," Will responded, pulling out a chair. As he sat, he looked around again, finding a console table along one wall with a few empty coffee mugs, a short stack of letter-sized notepads, and a cup with a couple of black pens. A map of the United States hung on one wall, a map of the world on another, and a large whiteboard was mounted on the wall at the head of the table.

"Coffee?" Harris asked unceremoniously.

"Two creams, four sugars," Will answered without thinking. Then he realized who he was talking to. With a sheepish smile, he added, "For me, it's always just been a vehicle for the cream and sugar."

"Sure," came the reply, and Harris turned on his heel to leave.

It was oddly quiet. Will pulled the chair so it rolled on its five casters, bringing him closer to the table. He swiped his fingers across the computer's touchpad and clicked on the "play" button. Instantly, the Russian pop song started sounding from the computer's speakers. He winced at the quality of the audio. The low frequencies were nearly nonexistent, and the high frequencies didn't fare much better. That left only the mids, which, without a balance with the highs and lows, made the song sound tinny and small. It didn't play for more than a few seconds before Harris returned.

Placing a steaming coffee mug on the table with one hand, Harris placed a pair of external computer speakers on the table next to Will with the other. "Thought you might appreciate these," he said.

Will smiled and looked up over his shoulder, for the first time noticing how tall Harris stood. Maybe six-foot-two? It was hard to tell from this angle. Regardless, he dwarfed Will's meager five-ten, and his shaved head and glistening black skin somehow made the dark suit he wore all the more intimidating.

"When you're finished, just let Robin know. She'll notify one of us and we'll take you back," Harris said with a nod. Then he left the room.

With a deep breath, Will got to work. As he often did when deep in thought, he began conversing with himself.

"Okay, Professor Driver," he said quietly. "Let's hear this song again."

He plugged the external speakers into the side of the computer and positioned them to his right and left. He then moved the mug of coffee to a spot between himself and the computer. Clicking "play" again, Will closed his eyes and listened.

The sounds washed over him. The incessant rhythm, the synthesized bass line, the perfectly auto-tuned voice. It was deceptively simple, he decided. The surface might have seemed all too conventional, but there were layers. The question was, what did those layers mean? And of all the sounds in a three-minute song, which ones were significant? Which ones signified?

"Let's start with the lyrics," he told himself as the song ended and the on-screen player stopped. He started it again, reaching for the pad and a pen from the console table behind him. The lyrics were grouped in double couplets, pairs of lines that formed the smallest complete unit of thought. Linguistically, most were in standard Russian, but he knew from the two times he'd heard the recording so far that the Russian-language words were interspersed with a few that, to the untrained ear, sounded Russian but weren't actually part of the language.

A smile crept across Will's face as he heard the first non-Russian phrase. Leaning forward, he dragged the slider on the computer screen back, rewinding the recording by a few seconds so he could hear it again. "Well, I can't believe it," he said out loud. "Ket!"

Then he paused, questioning himself. It's not like the identification of Ket as the language of the non-Russian lyrics was any big discovery. After all, that's the whole reason why he was there. His momentary sense of elation was quickly deflated. Time to get back to work.

Drawing a vertical line down the center of his paper, Will titled the left column "Russian" and the right column "Ket." At the top of the Ket column, he wrote the three words from the phrase he'd repeated from the recording. Then, just below it, a quick translation: *white bird flies below treetops*. Chewing on his lower lip, Will considered the phrase. Of course, it was way too early to make much of the words. It was just the first of what may end up being several Ket phrases in the song. Still, something gnawed at him.

The translation wasn't quite right. He crossed out "bird" and "flies," and above the scribbles wrote new words. Then he sat back, regarding the translated phrase: *white owl dips below treetops*. Was there significance to "owl" that wasn't there with "bird"? Why use the verb "to dip" instead of "to fly"?

Moving on in the song, Will began to transcribe and translate what seemed like important parts of the Russian and Ket lyrics. The former sketched a fairly conventional love-song narrative, with phrases like "his deep blue eyes," "his strong embrace," "his warm lips," and so on. Nothing there to distinguish this song from thousands of other Russian pop songs Will had heard in his years of north-Asian music research.

But the Ket lyrics, though numbering much fewer, offered a more lyrically sophisticated narrative.

> *Feathers ascend above the leaves*
> *Unseen and unheard*
> *Carrying treasure across the forest*
> *Tomorrow's brighter sunrise*

Joshua S. Duchan

Compared to the Russian lyrics, the Ket references were less concrete but more metaphorical. The problem was, to understand a metaphor, you need knowledge from two domains. There's the surface description—which in this case seemed clear, with references to the owl, treetops, treasure, forest, etc.—and then the other domain that those references are being used to describe. It was like a code, but, aside from the fact that the metaphorical basis of the Ket narrative was rooted in the natural world (which was not surprising given what Will knew about Ket culture), he just didn't know enough to crack the code.

Maybe a look at the other musical elements would help. Will slid the computer toward the head of the table, got up from the chair, grabbed the now-lukewarm coffee mug, and moved for the whiteboard. "Let's map it."

Placing the mug back down on the table, he picked up a dry-erase marker in his right hand and tapped the computer with his left, starting the song again. This time he wasn't listening for the words. Instead, he trained his ears on the patterns in the accompaniment. Specifically, he was trying to get a handle on the organization of the melody, his go-to first step in determining the piece's form.

Recalling his pre-tenure days teaching an introductory, general education course on music traditions around the world, Will smiled broadly and turned to the chairs around the table. "Remember, students," he lectured to the empty room, "in music, the term *form* has a specific meaning. It's the sequence of events over the duration of the piece. The sections and their relationships. What happens first, what happens next, and what happens after that. Most importantly, how are they related?"

Playing the song yet again, Will began to recognize when sections of the melody repeated. Often the background music would change with each section, too. Different instruments would join the band or drop out of it. The drums would provide an exciting fill, ending with a crash of the cymbals right at the moment—on the very beat—when the next section began. On the whiteboard, he began to write a string of capital letters.

"If you don't know the indigenous names for the various parts of the form, use letters instead. Go to the first available letter in the alphabet for the first section. Then, when a new section begins, ask yourself: have I heard this before? If the answer is yes, reuse the letter from the last time you heard that section. If the answer is no, use the next available letter." This was getting fun.

A B A B C B B

Looking at the string of letters on the whiteboard, Will frowned and let out a sigh. It wasn't that helpful. After all, the A section was the song's verse, the B section the chorus, and the C section the bridge. It was a classic popular song form, right down to the fact that the C section was only eight measures long. "The 'middle eight,'" Will said quietly. "Like some kind of Russian version of The Beatles." If the song's form was unremarkable, maybe there were some remarkable aspects of its other musical features.

"Alright, let's talk melody," he said to himself as he began drawing five parallel horizontal lines across the whiteboard. A musical staff. Turning around, he clicked the computer to play the song once more. This time he was listening not to the sequence of sections or the lyrics, but to the *pitches* the primary vocalist sang, the high and low sounds whose sound waves can be measured in cycles per second, or Hertz (the faster the wave, the higher the pitch, and vice versa).

In fact, the pitches repeated a lot—not unusual for a pop song—but he tried to notate on the whiteboard each pitch that was used. It didn't take long before he had an ascending line of dots on the staff, a few of which had extra little symbols next to them (for sharps and flats, when pitches are modified by moving them slightly up or down). It wasn't a transcription of the melody, but instead a reduction: each pitch from the melody appeared on the staff once, no matter how many times the singer used it. That way, he had a representation of the selection of pitches used to make the melody.

Laughing quietly to himself, Will resumed teaching to the empty room. (At least these imaginary students didn't respond with snarky comments under their breath!) "Remember, class, we don't usually use any and all pitches. That would sound pretty chaotic to most listeners. Instead, we organize pitches into particular collections we call *scales*. And the thing about scales is, they're not really defined by the particular pitches in them. Instead, they're defined by their *intervals*, the distances between the pitches. So, you can start a scale on any pitch, and as long as you use the same series of intervals, you will accurately reproduce the scale's structure." He paused, imagining the students furiously taking notes. "Any questions? Yes…" He chuckled. "Yes, this will be on the test."

Suddenly, Will wondered whether the room was bugged. Not by the Russians or Chinese, but by the ONI itself. Maybe there was a hidden camera somewhere? A microphone? What would Harris and Fisher think of him, lecturing to an empty room—and clearly enjoying it?

He didn't care.

"Let's hear it again," Will said confidently as he played the song once more. This time, he noticed when the singer used pitches that were decidedly *not* part of the usual Western major or minor scale. Certainly, there's no law saying that all songs must stick to the most common types of scalar structures in Western music, especially when the song comes from a place that is not only non-Western geographically, but also defiantly non-Western culturally.

Nonetheless, he began to observe where in the song these extra-scalar notes occurred. Which lyrics were sung on those pitches? It didn't take long for him to realize that these "odd" sounding parts of the melody corresponded exactly with the moments in which the lyrics switched from Russian to Ket. Coincidence? Will raised an eyebrow. He suspected not.

"One more thing," he said to himself. "Harmony." Playing the recording yet again, this time Will focused his listening on the simultaneous combinations of pitches produced by the background instruments, the *chords* they played. By this point, he'd heard the song enough times that he knew it well and began to quietly sing along. For most of the piece, the sequence of chords was conventional, sticking to combinations of pitches built on the first, fourth, and fifth notes of the scale. It was also predictable, following conventional patterns.

But there were moments when the harmonic progression surprised him. Upon further reflection, though, Will realized that he shouldn't have been surprised after all: the "odd" chords lined up perfectly with the "odd" parts of the melody, which coordinated with the Ket lyrics.

Taking a step back from the whiteboard and crossing his arms, Will observed his work. "Fascinating," he whispered. "But what does it mean?"

Chewing on his lower lip, Will took another look at the scale on the whiteboard, the pattern of harmonies he'd notated on his notepad, and the lyrics in the "Ket" column on the page. He narrowed his eyes as he thought. "There's got to be more to this," he said to himself.

The whole situation reminded him of his second year of graduate school, when he was required to pass a qualifying examination in music theory. He remembered growing nervous when he realized that his junior year abroad in

London had resulted in him missing some important theory and analysis courses as an undergraduate. What had he missed out on that all the other students already knew?

He had spent the entire summer before the test trying to teach himself some of the most advanced concepts in music theory. While his family and friends swam at the beach, he swam in a pool of terminology: set theory, neo-Riemannian analysis, quartile harmonies, integral serialism, spectralism. It became an intellectual soup that was equal parts music and mathematics.

Mathematics. Maybe that was it?

Rising from the chair at the head of the table, Will moved to the whiteboard, inspecting his scale more closely. (He let out a little chuckle at the idea that getting physically closer to the board would accomplish anything other than making the black smirches of dry-erase marker relatively larger.) What if there was some sort of serial procedure going on here?

"Okay, Professor Driver. Let the first pitch have a value of zero," he mumbled as he wrote the number above the first pitch in the scale, the one all the way to the left. "Then let the remaining scale degrees be designated by their distance from zero, expressed as the number of half-steps." He cleared his throat. "The first pitch was D-natural and the second is E-natural, a distance of two half-steps." He wrote 2 above the second pitch.

"Continuing on, the third scale degree is F-natural, a distance of three half-steps from zero." 3. "Then G-sharp, a distance of six." 6. Soon, he had a sequence of six numbers derived from the scale:

$$0\ 2\ 3\ 6\ 9\ 10$$

Stepping away from the whiteboard, Will let out a breath. This could mean something. "Hello, prime form," he said.

"If Arnold and Milton were here, we might transform you in fascinating ways. But I'm more interested in those coincidences with Ket lyrics…"

Without looking, Will reached behind him to pick up the pad from the tabletop. It was a bit farther away than he remembered, so he stretched backward, keeping his eye on his prime form on the whiteboard as if it might disappear at any second. Sweeping his hand back and forth above the surface of the table, he didn't realize until it was too late that the coffee mug was in its path. It was the sound of the mug shattering as it hit the tabletop that caught his attention. He spun around just in time to see the remaining coffee drain between the keys of the laptop computer.

"Well, shit."

Will closed his eyes and exhaled slowly. The government can afford to replace a computer, right? In fact, a dead computer wasn't really a problem at this point. As his heart rate came back down, he smiled and began to sing the song to himself.

And that's when he began to see how the Ket lyrics were the key to the entire puzzle. By identifying where, exactly, in the song the language switched from Russian to Ket, he could then examine the pitches used in the melody at those moments. None of them were drawn from the prime form! In other words, when the song switched to Ket, the melody completely ignored the intervallic relationships that governed most of the piece. Instead, a new set of numbers was revealed:

$$0 \ 1 \ 4 \ 5 \ 8 \ 11$$

Moreover, the unusual-sounding accompanying chords utilized the same alternative series of intervals. It was as if, for just a moment or two, he could glimpse an entirely new musical composition lurking beneath the glittery, smooth pop surface. He'd cracked the code!

Gathering up the coffee-stained pad, Will looked one last time at the whiteboard, still adorned with his analysis. Then he nodded to the empty room. "Class dismissed."

10

DOMESTICITY

IT WAS ALMOST midnight when Will finally made it home. He'd completely lost track of time while he analyzed the song at the ONI field office. What was that old saying about time flying? He hadn't felt that alive in years. He was putting his unique skills to work, he was making progress, and he was serving a higher purpose.

Ashley had left the light on over the kitchen sink, but otherwise, the room was dark. He quietly put down his briefcase and slipped off his shoes, peering around the doorway and into the living room, where he could see a faint yellow glow coming from the far corner. Stepping into the room, he saw his wife sitting at the far end of the couch next to the end table with the lamp they'd bought together for their first apartment.

"Nice of you to join us," she said, looking up briefly from the book she was reading. Marz, who tended to be more human and engaging late at night, sat at the opposite end of the couch, her eyes glued to her phone. Probably texting her friends. Ashley saw her husband's eyes move to their daughter and then back to her. "Jake's in bed. He's been asleep for hours."

"Oh," Will replied. Of course.

"Where have you been?" Ashley asked. Her tone was genuine, and she smiled softly while she watched Will and waited for an answer. Will didn't immediately provide one. "How was the day? How was your class?"

"Oh, the usual," he replied, sitting himself on the comfortable chair catty-corner to where Ashley sat. "Most of them didn't do the reading, so it was a struggle. Or maybe they did, but still they struggled. I mean, I know that semiotics isn't everyone's cup of tea, so to speak, but…" Will trailed off. He could tell that Ashley didn't really care about the challenges of teaching Saussurean and Peircian semiotics. That was nothing new.

She really did care about him and about his work. It's not that she didn't have the mental capacity to understand what he thought, wrote, and talked about all day. It's just that she had too much else on her plate to put that much energy into topics from classes she never signed up for.

It was an argument Ashley had made repeatedly over the years: she simply does more than he does, and so he should be more helpful to lighten her load. She wasn't wrong, although Will didn't like admitting it. She organized the family's schedule, stocked the kitchen, planned and cooked the meals, washed and folded the laundry, and so on. And on top of all that, she had her job at Green Stables Medical Associates over in Ardmore. As a physician's assistant, she saw a lot of patients each day in the clinic, diagnosing the common cold and occasionally something more exotic, like a broken bone or sinus infection. And since the practice had recently been bought by a statewide corporation, the PennWell Health Group, she'd been under pressure to increase the number of patients she saw each day. She still enjoyed her job, but she didn't enter the medical field because she loved the *business* of medicine. She did it because she loved *helping* people through medicine.

So it truly ruffled her feathers when she got the feeling that others weren't helping where they should. And although there was much about Will that she found attractive—including, among other things, his intellect—this was one of the things that had always bothered her about the man. He was content to do the minimum, if he remembered to do anything at all. Unless, of course, the thing he was asked to do was something he found especially exciting. Music was one of those things, or at least it used to be. But in all their years of marriage, she hadn't quite figured out what else would motivate him.

"And how was *your* day?" Will asked his wife, placing a hand on her knee.

"Fine," she answered quickly. "What time did your seminar end tonight?"

Will sighed. "Hours ago."

"So…what have you been doing since then?"

Will was afraid she'd ask that question. Harris and Fisher had sufficiently scared him and, despite whatever challenges their family dynamic was facing, he still loved his wife and children endlessly. If any of them were hurt (or worse) because he said too much, well, he could never forgive himself. "Nothing important," he said in as nonchalant a tone as he could manage. He wasn't used to lying to her face.

"Well, *that* doesn't tell me much," Ashley responded, pulling her knee back and out from under his hand.

"You really want me to tell you about the latest in poststructuralist thought?" he said, hoping that would end her line of questioning.

"I suppose not."

"Alright, then. Besides, it's not like you had much to say

about your day either."

"True…"

They heard a scoff from the other end of the couch. Both turned to look toward Marz, phone clutched in her right hand and staring at them with a contemptuous look.

Will shrugged. "What?"

Marz shook her head. "You two are so…weird." And with that, she stood and climbed the stairs, heading to her room for the night.

THE PHONE IN Harper's cabin buzzed. Fortunately, he wasn't too busy. Frankly, he was actually a little antsy. Crew fitness reports weren't exactly the most compelling reading. He didn't mind an interruption.

"Skipper," he said, pulling the receiver from the bulkhead to his ear.

"Skipper, conn," Hargraves replied. "Sorry to bother you, sir, but we have a ship-to-shore call for you from the Pentagon. They claim it's urgent."

Harper closed his eyes and took a deep breath. "You'd think things would be quiet when we're all tucked in and tied up at home, but I guess not."

Hargraves didn't know what to say to his captain; he couldn't tell whether the skipper was annoyed or amused. "Uh, yes, sir. Shall I—"

"Yes, yes. Patch it through, Hargraves."

"Yes, sir. One moment."

Harper heard a few clicks as the call was connected through the base's switchboard and routed to the Royal Oak through its pier-side umbilical. It wasn't long before the process was complete. "USS Royal Oak, actual. This is Commander Harper."

"Good evening, Commander," said the voice on the other

end of the line. "This is Lieutenant Donovan with the ONI."

"What can I do for you, Lieutenant?" As much as Harper enjoyed a break from reviewing the stack of reports in front of him, he never really liked formality for the sake of formality.

"Sir, I'm calling to follow up on the orders you received earlier today. I have additional information about the additional personnel you'll be taking to sea with you."

"Personnel?" Harper asked, feigning irritation. "My orders said *one*. One person. This is a submarine, Donovan, not a resort hotel."

"Yes, sir," Donovan said, clearly thrown by the skipper's tone.

Harper smiled to himself. Not that he enjoyed picking on the Navy's paper-pushers and spooks, but sometimes he couldn't help himself. "Well, out with it, Lieutenant. What can you tell me?"

"Sir," Donovan said, collecting himself. "The ONI has identified a civilian asset and plans to impress him, embedding him with your crew. We've made initial contact and our agents have completed a preliminary assessment. I'm pleased to report that he seems highly skilled, highly cooperative, and highly...compliant."

"I see," Harper responded, intrigued. "When can we expect him to embark?"

"We have a few more steps to complete here, sir. It should only take a few hours or so. We anticipate being able to send him your way after that, with a stop here at the Pentagon first. The admiral would like to look him in the eye before placing him on one of our boats."

"Alright," Harper said. If only the Pentagon would allow *him* to look this civvy in the eye before accepting him on *his* boat.

"Between transport to Arlington for the briefing and then to New London, I would anticipate his arrival the day after tomorrow, early to mid-morning."

"Fine, fine."

"Thank you, sir. If you don't have any questions—"

"Lieutenant," Harper interrupted. He wasn't going to let Donovan get off that easy. "I'm glad you found your man. Now tell me, what's his name?"

WILL SAT DOWN at the kitchen table in front of his computer, his checkbook off to the right and a cheap beer to the left. The house was all quiet now; Ashley had gone up to bed and was probably asleep, while Marz was probably not asleep but cocooned in her bed with her phone still attached to her hand.

He had planned to use some time this evening to prepare for the following week's seminar meeting. He wasn't completely fibbing when he mentioned poststructuralism to Ashley. After all, that would be the topic of conversation. They'd be reading some case studies and applications of semiotic theory to some real music traditions in various parts of the world. (Semiotics was a manifestation of poststructuralist thought, Will intended to show.)

But class prep just wasn't doing it for him tonight. He had little motivation to work for this particular crop of students when it was quite clear that few of them were working. They weren't holding up their end of the bargain. Besides, teaching didn't hold the appeal it used to. He just wasn't as excited about it as he once was.

That Russian pop song analysis was another story, however. He closed his eyes, remembering the sound of the secret door as it clicked and slid open, the taste of the coffee, and the feel of the dry-erase marker in his fingers as his brain worked faster than his hand could write on the whiteboard. He had known it at the time, but it was even clearer now: conducting that analysis was the most fulfilling thing he'd done in a long time. A *very* long time.

It was done, though. Over. He didn't expect to hear from the ONI again. After all, his analysis had revealed some interesting turns of phrase in the little-known Ket language, as well as some fascinating, if obscure, intervallic relationships that corresponded closely with the linguistic idiom. But that was as far as he'd been able to take it. What more could be said about those Ket phrases? And what did the strings of numbers produced by reordering the melodic intervals signify?

He inhaled slowly, then exhaled even more slowly. Taking a sip of the beer, he spotted the checkbook beside him on the table and remembered that there were still bills to pay. That would distract him from class prep, at least for a little while. Long enough so that, by the time he made it upstairs to bed, Ashley would be in a deep sleep. He wouldn't face another inquisition.

Opening the computer's web browser, he clicked on the bookmark for his bank's website. As usual, he entered his username and password, waited for his phone to receive the code for two-factor identification, skipped past the bank's annoying advertisement for yet another credit card or mortgage or something-or-other, and finally landed on the page showing his family's accounts. As if on autopilot, he moved the mouse over to the list of functions along the right side of the web page, aiming for the one labeled "Pay Your Bills." But before he got there, something caught his eye.

It was the checking account labeled "Primary." That's where his paycheck and Ashley's were directly deposited every two weeks. Their family finances were pretty predictable these days, so he usually had a good idea of the approximate account balance, which would fluctuate a little bit depending on whether they were paid this week or last, as well as the monthly cycle of credit card and utility bills.

But tonight, the balance was not what he expected. Indeed, it was a whopping $10,000 more.

"What the..." he whispered to himself as he moved the mouse back toward the list of accounts. "Primary" lived at the top of the list, above "Secondary," "Savings," and "Mortgage." All of those balances were more or less where he expected them to be. But not "Primary."

"Bank error in your favor?" Will asked himself, smiling at the reference to the classic tabletop game of Monopoly. "That would be one hell of a bank error, though."

He clicked on the link to view the account's transactions. There it was, at the very top of the list: a deposit of $10,000 with today's date. The short text descriptions next to each transaction were not usually all that descriptive, but he could sometimes figure them out. A string of numbers with "PLP" in the middle, for example, typically meant a payment to Pennsylvania Light and Power, the local electric utility. But there was nothing about the description of this deposit—"ONIFO-P-1946XXXX25"—that he recognized. At first.

Then it hit him. ONI. *Office of Naval Intelligence.* FO-P. *Field Office, Philadelphia.* It was a little bit of a stretch, perhaps, but it seemed the most likely solution to the problem. Was this some kind of compensation for his work on the Russian pop song? He hadn't given them his bank account number, routing number, or any other information they could have used to locate his account.

"You idiot," he chuckled to himself. "They're an *intelligence agency.* If they want to know your account number, they can find it."

He sat back in the chair, running both hands through his hair and exhaling loudly. "Well, that's a nice surprise," he said to himself. "Nice work if you can get it..."

For a few of the most fulfilling hours of his life, he had been very well compensated. Naturally, this raised the question: how could he do more of that?

11

CRYPTOGRAPHY

FISHER WALKED THROUGH the hidden door and reentered the field office. Harris met him, coffee in hand. "The drive back was okay?"

Taking a sip, Fisher nodded. "No problems. Thanks for this, by the way. How're things looking in the conference room?"

"Well, there's good news and there's bad news," Harris began. "The good news is our professor came up with a lot of stuff that you and I, and even our friends in D.C. and Langley, would never have found in that song. The bad news is it's incomplete: we've got information, parts of a story, and some numbers. But we don't know what they mean."

"I see." Fisher started toward the conference room.

But Harris didn't move yet. "And, in other news, we're going to need a new computer."

Fisher rolled his eyes, and then the two of them entered the conference room and looked over the whiteboard. Harris picked up the coffee-stained pad with the Russian and Ket lyrics. There was a moment of silence as the two men regarded the results of Will's analysis.

"I see notes here about owls, treetops, and sunrises, but it looks like some kind of poem that I don't understand," Harris said. "I wasn't an English major, you know."

"And I wasn't a math major," Fisher replied, unsure what to make of the two rows of numbers, scribbled Roman numerals, and a few key lyrics he was looking at on the whiteboard. "I think we need to put in a call to Kevin Park."

"The Kevin Park in cryptography?"

"Yeah, you know him?"

"Sure," Harris said with a smile. "When I was at the D.C. office, he was captain of the office baseball team. A real good pitcher, in fact. Kind of an ass as a coach, though. Acted like he was the only one who knew how to play the game."

"Well, this time you don't have to talk about baseball. We'll stick to...well, whatever this is," Fisher said, gesturing over the table and toward the whiteboard. "I'll see if he's still in his office. When we were roommates in college, he was a real night owl."

"IT'S BEEN A long time, Nate!" Kevin Park's voice came through the computer's speakers a little faster than his mouth moved in the video, but the connection soon stabilized. "How's it going? How are things in Philly?"

Fisher smiled. "Hey, Kevin. Good, good. Thanks for taking my call—"

"Are you kidding? I mean, I was a little surprised since I haven't heard from you since...when was it? Oh yeah, graduation! But seriously, it's no problem, buddy."

Fisher took a breath rather than respond immediately. He didn't consider the two of them buddies, but he'd let that slide for now. "Kevin Park, this is Rich Harris. I think you two might have crossed paths a few years ago, when—"

Again, Park interrupted Fisher. "Oh yeah! My favorite right-fielder!" He smiled broadly. "How've you been, man?"

"Just fine, Park, thanks." Harris could tell Fisher was eager to get down to business. "We called because we thought you and your crypto team might be able to help us out with a case we're working on."

Fisher leaned in closer to Harris, in front of the computer camera. "I just emailed you a few files. It should be some audio and some pics of an analysis conducted earlier this evening by a new informant, a professor of," he turned to Harris, "what was it again?"

"Ethnomusicology," Harris said.

"Right. That."

Park looked to his side, away from his camera. Fisher and Harris figured he had another screen there. "Just pulling up your files now." After a moment, he began to lean closer to the off-screen monitor. "Huh."

"What do you think?" Harris asked.

"It's been a long time since I took a music analysis class," Park started.

"Yeah, us too," Fisher put in jokingly.

"No, seriously. I took several music theory courses in college, remember? I didn't always love the music aspect of it. But the math behind it all, now *that* was interesting." Another moment passed, as Fisher and Harris looked at each other and shrugged.

Then Park spoke up again. "Okay. I think I see what your professor was doing here. He's got some tone rows, and based on the looks of his harmonic analysis, it looks like some weird harmonic things are happening at the same time as the song switches from one row to the other. And those tend to line up with the change in language in the lyrics. Nice—this music theorist or ethnomusicologist, or whoever he is, did some really sophisticated stuff here." Park seemed genuinely impressed, dropping his "cool" attitude in favor of straight-up praise for another's work. A rarity.

"The really clever part," Park continued, "was the decision to investigate the melody in terms of serial techniques. I'm not sure I would have thought of that. At least not quickly. But I think it's paid off. I mean, these tone rows are solid."

Harris cleared his throat. "Agent Park, can you put that into English for the uninitiated?"

"Of course, of course. The *tone row* is a series of numbers, each representing an *interval*, a…distance between the first pitch and each of the other pitches in the scale. In the twentieth century, some composers really went to town with these things, running them backward and forward, starting them on different pitches, and using them in sequence and in simultaneous clusters of chords. Your professor friend," he looked directly at the camera and pointed at Harris, "found two different tone rows at work in this song. One for the Russian lyrics and another for whatever this other language is."

"I think I understand," Fisher said, nodding. "You see, we suspect this song contains some kind of code to it. Now, it wouldn't be a really effective code if it depended directly on the Russian language. They know there are very good Russian speakers all over the world, and especially in our intelligence community. So, my guess is we need to focus on the other language."

"I agree," Harris added. "So, Park, as the best cryptographer on this conference call, what do *you* make of the, uh, tone row under the non-Russian lyrics?"

Park stroked the stubble on his chin. (Did he miss Harris's dig?) "Uh… I'm going to have to call you back. Don't go far."

The screen showed Park reaching forward, and then it

went black.

"Alright, children," Park said to Fisher and Harris when they reconnected thirty-five minutes later. "This was a tough one, but I think I've got something."

"Took long enough," Fisher teased.

"First, let me tell you, I have no idea what these weird words are telling us. From a cryptographic standpoint, I just don't have enough info about the language and culture—hell, I don't even know the *name* of it—to do any real decoding.

"The tone rows are another story, though." A smile began to creep across Park's face. "At first, I thought it was some sort of algorithmic thing, maybe a regression or transposition, or possibly both. But I got nowhere fast with that one. Then I figured, each row has six numbers. It could be some weird-ass variation on a tetrachord or something like that, but it sure as hell isn't a straight-up twelve-tone system. And I asked myself: what kinds of systems have I seen that rely on base-six numbering?"

Harris shook his head. "Whatever it is, it's a system I sure don't understand."

"Oh, buddy," Park replied, chuckling to himself as he saw Harris bristle, "you're selling yourself a little short here, no?"

Fisher looked back and forth between the screen and his partner. "Is someone going to tell me?"

"Cartography," Harris whispered. Then, with more confidence: "It's a friggin' map."

"Close," Park corrected with a touch of glee and a finger pointing at the camera. "It's not the map, per se, but rather *coordinates* on a map. And you know whose maps use a six-number coordinate system, right?"

"The Russians," Harris and Fisher said at the same time.

Park nodded. "Nicely done, children. I think you're learning!" He teased.

"So let me make sure I understand what you're telling us, Park," Fisher said seriously. "You're saying that the sequences of numbers refer to spots on a map?"

"Basically yes," Park answered. "To be clear, only the second set of numbers, the ones that occur at the same time as the weird non-Russian lyrics, are cartographically important. The others are meaningless. Red herrings. And the song doesn't use all six numbers in the system at the same time. It uses various combinations of three, like trichords, or as the musician might say, chords.

"So, essentially, whenever the singer switches her language, that's a trigger, a cue that something is happening in the music that some Russian soldier or sailor should pay attention to. There are still a few unknowns, though. First, we need a more precise mapping of musical coordinates with cartographic coordinates. I can keep working on that for you.

"But second, we need someone who knows something about this language, preferably someone who also knows something about the culture and society of the people who speak it. We need that kind of insight to answer the most important question."

Fisher leaned forward, his eyes rolling before he even began to speak. "And what, mister teacher, is that?"

"Once the Russian gets to the right spot on the map, what will he actually do there?"

12

THE TAVERN

THE MORNING AFTER Will's financial discovery, he was up earlier than usual. A quick run on the treadmill in the basement and an even quicker shower, and then he was in the kitchen, dressed in casual khaki slacks and a blue button-down Oxford shirt, with two steaming cups of coffee. One was in his hand, the other was on the counter when Ashley walked in, wearing a black blouse over taupe slacks, ready for work. She looked nice. Really nice. She smelled nice too.

With a double-take, she asked, "For me?"

"Mmm-hmm," Will responded, his mouth full of java.

"Isn't this a nice surprise?" she said, picking up the cup and giving him a peck on the cheek.

Will quickly looked at his watch. "I'd better wake the kids before we're all late." He started toward the stairs but stopped himself in the doorway and turned back to face his wife. "You know what? I'll take them both to school today. You don't need to do it. Enjoy your coffee and a few minutes of quiet before work."

The smile on her face was genuinely heartwarming, and Will bounded up the stairs two at a time, knowing that he had more surprises in store for her. Funny how a sudden influx of money can put you in a good mood.

Of course, he wasn't completely ignorant of her frustrations with him, and he knew that the previous evening's conversation didn't exactly help. But how could he ever explain it to her without putting her life, or the lives of their children, at risk? The best he could do, he figured, was to try and compensate, to balance out the frustration with loving kindness.

After finishing his online banking the night before, he had decided to arrange for a delivery of flowers to Ashley's office. An impressive bouquet of roses, her favorite. The "deluxe package," according to the florist's website. Was it a bit of a splurge? Sure. But they could afford it and she was worth it.

What's more, he'd made a dinner reservation for the two of them at Tavern by the Brook, one of those fancy restaurants whose chef had been on one of those cooking shows. He couldn't remember the chef's name or the name of the show, but he knew Ashley would be thrilled. She'd been salivating at the idea of eating there since it opened two years earlier, but the menu wasn't what either would have called "budget friendly." Another splurge? Yup. But, again, they could afford it.

And she was worth it.

"UH, ASH?" THE voice of the receptionist called around the corner, where Ashley sat at a small desk in a little alcove. From there, she was hidden from the check-in window's parade of patients. And although she could still hear the music playing over the office's speakers, it was as quiet a place as she could find in an otherwise busy medical practice.

"Yeah," Ashley replied without turning around. She was typing furiously on the computer in front of her, filling out another pre-authorization peer-to-peer insurance request. Her fourth one today. The insurance company would reject her request, she was sure, but she had to go through the motions anyway, asking to chat with a physician from The American National CoreHealth Insurance Company so she could explain why she needed to prescribe a liquid version of the ADHD medication her four-year-old patient needed. Had she prescribed pills, it wouldn't be an issue. But you can't do that for a patient who doesn't know how to swallow pills yet. She'd never get the chance to actually say that to a human from TANCHIC, though, because their computer system would automatically determine that such a conversation was not warranted. More like, such a conversation was a waste of their time—or, more precisely, a waste of the money they would need to pay the poor doctor who would have been happy to chat but whom company thinks is overpaid and eating away at their profits.

Ashley sighed. Filling out this pointless paperwork, even if it's an online form and not actually on paper, took up time that she could be spending with actual patients. That would make her happy—talking with living people was why she went into medicine to begin with—and would also help satisfy her own corporate overlords.

The receptionist, an older woman whose voice, over the past year or so, had acquired a bit of a shake to go with its hoarse quality, continued. "You'd better come see this. It's pretty…impressive."

Ashley stopped typing and looked up. Those words could either describe some kind of injury or, well, she wasn't sure what else. Getting up from the chair, she poked her head around the corner.

"Oh, my!" Ashley exclaimed as a smile crept across her face. There on the desk was a large glass vase with two dozen velvety, deep-red roses. "Who are *those* for?"

The receptionist turned around, a smile on her thin lips. She didn't say anything, but her silence spoke volumes.

"For *me*?" Ashely asked, a hand on her chest. "Oh, my goodness!" She reached for the vase and smelled the flowers, closing her eyes so as not to be distracted. That scent was one of her absolute favorites and always filled her with joy.

She opened her eyes and they immediately fell on a small, cream-colored card perched between the flowers. Placing the vase back down on the desk next to the receptionist, she didn't even notice the patient on the other side of the sliding glass door, standing in the waiting room, eyes wide at the sight of the bouquet.

To my love, the card read, *whose brilliance and beauty surpasses even those of these roses. Please join me as we dine at Tavern by the Brook at seven o'clock this evening. (Marz has already agreed to babysit Jake, at a premium rate, of course!) All my love, Will.*

Overjoyed and excited, Ashley could feel the heat from her cheeks, which had turned a shade of red that rivaled the flowers. Tavern by the Brook?! A Charlie Coopersmith restaurant—the one they used as the setting for the second season of *Cooking in Charlie's Kitchen*! She'd wanted to go there for years!

As if in a daze, Ashley carefully carried the vase back to her alcove.

"You're welcome..." the receptionist said quietly as Ashley walked away.

But Ashley didn't hear her. She slowly lowered the vase down onto the surface of the desk, smelled them again, and resumed her seat.

That's when it hit her. To what did she owe this pleasant surprise? Will wasn't above unexpected, and occasionally grand, gestures. But this was his biggest yet. Was there some good news he had to share? Perhaps related to his mysteriously late return home last night? Then her face grew a bit darker. Or maybe it was bad news—also related to staying out late last night—and he was trying to proactively (prophylactically?) soften the blow? She didn't want to make too much of it or ruin the moment. But he certainly had some explaining to do.

"YES, MADAME, I believe your dinner companion is already here," the Maître d'hôtel said as he turned on his heel to lead Ashley into the restaurant. She had just barely had time to make it home, change into an outfit more becoming of the venue, and get here. Like a kid in a candy shop, she looked around, wide-eyed, at the beauty of the place. True to the theme, there was plenty of greenery and a waterfall in the small waiting area, just behind the podium, which led to a stream that wound its way through the dining room, lined with subtly sparkling gray rocks. Some kind of classical music was playing quietly overhead. A string quartet? She wasn't sure and didn't care. It simply added to the atmosphere, and she loved it.

Will rose from his seat as his wife approached, and then quickly pulled out her chair before the Maître d' could do it. With a smile and a nod, she sat and let her husband slide the seat closer to the table.

"Well, isn't this nice," Ashley said quietly, a smile lighting up her tastefully made-up face.

Will nodded gently. "Indeed. I take it you received my invitation."

"And the bouquet it was delivered in."

"Wonderful! I thought you might like that. How was your day, honey?"

"Oh, you know," she answered with a sigh. "Some paperwork, some patients…some flowers from a suitor…" Her smile grew mischievous as she giggled.

"Oh?" Will asked, returning the smile. "I hope this one is well-monied!"

Ashley laughed out loud. Then her expression became more serious. "Speaking of which. How did you make all this happen?"

"What do you mean?" Will responded, taking a sip of water from the large glass on the table in front of him.

"I mean, how can we—"

Ashely was interrupted by the waiter, a tall, lanky man in a gray suit, arriving and introducing himself. He asked about drinks; they each ordered one. Then he reviewed the day's specials, including the catch of the day (bay scallops) and the soup du jour (Boston clam chowder).

As the waiter left to allow the couple to consider their culinary options, Will spoke up quickly to make sure the subject was changed. "This place is amazing, isn't it? I feel like we're at some sort of resort, not in West Chester."

"I know!" Ashley replied enthusiastically. "The water, the greenery…the light in here is, shall we say, de*light*ful?"

Will chuckled. "Why Ashley, that was terrible. How about you let me handle the dad jokes this evening, okay?"

"Yes, okay," she said, flashing a devilish grin.

Once again, however, the grin promptly disappeared as Ashley continued. "But, Will, as I was saying. This isn't the sort of place we just casually wander into for a quick bite. This place is…really nice—"

"Only the best for—"

"—and I want to know," she pressed on, not allowing him to interrupt, "how we can afford it." There. She'd said it. Lifting her glass of water, she looked him in the eye.

Will sat back in his seat, looking down at his lap, hoping to buy himself some time. Maybe he'd figure out what to say.

Maybe that waiter would stop by and enter the conversation again.

A beat passed. No waiter.

"Will? Are you with me?" Ashley asked, leaning forward and gently waving her hand over the table toward him.

He forced a smile. "Yes, of course I'm here."

"Okay, so?"

He paused before speaking. "Let's just say we've come into a little bit of money. And my first thought was to spend it on you, alright? I'd think you'd be flattered."

She shook her head. "Of course, I'm flattered, Will. I just thought that you'd talk with me about something like this, some sudden windfall. We're supposed to be partners in this marriage." Her voice was gaining an edge. Then, she added quietly: "Not that it's felt that way lately."

Will held up a hand. "Woah, let's stop right there, okay? I worked hard for this money and—"

"How much are we talking about here, Will? A few hundred? A thousand?"

He didn't answer.

"More?" She asked, a bit surprised. "Two thousand?" She raised her eyebrows as she tilted her head.

He remained quiet. On the other side of the dining room, at the bar, Will saw a television mounted in one corner. The newscaster was standing, talking into a microphone, in front of the Pentagon. Not an uncommon sight these days.

"Five?"

He shook his head.

"Ten?"

He nodded.

"Ten thousand dollars? My goodness, Will! No wonder we're eating at a restaurant where the house salad costs..." she looked down at the leather-bound menu on the table in front of her, "nearly as much as a house payment!"

Will forced himself to smile but didn't speak.

"What did you *do*, Will? How did you suddenly come into ten thousand dollars?!"

He continued to keep his mouth closed, looking down at the napkin in his lap.

"I don't understand, honey," Ashley went on after a moment. "And I *want* to understand. We're in this together. Please. *Help* me understand what's been going on. Does this have something to do with why you were out so late last night?"

Will turned his head to the side, watching the other diners. The waiters. The busboys. Heck, anything that would avoid her questions—legitimate though he knew they were. The words on the bar's TV crawled across the bottom of the screen. Something about a new Russian technology that allows missiles to be launched from either submarines or from land-based vehicles. He let out a little chuckle. Those missiles couldn't do nearly as much damage to him as his wife could.

Suddenly Ashley's voice was lower and quieter. "Is it another woman? Oh, fuck, it's another woman, isn't it?"

He returned his eyes to hers and, for the first time since this round of interrogation began, leaned forward to speak. "There is absolutely *not* another woman, Ashley," he said as firmly as he could.

Her eyes grew wide. "Another man?"

He laughed. "No, honey. I don't work that way. You know that." He could see her breathe in what he hoped was relief. Maybe he could end this conversation faster than he expected? "Not that there's anything wrong with that," he added quickly, quoting her favorite old *Seinfeld* episode.

She smiled. It wasn't a laugh or even a giggle. She got the reference, the joke, but it wasn't enough.

"I'm not satisfied, Will." She said, looking him squarely in the eye. "Getting some money is nice. But not knowing where it came from or where you've been is, well, not. And you're clearly doing everything you can to avoid telling me. The worst part is, I don't even know why."

He could see the tears gathering in her eyes and reached out, placing his hand on her upper arm in the best comforting gesture he could muster.

"I'm not stupid, Will," she continued with a sniffle. "You know I'm not stupid. I know things haven't exactly been perfect between us lately, but I didn't think you were capable of keeping secrets like this. To the tune of ten thousand dollars."

"Minus the cost of your side salad," Will said, trying to lighten the mood.

"Don't," she responded angrily. "Don't do that. Don't try to weasel your way out of this conversation with a pithy little joke like you do with all the others. This ends here."

"Wait," Will said, protesting and removing his hand from her sleeve. "What are you saying, Ashley?"

"I'm saying you need to come clean. Whatever it is. Or you're sleeping on the couch tonight. Or wherever, I don't care, just not next to me. Not until I can trust you. It's time to be honest, for once." She crossed her arms across her chest as a tear ran down her right cheek. "What's going on here?"

It was like a battle—no, a war—going on in Will's head and heart. He so desperately wanted to tell her the truth. About Harris and Fisher. About the Russian song that wasn't entirely in Russian and wasn't just a song. About how amazing it felt to be doing something useful with his training, with his talent. About how much fun it had been. And how lucrative.

But he had Harris's voice ringing in his head: *This material may be so sensitive that agents of foreign governments would attempt to bribe, blackmail, kidnap, extort, or even kill to get it. Your friends and loved ones will be safer if they don't know anything about this. So do not speak of it to anyone. Not to your wife. Not your kids. Not your parents. Not even your goldfish.*

Ashley dabbed the corner of her eye with the white linen napkin from her lap. Then she neatly folded it and gently placed it on the table. Finally, with a sniffle, she rose from her seat and walked toward the exit.

13

Picked Up

Will sat there, staring at the bright white napkin Ashley had deposited on her empty plate minutes earlier. She had actually done it. She had walked out on him. He wasn't sure whether he was more surprised, shocked, or upset. What did this mean? For his marriage? His family? His life? He could feel a tickle in his throat warning him that tears were on their way; he suppressed them.

The couple at a nearby table, who looked about his age, had stopped staring into each other's eyes and talking, and were now looking his way, trying not to stare but clearly waiting to see what he would do. Glancing around, Will spotted the waiter across the room, watching him from the bar. He was drying some wine glasses with a dish towel in a poor attempt to appear busy. The string quartet took an ill-timed break, revealing the low din of diners' voices and the babbling of the waterway that wound through the dining room and past ogling patrons.

Now Will was growing angry. He wasn't putting on some

kind of show. His life wasn't a melodrama for others to enjoy. He could feel his hands forming into fists, his face becoming warm and flushed. Was he angry with these people or with his wife? Or himself?

Slowly, he relaxed his right hand and reached for his water glass. He hadn't realized how thirsty he'd become. Bringing the glass to his parched lips, he took a moment to collect himself and to try to ignore his audience. He swallowed a big gulp as he replaced the glass. Deep breath.

Finally, Will picked up the napkin from his lap and stood, pushing his chair with the back of his knees. Tossing the napkin onto the table, he turned toward the door and spotted the waiter walking toward him, trying to act casual.

"Sir?" the waiter called from a few feet away, a look of feigned confusion on his face. As if he didn't know what just transpired.

Will began walking and held up his left hand, palm toward the approaching waiter, fingers straight up. He shook his head. He was in no mood to talk.

The air outside had cooled off a bit since they'd arrived at the Tavern. It was somehow fresher, almost happier—as if adding insult to injury, causing Will to feel even more alone, sadder. A group of thirty-somethings standing on the sidewalk nearby burst into laughter. He knew they weren't laughing at him, but it sure felt that way. He took the evening's pleasant atmosphere as a personal affront.

With a shiver not entirely justified by the ambient temperature, Will grabbed the lapel of his blazer and yanked it up around his neck. Then he walked. He wasn't sure which direction he should go; it didn't really matter. He just wanted to disappear into the dusk and get away from this place, these people.

Maybe he could spend the night in his campus office. He'd considered it on other occasions—there was a rather old and slightly smelly couch he could sleep on—but had always rejected the idea. Too professorially cliche.

By the time he reached the next block, Will was instead thinking about a hotel room for the night. There were several mid-range offerings not far from the restaurant. And it's not like Ashley would cancel his credit card so fast, right? He hoped not.

A light, misty rain had begun to fall by the time Will had walked three blocks from the Tavern. Ignoring the precipitation, he could feel his mood sinking toward depression. It was becoming too much effort to even think about what had happened with Ashley.

Maybe he'd call Roger, himself a divorcé, to see what he thought of the situation? Nah. Best not to mix work and personal matters. Perhaps he should call his father? He shook his head at the thought. Definitely not. For all his wonderful traits, his father had never been the shoulder-to-cry-on type.

The rain grew harder.

At the end of the fourth block was a stoplight, which was, of course, red. As he waited for his turn to cross the busy intersection, a large black SUV slowly pulled over, just shy of the corner and right next to Will. If it had been driving any faster, it would have splashed rainwater from the gutter into his face. The front passenger window slowly rolled down.

"Want a lift?"

The voice was oddly familiar, and it took Will a moment to place it. The speaker was inside the vehicle, hidden by the shadow of a nearby streetlamp. Then he heard it again.

"Professor? Would you get into the car please?" the voice asked, using a tone that suggested it wasn't really a question. More like an order.

Fisher.

"Is that you?" Will asked, shouting through the now-pounding rain and squinting his eyes as water flowed down the lenses of his glasses and dripped off to join the river quickly forming at his feet.

"Yes, Dr. Driver, it's Agent Fisher. Let's get you out of the rain and into the car. Something's come up. We have to get to a meeting."

With a small sense of relief, Will reached for the handle of the nearby rear door, yanked it open, hoisted himself up into the vehicle, and slid onto the seat. He pulled the door closed behind him just as the light turned green. Harris quickly drove away from the curb and into the evening's traffic.

Harris lifted his head to glance at Will through the rear-view mirror. "Some night for an evening stroll, huh Professor?"

Will looked out the rain-streaked window. The tinting made the night seem even darker. "Not really by choice," he replied through girded teeth. Then he shivered.

"Mmm," Harris responded. "There should be a few towels in the trunk behind you, maybe another jacket or something you can put on." In the mirror, he could see Will turn around and reach into the vehicle's large trunk. Returning his eyes to the road, he turned and followed a ramp onto the highway, heading south. "You have a little time to clean up before the meeting."

"Thanks," Will said, rubbing the towel over his head. He suddenly froze, a question forming on his lips. "Hang on. How did you know where to find me?"

"We have our ways," Harris replied with a slight smile.

Will nodded slowly. "I guess I should have figured." He finished drying his hair and wiped his glasses on his tie. Then he wriggled out of his soaked blazer and slipped his arms into a windbreaker he'd found in the trunk. "Where are you two headed for your meeting, anyway?"

Fisher turned his head to answer. "Not *our* meeting," he said, looking backward between the two front seats. "*Your* meeting."

A moment passed. Fisher turned to face forward again. Only the roar of the eight-cylinder engine and the tinkling of the rain, which was beginning to slow, could be heard.

"I'm afraid I don't understand," Will said, genuinely confused.

"The ONI was very impressed with your work the other night," Fisher said. "And while we'd like nothing more than to file away the results so some future analyst can reference them while working some other case, that's no longer possible."

"What do you mean, 'no longer possible'?" Will asked, noticing through his window a green exit sign with white lettering: *Philadelphia International Airport, 1 Mile. Cargo Terminal, Stay Left*.

Harris cleared his throat. "Circumstances have changed, Dr. Driver. The information you were able to provide was helpful but left many questions unanswered. Meanwhile, one of our assets has intercepted another, um, song. Based on our incomplete knowledge of the code, we can tell something is happening, but we can't determine exactly what. We need more context. That's where you come in." Harris let this information sink in before adding, "Again."

Will thought for a moment, then asked. "So, where are we going? The airport?" The rain just about stopped.

"We need to get you on a helicopter, Dr. Driver," Fisher said with a hint of urgency.

"A helicopter?!" Will's eyes widened and he grabbed an overhead handle as the SUV took the exit at high speed. The airport's cargo terminal loomed in the windshield with a large commercial cargo plane standing in front. "Why? Where's the meeting?"

Harris steered the vehicle onto the concrete apron and stopped in an empty area near a hangar. A helicopter sat in the center of a large circle painted on the tarmac. Its large rotors were already spinning. Loudly.

"Fisher! Harris!" Will yelled as the three of them opened their doors and stepped out of the SUV. "Where the hell is this meeting?!"

Harris turned and looked Will in the eye as he shouted his answer: "The Pentagon."

Part Three

Wider Scope

14

THE PENTAGON

THE FLIGHT FROM Philadelphia to the Pentagon was surprisingly brief, as happens when you dispense with all the security lines, boarding procedures, and safety speeches. Instead, the helicopter lifted off just as Will secured his harness and put on the headset the copilot handed to him. As they were flying at night, Will could see the city's lights splayed out below and was able to follow their progress as they passed by Wilmington, Baltimore, and Washington D.C. on their way to Arlington, Virginia.

Just north of the massive five-sided building and wedged next to the junction between state route 27 and Richmond Highway, the chopper landed at the Pentagon helipad. It took only a moment from touchdown until Agent Harris swung the door open, revealing two uniformed personnel standing outside the safety line painted on the concrete. The rotor blades were beginning to slow, and the whine of the helicopter's engine was dropping in pitch and volume as Will stepped out onto solid ground.

Harris followed closely, stepping up to Will's right side and gesturing toward the welcoming party. "This way, Dr. Driver," he said loudly.

Will nodded and walked toward the waiting figures. As he drew closer, he could see one man and one woman, both in smart, blue uniforms with American flag patches on their shoulders, a few colorful pins on their breasts, and name tags reading "Anderson" and "Donovan."

"Professor Driver," the woman reached out to shake his hand, "welcome to the Pentagon. I'm Lieutenant Anderson, Admiral Carter's staff secretary."

Will took her hand. "Thanks. Now, what's so important that you had to—"

"If you'll follow us, please," the man wearing the "Donovan" name tag said forcefully.

"Okay," Will agreed with a nod.

Anderson and Donovan spun around and began moving briskly toward the large building at the end of a long walkway. Will followed, and Harris and Fisher fell in behind him. Behind them, the chopper's engine grew louder as it prepared to depart. The breeze from the rotors became stronger, pushing at Will's back as if encouraging him to keep up.

When they reached the door, Donovan pulled a plastic card from inside his uniform blazer and waved it in front of a sensor. With a click (audible now that the helicopter had flown away), the door unlocked and Donovan swung it open, revealing a wide corridor extending right and left. It was brightly lit, which seemed to Will to be comically incongruent with the fact that it was the middle of the night. Several people walked purposefully past the open door without even looking through it. Just another day (or night) at the Pentagon, he supposed.

Anderson led the way inside, turning left, and Will and the rest of the entourage followed. She stared straight ahead, but he looked around, taking it all in. Along the right side of the hallway, he saw gray metal doors with multi-digit numbers and cryptic acronyms painted on them. ONPIP. SPP-NC. USAFPO. They seemed to walk for several minutes. Will didn't know exactly how long; he was tired enough that his body was beginning to have trouble keeping track of details like that.

Then Anderson turned right and led them into an open area, a junction between the corridor they had come from (which followed one of the outer rings of the Pentagon complex) and a perpendicular one that led toward the inner rings. At the intersection was a bank of elevators, and she pressed a button to call for one. It didn't take long before the doors slid open and the party stepped in.

Will continued to look around. He was disappointed: the elevator wasn't all that different from one he could ride in any campus building. The only difference was that posters of smiling students advertising campus housing or various degree programs were replaced with images of alternatively smiling and serious service members posing with various pieces of equipment. A tank, a plane, on the deck of some kind of ship.

The elevator jerked as it began rising two, three, and finally four levels before stopping with a similar jolt. Will caught Fisher giving Harris a look, which he imagined to be the equivalent of *they still haven't fixed that?* With a smirk, he stepped out of the elevator into the hallway, which he immediately noticed was much nicer than the one several floors below. It was carpeted and there were tasteful sconces along the walls. As Anderson turned right, toward the inner rings, and eventually turned left, Will also noticed that the doors to various offices and suites were darkly stained wood rather than utilitarian gray metal.

After a few moments, Anderson stopped in front of one of the wooden doors. This one bore the sign: *Admiral J. Carter*

III, Director, Office of Naval Intelligence. Once again, Donovan produced a security card, unlocked the door, and held it open. Anderson led them through the outer office and toward a set of grand, double doors that led to the Admiral's inner office. She pushed them open and announced, "Professor Will Driver and agents Fisher and Harris, sir."

Will stepped into the nicely appointed inner sanctum. There, in front of a large window that overlooked the courtyard at the center of the Pentagon complex, stood a large mahogany desk. Opposite the desk were three chairs. On the other side of the room was a matching mahogany conference table with seating for eight, plus a couch and three tall, wingback chairs with accompanying coffee table. One of the walls was lined with bookcases full of tomes and the occasional framed photo. The other featured large oil paintings of centuries-old sailing ships. The last wall, at the far end of the conference table, had a console table topped with an array of glasses. Above it was an oversized display screen, which was currently showing a map of the world.

A white-haired, be-speckled, and slightly portly man rose from his chair behind the desk. His uniform blazer was unbuttoned, but the three stars on his shoulders were clearly visible. He rounded the side of the desk and walked up to Will, who had stopped only a few feet from the doorway to take in the room.

"Professor Driver, I'm Admiral Jack Carter, Office of Naval Intelligence." He shook Will's hand with surprising strength, drawing the professor's gaze back from the art on the wall. "Thank you for coming in on such short notice."

Will returned the handshake and smiled. "Not that I had much of a choice, Admiral. I'm sorry if this thing—whatever it is—got you out of bed in the middle of the night."

Carter let go of Will's hand and, with a gentle wave, responded, "Bah, I practically live in this office anyway. Come, sit." He gestured to the couch.

"Thank you, sir," Will said, carefully setting himself down at one end of the sofa. It was plush and soft, and he was so tired he worried he'd fall asleep right then and there. That would probably be a violation of a bunch of military rules, he figured.

SITTING IN THE crew's mess, Alex Burke stared at the three-ring binder lying open on the table in front of him. He knew it contained the detailed procedures for testing various fluids around the boat. One section covered potable water, another the liquid used to cool the sub's nuclear reactor. Both had to be checked multiple times a day.

Burke knew there would be a lot to learn when he joined the submarine service. In fact, he figured out pretty early on that a lot of his early advancement through the enlisted ranks depended on taking and passing various exams covering all sorts of things on the boat. He also figured out pretty early on that those exams were going to pose a challenge for him.

Fortunately, he had befriended one of the petty officers on board, Frank Woodley. They were both in the engineering division, and both came from humble backgrounds. Woodley took him under his wing, and after a few weeks aboard the Royal Oak, the chief engineer made it official: Woodley would be his mentor, helping him prepare for his first set of qualifying exams.

Woodley had a good sense of humor, which Burke appreciated right away. But Woodley wasn't trained as a teacher, a hurdle they could have overcome if it weren't for Burke's learning disability. That was something Woodley just didn't know how to handle. He didn't give up on the new seaman, though.

"Potable water or nuclear coolant?" Woodley asked as he

approached Burke with two mugs in hand.

"How do I know which is which?" Burke responded, looking from one mug to the other. "They look the same to me."

"Well, you don't want to mix them up, Seaman Burke, no matter how similar they might look!" Woodley put the two mugs down on the table and sat opposite Burke. "Fortunately for you, these two are just coffee."

"Right," Burke said with a nervous laugh.

"But seriously, don't try to take a shower in reactor coolant, and don't try to cool a reactor with drinking water," Woodley said with a smile.

"Right," Burke said again. "Now, let me know if I've got this down good. The chlorine tests are used to figure out if we need to treat the reactor coolant, and the radium tests are used…" His voice trailed off when he noticed Woodley shaking his head.

Burke sighed with frustration. "Why do I need to know all this stuff, huh? We've got the most advanced technology in the navy on these boats. They can practically run themselves!"

"That's true," Woodley replied. "But these boats are also warships. And in war, things go wrong. Stuff breaks. Maybe because it's overused or used beyond the way it's designed. Or maybe because it's damaged in battle. And when stuff breaks on a submarine, we need to be able to fix it ourselves. And we need to be able to run the boat ourselves until we can get the thing fixed. Not only that, but we *all* need to be able to do each other's jobs, even if only on a basic level, just in case the person whose job it is is, well…"

"Hurt," Burke said, nodding. "Or worse."

"Yeah. All our lives may depend on it. We have to work together, and we need to have confidence that every man on the boat has at least some familiarity with every system aboard."

"Huh," Burke said. "I guess I never thought about it that way before."

"Well, welcome aboard, Seaman Burke," Woodley said with a hint of sarcasm. "After we're done with this test, we get to move on to air handling and carbon dioxide scrubbing technologies before tackling electrical distribution systems. So get your nose back in that book."

CARTER'S TWO AIDES slipped out of the room; Anderson gently closed the door on her way out. Harris and Fisher sat on two of the wingbacks. Carter sat in the third.

"I'm sorry we had to nab you after your dinner," Carter started.

"Actually, sir—" Will began.

But the admiral kept talking. He wasn't used to being interrupted. "I'm afraid we had to do it. It's this thing with the Russian music. I believe Harris and Fisher, here, have already shared one of the recordings with you?"

"Yes," Will replied.

Carter looked to Fisher. "Which one?"

"Disco three, sir," Fisher replied quickly. "The last one picked up by the Royal Oak on her previous deployment."

Will smiled at the label—Disco? None of them seemed to even snicker at the word. Had these people no sense of humor? Or knowledge of music history?

"What about Discos four and five?" Carter asked.

Harris leaned forward to answer. "Poseidon Six-Two just sent those in a few hours ago. It'll be a few more while crypto conducts their analysis. Then we can take a crack at them."

"Ah," Carter nodded. Then he turned back to Will. "As I'm sure you can tell, we've got more music for you. Our cryptography team has been able to use some of the information you provided, especially the numbers you found."

"The tone rows," Will said. He couldn't help it, he was a teacher at heart. Carter didn't seem to notice, or he ignored the correction. Will supposed that a man didn't earn three stars on his shoulders by dwelling on the little things.

"As best we've been able to tell, they are references to locations on a map, using a geolocation system tethered to the recent GLONASS upgrade." Carter stopped, observing the confused expression on Will's face.

"It's the Russian equivalent of our Global Positioning System, which most people know simply as 'GPS.' Essentially, the Russian Navy is using these songs to send instructions to their ships. The songs include this location information, the place in the ocean where they will execute their orders."

Will raised his hand slowly, as if he were a student in the admiral's seminar—an irony that was not lost on him—and looked around at Harris and Fisher, the other "students" present in the class.

It was the first time Carter seemed even a little thrown off his track. "Uh, yes, Dr. Driver?"

"Thanks, um, sir," Will sputtered. "One quick question: how do we know what their orders are?"

"*That*," Carter replied, pointing a finger at Will, "is what we need you to help us find out. According to crypto, they're using some other language—"

"Ket. It's called Ket, sir," Will offered.

"—this…Ket…to send the operational commands. You kindly provided translations of the Ket text, but they appear to be, well, metaphorical in nature. And my officers in crypto tell me that that's not the sort of thing they can decode without considerable knowledge of the culture the text comes from."

For a moment it was silent. Will realized that all three

naval officers were looking directly at him. "And...I take it you want me to provide that context, given my familiarity with the Ket people."

Carter nodded. "Yes, your familiarity and," he rose from the chair and walked over to his desk, where he picked up a large book. It was bound as if it came from a university library. As if it were, Will realized, a dissertation. "And your experience." Carter turned the book around to show Will the cover: *Music, Politics, and Resistance Among the Ket of the Central Krasnoyarsk Siberian Lowlands*, by William Driver.

"Ah," Will said, smiling a little as he recognized the title. "So, you're the other person in the world who read that, aside from my mother." It quickly became clear that Carter didn't get the joke. Or didn't care for jokes at all.

"There's one more complication," Carter pressed on. "We've determined, based on the work of our aircraft, Poseidon Six-Two, that the Russians are using a narrow-beam transmission to send these new signals."

"What does that mean?" Will asked.

As Carter returned to his chair, Harris leaned forward to answer. "It means, Professor, that there's basically a straight line from wherever the message is being sent from to the recipient. The only way you get to hear the message is if you're somewhere on that line."

Will shook his head, furrowing his brow as he listened to Harris's explanation. "But the admiral just said an *aircraft* determined this narrow thing. If the messages are being sent to ships on the surface of the ocean, how did an airplane intercept it?"

"Luck, Dr. Driver," the admiral answered. "Poseidon Six-Two was beyond the intended recipient, a Russian frigate, flying unusually low to try to avoid the frigate's radar. That put it at the right altitude to catch the signal. And they just happened to be in the right position, relative to the transmission's source, to pick it up as it passed the frigate."

Fisher shrugged his shoulders. "Sometimes, in this business, we get lucky."

"I'll say..." Will responded. "But if you have to be somewhere along this transmission's straight-line path in order to hear it, how are we going to pick up more transmissions? I mean, the chances of me figuring out what these metaphorical Ket lyrics mean will go way up if I have more data, more songs."

"Poseidon Six-Two just happened to be in the right place at the right time," Carter said, "and she was lucky enough to copy Disco Five and Disco Six. But she also gave us enough information to figure out another piece of the puzzle: the location of the transmitter. It's a newly constructed radio tower just outside of Tsypnavolok, a town on a peninsula at the northern tip of the Murmansk Oblast. It's in the Arctic Circle, a short distance from the Russian Navy's base at Polyarnyy, and, from its position there at Tsypnavolok, it can aim its broadcast in a wide arc covering most of the Barents Sea.

"That may seem like a limited range to you, but we suspect this transmitter is simply the first one we've found. There could be many more all around the Russian shoreline —or the shores of their allies. So, we need to crack this code before this potential communication system becomes fully operational. And cracking the code means hearing the code.

"You see, Dr. Driver, if we know the location of the transmitter, and we know the location of the recipient—a Russian warship—then we have a good idea of where you will need to be in order to intercept these coded songs."

"Forgive me, admiral," Will said. "But where exactly do you need me to be?"

Carter looked to Harris, who answered. "The Barents Sea, off the coast of Murmansk Oblast."

Will swallowed hard. "And...how do you intend to get me there? I assume that, unlike my dissertation fieldwork, we can't just ask the Russian government for permission to be there. How can you get me there without the Russians knowing about it?"

Carter shifted his gaze to Fisher, who answered this time. "Professor Driver, you'll be stationed on the USS Royal Oak."

Will's brow furrowed further. "Don't you think the Russians will notice an American warship lurking off the coast of one of their naval bases?"

"Not *this* warship," Carter replied.

15

THE MISSION

"MOM? WHERE'S DAD?" Jake Driver asked his mother as she entered the house from the garage. It was about eight o'clock, and though it was getting close to his bedtime, he technically didn't need to be in bed for another half hour. And he knew that.

Ashley sighed as she dropped her car keys into a little wicker basket near the door, slipped out of her coat, and stepped out of her shoes. She looked through the kitchen to her son, who was sitting on the couch in the family room just beyond.

"I'm not entirely sure, buddy," she said. "We...we went different ways after our dinner ended."

Marz came down the stairs, stopping on the bottom step and leaning around the banister. "Kind of a short dinner, Mom. Wasn't your reservation only, like, an hour ago?"

"Nothing gets past you two," Ashley said as she opened a kitchen cabinet and removed a wine glass from one of the shelves. Tonight's events certainly called for it.

Not satisfied with her mother's response, Marz pressed. "I take it Tavern by the Brook didn't live up to your expectations?"

"The restaurant was lovely, and I'm sure the food is fine," Ashley replied, trying to be cagey but honest with her children.

"Mom." Marz wasn't asking again.

"We didn't..." Ashley began, searching for the right words. Sure, her daughter was thirteen years old and could probably handle it if she told her the truth. But thirteen-year-old girls were also notoriously emotional, as Ashley well knew from her patients at the clinic, and she was hesitant to add fuel to a hormonal fire.

"Fine," Marz said. She wasn't patient enough to wait for her mother to find the right words. "I get it."

"Don't make assumptions, Margaret," Ashley said, looking through the wine glass as she took a sip of merlot.

"It's not like you leave me a lot of choice, Mom," Marz retorted. "All you're willing to say is that the restaurant was nice. You didn't eat the food. You didn't stay long. And you didn't come home with Dad. What do you think I'm going to assume?"

"Margaret," Ashley said, growing frustrated and tired.

"It's no secret you two aren't getting along," Marz said, pushing harder.

Jake walked into the kitchen. "Is Dad going to be here later?"

Marz looked down at her younger brother. "Who knows? It's a friggin' state secret." She looked up at her mother, sending daggers with her eyes.

Ashley exhaled slowly, looking as softly as she could at her ten-year-old son. "I'm not sure, buddy. I don't know what his plans are."

"Okay, but will he bring me to my soccer game tomorrow?"

Ashley moved her eyes from Jake up to Marz, who met her gaze and held it. Marz could see a single tear dripping down her mother's cheek.

"A SUBMARINE," WILL said, hoping he'd heard the word wrong.

"Yes," Admiral Carter said. "A Virginia-class nuclear attack submarine, although she's been modified for intelligence gathering and has modular space that can be adapted to suit your needs."

"You want to put me on a submarine?" Will asked. "You want to put me *inside* a submarine? Underwater?" The pitch of his voice rose with each question.

"Yes," Carter said again. "It's the only way to accomplish this mission given the constraints."

Will was flabbergasted. "But…how…what about my family?"

"They cannot know about this," Harris warned. "It could compromise the mission—"

"And put their own safety at risk," Fisher added.

With a gulp, Will looked from Fisher to Harris and back to Carter. "What *can* I tell them?"

"Tell them you…have to attend a professional meeting or something of that nature," Carter suggested.

Will knew that, with the level of trust in their marriage already low, it was extremely unlikely Ashley would believe that story. Or *any* story.

"And what about my job?" Will asked. "What are you going to tell the University?"

"Leave that to us," Carter said.

"In the morning," Harris added, "we'll reach out to your supervisor, one…" he looked to Fisher.

"Professor Jacqueline Fletcher," Fisher offered.

"Yes, Professor Fletcher. We will offer to cover the costs associated with your absence." Will watched as Harris started the smile. "Plus, a nice donation to your department's research fund."

With the smallest of chuckles, Will nodded. "I can't imagine Jackie saying no to that…"

"Good," Carter announced, clearly wishing to bring the meeting to an end. He looked to his officers. "Harris. Fisher. You will return to the Philadelphia field office in the morning. Good work."

"Thank you, sir," the two agents said at the same time.

Carter turned back to Will. "And you, Dr. Driver, will find that my aides on the other side of that door will take you somewhere where you can get yourself a clean set of clothes before your flight."

"Okay," Will replied. Then his exhausted brain caught up. "Um, flight?"

"You don't think we can drive a nuclear submarine right up the Potomac River to come pick you up, do you?" Carter chuckled as he got back up from his chair. "You've got a flight out of Andrews departing in about an hour. Better hop to."

FISHER AND HARRIS snapped quick salutes to Admiral Carter and shuffled out of the office. Will thought he saw Harris wink at him on his way out, but it was so quick, he wasn't sure. Will looked to Carter to see if he'd noticed, but the admiral had his back turned as he slowly ambled toward his desk. Through the window beyond, he could see a dark sky but, given the amount of light pollution coming from the Pentagon and D.C., just across the river, no stars could be seen.

Looking back toward the door, Will could see Donovan

standing there, waiting for him. He nodded to the lieutenant and followed him through the outer office. Donovan turned left before reaching the outer door, leading Will down a carpeted hallway with portraits adorning the walls. They all looked similar: older, white men wearing navy uniforms, two or three stars on their shoulders, and with rather serious expressions on their faces.

Donovan stopped at another wooden door and, with a wave of his keycard, opened it and held it for Will. "I think you'll find everything you need here, sir," the officer said. "I'll be back to collect you in about twenty minutes."

Will peered around the corner and slowly entered. The room wasn't large, but it sported a small daybed, a desk, a dresser, and another doorway to an en suite bathroom. The whole setup reminded Will of his dorm room in college. On the daybed, someone had laid out a navy uniform, although without any indications of rank and no colorful or fancy pins. It looked to be pretty close to Will's size.

"I guess this will help me fit in?" Will asked aloud and turned to look over his shoulder at Donovan. But the lieutenant had already left and shut the door behind him, leaving Will alone.

With a sigh, Will entered the bathroom and splashed some cold water on his face. He wished he could take a quick shower, but he didn't think he could do it in twenty minutes. A clean face, some water through his hair, and a change of clothes would have to be enough.

Twenty minutes went by quickly, and soon there was a knock on the door. Will had just finished getting dressed and was sitting on the daybed, closing his eyes and enjoying a moment of quiet. He knew it wasn't going to last long.

Donovan led him out of the office and through the labyrinthine corridors of the Pentagon until they arrived at an underground parking area. There, Donovan unlocked a black Chevy SUV and the two of them got in. "This will take us about thirty minutes," the lieutenant said as they buckled their seatbelts.

Soon they were crossing the Potomac on the Arland D. Williams Memorial Bridge. The roads were mostly empty. Will glanced at the clock on the dash: 2:35 AM. No wonder. Just looking at the time reminded him of how tired he was, and the next thing he knew, they were arriving at Andrews Air Force Base. Donovan drove right onto the tarmac, where a small passenger jet stood waiting.

Before Will could open the door, Donovan turned to him, a serious look on his face. "I'm going to remind you, Dr. Driver, that you're going to embark on a mission on behalf of the United States Navy and will have access to some highly classified information and equipment. The nondisclosure agreement you signed in Philadelphia still applies, as do the warnings about keeping quiet for the sake of your safety—and the safety of your loved ones. Do you understand?"

"I understand," Will responded. Then, steeling himself for the next leg of his adventure, he opened the door.

Lieutenant Anderson was standing at the bottom of the staircase that extended down from the plane's door. "Dr. Driver," she called, gesturing toward the steps with a smile. "This way, sir!"

Inside, the passenger cabin had only ten seats, some of which were facing each other across a table. In one corner was a couch. Aside from Anderson, who had followed him up the stairs, and the two men in the cockpit, Will was the only passenger on board.

"Sit anywhere you like," Anderson said gently.

"Oh," Will said. "I see. I'm not used to this sort of treatment. Usually, when I fly, I'm crammed like a sardine in the last row, next to the bathroom. What luxury!" He smiled at the lieutenant. She was in the same uniform as when he first arrived at the Pentagon an hour or two earlier, but now he could focus on her, with her beautiful, girl-next-door sort of look. It was complemented by her light brown hair, which was pulled back in a tight bun, although a few strands had escaped and now framed her face. He guessed she was in her late twenties—he'd never been very good at estimating things like that. He quickly looked around the cabin again, hoping she hadn't noticed him staring.

She smiled broadly as she spoke. "Compliments of the United States Navy."

He found a row nearby and slid across, so he was in the window seat. It was decidedly wider than the typical cattle car he was used to flying in. And certainly more plush. Through the window, he could see one or two other aircraft taxiing to or from the runway, and a few personnel moving around his plane.

Anderson found a seat somewhere behind him.

"Professor Driver, Lieutenant Anderson, this is Captain Marks up in the cockpit." Will could hear the man's voice through the small speaker above his seat. He looked up to it instinctually, as if he could see the pilot. "We should be wheels up in approximately five minutes and we'll get you up to Connecticut as quick as we can. Not too much commercial traffic this time of night, and the weather looks clear, so I'm not expecting any surprises. Although, I suppose, one never does."

Will smiled. It was just the kind of joke he would make. Marks continued. "Anderson, if you don't mind, please stow the aircraft door. Then we'll be on our way."

Will watched Anderson's form as she walked past his row, toward the front of the cabin. Then he felt a pang of guilt as he realized his eyes were focused on her backside.

What was he thinking? Not just about the direction of his gaze, but about this whole venture. It certainly would not earn him any credit from Ashley, what with his total disappearance and lack of communication. Not that it would make any sense to call her at three o'clock in the morning, anyway. But more fundamentally, what did his willingness to accept this mission say about his commitment to his wife?

He could feel the tears welling up in his eyes, so he turned to once again look out the window into the darkness of the airfield. He was doing something he knew *he* would enjoy. It would make him feel useful. It would be an opportunity to serve his country using his unique skills. He could be proud of himself for the first time in years. But at what cost?

As the small jet rolled down the runway, picking up speed, Will squeezed his eyes shut, wringing out the tears. Keeping his eyelids closed, he relaxed the muscles in his face and leaned to the side, resting his head on the bulkhead next to the aircraft's window. He was asleep before the plane left the ground.

16

GROTON

SKIRMISHES IN SCANDINAVIA AS TENSIONS REMAIN HIGH

By Gregory Bowers, New York Star-Gazette

Allied and Russian troops exchanged gunfire for about thirty minutes yesterday in the second such incident in two weeks. The fighting broke out near the Vaalimaa crossing, on the border between Finland and the Vyborgsky District in Leningrad Oblast, Russia. Both the Finnish and Russian governments say the exchange was brief, and each blames the other for the provocation.

The Vaalimaa crossing, one of several linking Finland and western Russia, is guarded by several platoons of British and Finnish soldiers. They have been on high alert since the skirmish last week at Imatran-Rajatarkastusasema, about sixty miles northeast and just across the border from the Russian city of Svetogorsk.

A spokesperson for the Finnish Border Guard told reporters in Helsinki that three soldiers were injured, two Finns and one British. All three were evacuated to Helsinki for treatment and are expected to make a full recovery. The Russian Army declined a request for comment but issued a written statement praising its soldiers for their "bravery in the face of Western aggression."

Analysts are not convinced the British and Finnish troops are to blame. "It's not a major military installation," Alvi Riikonen, a Finnish fellow at the London-based Brinkman Institute. "Vaalimaa certainly has more guards than before this conflict, but they are in a defensive, not offensive, position."

A Pentagon official, speaking on the condition of anonymity, told a reporter, "They're testing us, you see. The Russians are probing our defenses, trying to see where we're weakest. I'm glad the Finnish Border Guard and the British Army held them back. We can't show weakness at a time like this."

Others are less enthusiastic in their assessments of the battle. "It's good that it was brief," Ronald Jamison, an analyst with the Global Peace Initiative said. "Our hope, of course, is that this entire situation can be resolved through diplomatic means and that tensions all over the world can ease. At the same time, our fear is that one of these isolated incidents will get out of hand, lives will be lost, and one or both sides will feel as though they have no choice but to retaliate and escalate the conflict."

"DR. DRIVER," LIEUTENANT Anderson's voice cooed quietly as she leaned over Will, her hand gently shaking his shoulder.

"Dr. Driver, we've arrived. It's time to go now."

Will opened his eyes, slowly coming out of a deep sleep. As the image of Anderson's face came into focus, he smiled. "Hi..."

"Good morning, Dr. Driver," Anderson said with a quiet chuckle. Did she just blush? "I'm sorry to wake you, but we've landed at Groton-New London Airport. The car is waiting to take you to the naval base."

Will sat up straighter and looked out the window. He could just see the first rays of dawn peeking over the horizon, which was filled with the dark blue-gray color of the North Atlantic. He had to admit, it was a beautiful sight. The only other time he'd been to the Constitution State was for an ethnomusicology conference at one of its fancy liberal arts colleges somewhere in the middle of the state, nestled among tall, green trees. This ocean view was much nicer.

But he wasn't here to sightsee. With a deep breath, he stood and followed Anderson out of the small plane, descending the tiny staircase to the tarmac, where a gray Ford SUV sat waiting. Anderson stood at the foot of the stairs as he came down.

"This is where I leave you, Professor," Anderson said with a sad smile and an outstretched hand.

Will took it and smiled back. "Thanks, Lieutenant. Hopefully, our paths will cross again."

She nodded quickly, still smiling, and then turned and walked back up the steps.

With a sigh, Will turned the other way and walked toward his next ride.

"So, you're our new passenger," Randy West said as he alternated between looking at Will, standing on the pier in front of him, and looking down at his clipboard. The trip from the airport took all of fifteen minutes, plus another five getting through the base's gatehouse, which was the only time they hit any traffic.

There was a slight breeze here on the water. The sun was part way through its morning ascent, casting long shadows with its golden rays. Some of those rays illuminated the long, black hull of the USS Royal Oak, which was moored at the pier behind West. It sat rather low in the water, with its deck only a few feet above the surface. Its sail, on the other hand, rose from the hull about two stories. Two men were visible, at least from the torso up, in the top of the sail. One held binoculars and was scanning the horizon. The other looked down at the pier, watching West and the new arrival.

If he hadn't been told it was the Royal Oak, Will would have known by the banner hanging from the side of the brow, the narrow gangplank connecting the pier to the deck of the boat. A sailor stood on the pier side, just in front of the brow, to control who went across. At the moment, there were four or five sailors carefully walking from pier to deck, each carrying a wooden crate of what looked like fruits and vegetables.

"Uh, yes," Will said, moving his gaze from the sailors carrying provisions to the one standing in front of him. "William Driver, ethnomusicologist, University of Philadelphia. Reporting for duty." He brought up his right hand in a salute.

West didn't move. "Don't do that, Mr. Driver. They may have put you in a uniform, but you're not navy."

Will dropped his hand quickly. "Ah, yes, I see—"

"Well, your paperwork checks out," West said, looking one last time at his clipboard and then finally back to Will. "Kind of strange, having a civilian on board. But if that's what the brass says needs to happen, we make it happen." He looked Will up and down and then scanned the area around his feet. "No bags? No gear?"

"No, sir," Will replied quietly. "There wasn't really time to
—"

"I'm the Chief of the Boat, Mr. Driver. Enlisted. Not an
officer. No need to 'sir' me," West said matter-of-factly.
"Alright, if you don't have any luggage, you can follow me
aboard." He turned on his heel and started for the brow, still
talking. His gruff attitude and curt demeanor were starting
to annoy Will, who, lacking a good night's sleep, didn't have
a lot of patience.

The COB continued. "Some equipment was delivered last
night for you. Our engineers connected it all to the boat's
network this morning. Pretty straightforward job."

Will shuffled along quickly, trying to keep up with the
COB as he walked across to the deck. "Thanks, I guess. And,
by the way, I'm a doctor."

For a moment, West gave no indication that he'd heard
Will's correction. But then he stopped, halfway across the
brow, and looked back down at his clipboard. "It says here
you're some kind of music professor?"

"Yes, that's right," Will responded.

"And you're also a doctor? Like, you heal people with
music?" West contorted his face with confusion.

"Well, that would be music *therapy*, but that's not what I
do."

"Then what kind of doctor *are* you?"

"A doctor of philosophy, Mr. West." The COB stared right
at him. "A Ph.D."

"Oh," West said. Then, with a shrug, he added, "Good for
you, *doctor*. Let's get you below. We'll be getting underway
soon."

And with that, he turned back toward the submarine,
leading Will across the other half of the brow and onto the
deck. Will hadn't realized that there was a door in the sail,
the part of the boat that extended up from the long
cylindrical hull. That way, one could enter from the deck

rather than having to climb up the outside of the sub, hop into the bridge at the top of the sail, and then climb down inside. West led him through the door, which he later learned was called a "hatch." It opened to a small landing inside the sail, from which a ladder went up (to the bridge) and down (to the sub's interior). West began climbing down.

The ladder ended in an alcove just aft of the sub's control room. On the bulkhead was a matte brass sign that read *USS Royal Oak, SSN 812*. Will followed West slowly out of the alcove and into the control room proper. It was not large by any stretch of the imagination. In fact, Will was impressed the Navy managed to fit the number of men and the amount of equipment they did into the space. Along each side were stations with consoles, buttons, lights, and screens. So many screens. It was nothing like the last submarine movie he'd seen.

In fact, where Will had expected to see a giant cylindrical tube in the center of the control room, which he had expected to house the ship's periscope, was merely an empty space. Well, not quite empty. There was a table there, which Will suspected was for charts and navigation. As he peered at it from the back of the room, he realized that the entire top of the table was actually another screen. Beneath the screen, on the side of the table, were the letters *ECDIS*. He'd have to ask about that later. As his eyes scanned the room, they landed on the forward bulkhead, on which was mounted the largest screen of all. At the moment, it appeared to show a view looking forward from the top of the sub.

"Not what you expected, doctor?" West asked with a smile.

Will nodded slowly. "Impressive. But not what I thought it'd be like. Not quite like the movies."

West laughed aloud. "No, sir, it's not at all like the movies. It's better."

Will smiled, feeling for the first time like West might

actually like him.

West gestured toward the back of the sub, toward an opening in the bulkhead that led to a narrow passageway. "We'd better let the XO know you're aboard."

"I'm sorry," Will said quickly. "X? O?"

West spoke as he walked down the passageway. "The Executive Officer. First mate. Second in command. The man whose fan the shit hits, if you know what I mean," West smiled, then stopped in front of a narrow door. "In our case, it's Lieutenant Commander Robert Worth."

He rapped quickly on the door with his knuckles and a muted voice responded, inviting him in. Swiftly opening the door, he announced, "XO, this is *Doctor* Will Driver, a music professor of some sort and our passenger for this next little voyage."

Worth looked up from the minuscule desk at which he was sitting and gently closed the lid of the laptop computer he'd been typing on. "Dr. Driver, welcome aboard. Please, come in, have a seat. Thank you, COB. Please inform the skipper once all personnel are on board and accounted for. I'm sure he'll want to get underway as soon as possible."

West nodded and closed the door. Will stood there awkwardly. Where to sit? Worth was occupying the only thing that resembled a chair.

"The rack is fine," Worth said, as if reading Will's mind. He pointed to his bunk.

It seemed a little strange for Will to be sitting on another man's bed, especially since they'd just met. But he'd already seen how tight the space was on the Royal Oak, so he figured close quarters were probably not something a submariner complained about.

"Uh, thank you, sir," Will said, taking a seat on the thin mattress. "It's a fine ship you have here."

"Boat," Worth corrected.

"Pardon?"

"We call a submarine a *boat*, Dr. Driver. Surface vessels are ships. Subs are boats."

Will frowned and nodded. "Huh. I didn't know that. Well, it looks like a fine boat, then."

"Thank you," Worth said quickly. "Now, as you heard, we are eager to get underway as quickly as possible, so—" he was interrupted when the phone, attached to a nearby bulkhead, buzzed. He swiftly grabbed it. "Worth. Yes. Good. Very well. Underway in five."

"Bad time?" Will asked, trying to lighten Worth's rather serious mood with some humor.

At first, Worth didn't know what to make of Will's comment. Then the left side of his lips curled up ever so slightly. "I think you and I are going to get along just fine, Dr. Driver. Your dad jokes will be right at home." Then he was serious again. "Just do not, under any circumstances, distract my crew with your wisecracks. It's one thing to be friendly—hell, on a submarine, you have little choice—but another to be in the way. Be friendly, Dr. Driver, but don't be in the way."

The XO rose, stowed the computer on a small shelf, and folded up the desk, which was hinged at one side so it could lay vertically, flat against the bulkhead. "It's not a bad time at all," he added. "Any time we get to take this boat out on a mission is a good time. Only time better is when we bring her back home again.

"Now, I've got you assigned a rack across the hall in the VIP stateroom. One door aft of the SigInt suite, which itself is just aft of the mission space, which is just aft of the conn—that is, the control room—and across from the skipper's—that is, the captain's—quarters. You know what 'aft' is, right? The back of the boat." He was speaking so quickly now, Will was struggling to keep up. And Worth could tell. "Why don't you settle in while we steer this little runabout out of Groton and down the Thames. Shouldn't take more than an hour or so. Then I'll have the COB come get you in time to join me and the skipper for an early lunch. Sound good?"

He didn't wait for Will to answer before opening the door and gesturing Will out into the narrow passageway again. There, directly across the hall, was an identical door. Someone had scrawled the letters "V.I.P. Doctor" on a scrap of paper and jammed a pin through it into the exterior side of the door.

Will looked to Worth and shrugged. "I guess this is me," he said meekly.

"SOME VIP SUITE. It's hardly the Ritz, but it'll do," Will muttered to himself as the door to his cabin closed behind him. The room was identical to the XO's cabin across the hall, only without the family photos, books on the shelf, or clothes in the closet. There was, however, an attached bathroom with a sink, toilet, and shower. He could also see that the bathroom opened, on the other side, into the neighboring stateroom. "A Jack-and-Jill," he remarked as if evaluating real estate.

Sitting down on the bed, Will pulled his phone out of his pocket. It said the time was 8:42 AM. He thought about calling Ashley, figuring he might be able to catch her before her first patient of the day. The battery was running low, but it should have enough juice for a brief call, he figured. After tapping the screen to find her name in his list of favorite contacts, he brought the phone up to his right ear. She answered after the third ring.

"William!" Ashley exclaimed. He could tell by the lower quality of the audio that she was in the car. Probably on her way to the office. "Where the hell have you been?!"

Will cleared his throat. "Oh, so *now* you care about my whereabouts? Last time you spoke to me you said I'd be lucky if I could land an overnight spot on our couch." He hadn't planned on fighting with her, but it came so easy these days.

"Of course I care, Will. I was just upset." Ashley's voice sounded a tad calmer. "Where did you go?"

Shit. He was hoping she wouldn't ask that question. "I, uh...I had to leave town for a work thing. Should be back in a week or so, I hope."

"Huh," Ashley responded dramatically. "That sounds awfully vague. Since when do tenured professors of music get called away at the last minute? As if you were on some top-secret government mission or something crazy like that?"

Will didn't say anything. If only she knew how close to the truth she was.

"William?" she asked. "Are you still with me?"

He could feel a vibration; the boat's propulsion system must have engaged. With a gentle shake, he could feel the Royal Oak moving slowly.

"How do you mean?" Will asked. After all, was she asking if he was still on the line or was she asking if he was still committed to their marriage?

"I mean you've gone silent on me again," she said, the tension returning to her voice.

"Sorry about that," he said.

"I'm not sure you really are, Will," she replied. The edge was definitely back in her voice now. He imagined her face getting redder.

Will sighed. "Look, clearly we have a lot we need to talk about—"

"*You*, Will. *You* need to talk. I'm not the one keeping secrets."

"Okay. Clearly, we need to talk. But now's not the time, Ashley. Can we have a nice, calm discussion when I get home?"

Ashley exhaled loudly. "Fine. But do me one favor, okay?"

"Sure, what?"

"Call your kids, please. They might not admit it, but they need to hear from you."

Will closed his eyes tightly, fighting back tears. This whole situation wasn't fair to them. In fact, it was probably hardest on them, and they understood it the least.

"Yeah," he said, his voice cracking. He cleared his throat again. "Yes, Ash. I can do that."

He could almost hear Ashley nod her head as she drove, taking the win, however small it was.

"Good. Thank you. I'm not going to insist you tell me all the details of your trip right now, but I expect you'll have a good, long explanation when you return. Until then—"

He interrupted her: "I love you, Ash."

She stopped talking in what seemed to Will to be a moment of surprise. After a brief hesitation, she responded. "I love you too, Will. Be safe, wherever you are."

THE KNOCK AT the door woke Will with a start and a gasp. He hadn't even remembered falling asleep. That hour or so on the flight from Andrews to New London was clearly not enough shuteye. A quick glance at his watch and he saw it was 11:30 AM.

"Uh, yeah!" He called toward the closed door. Before he could get up from the bunk, the handle rotated and the door swung open. "Oh," Will said, "I guess you guys aren't really into privacy and personal space, huh?"

The COB leaned into the small cabin and smiled. "Nope, not really, Dr. Driver. Not on a United States submarine!"

There was a moment of awkward silence as Will cleared his head and the COB stood there smiling. Finally, the COB spoke. "The XO asked me to invite you to lunch with him and the skipper. I can take you to the wardroom if you're ready."

Will stood. "Lead the way, COB."

West led Will aft, through the narrow passageway and down a flight of stairs. From there, Will could see a large, open space—at least by submarine standards—with several long tables and benches. The crew's mess. On one of the short sides of the rectangular room was a small buffet, which at the moment was being set up with cold cuts and fresh fruit for lunch. On the other side of the buffet, Will could see, lay the galley.

But they weren't headed for the crew's mess. Instead, West walked forward, past the galley, and turned into a wood-paneled room with a large table in the center, seating all around, a large screen on one wall, and a doorway that (since it was open) led back into the galley. The room was decorated with photos, flags, plaques, and other memorabilia, presumably from missions past. Seated at the table was the XO and, to his left, Harper.

West cleared his throat. "Skipper, this is Dr. Will Driver, a professor from the University of Philadelphia. He's our VIP on this cruise."

Harper extended a hand and Will took it. "Pleasure to meet you, captain."

"Welcome aboard, professor. I'm Commander Jim Harper, skipper of this fine boat."

"Finest in the navy," the XO added. Harper nodded.

"Sit, Dr. Driver. We have several issues to discuss," Harper said gently as the COB slid onto the bench seat.

Will sat in one of the chairs, opposite the skipper, who began to speak while a young-looking sailor placed plates of cold cuts and bread on the wardroom table. "After we're done here, check out the mission compartment just forward of your stateroom and close to the SigInt suite. That's where you'll be doing your work."

Taking a bite of his sandwich, Will nodded. "I'm a little surprised," he said, swallowing a mouthful of smoked turkey and provolone cheese, "that the sub has an entire compartment to devote to my analyses. It seems space is tight around here."

Seeing that Harper was chewing on his sandwich, the XO responded. "That's life on a submarine. You want space? Take a cruise on a surface ship. Here, you're on a Virginia-class boat, Dr. Driver, the newest class of nuclear-powered attack submarines in the Navy. The Royal Oak has been modified, however, to conduct surveillance and intelligence gathering missions."

Harper nodded. "We gave up a little room in weapons storage and crew berthing, but gained the mission space you'll use and a more sophisticated SigInt suite. Both can be very useful for our kinds of missions."

"Forgive me, captain," Will said, "or skipper...sir. I've heard the term 'SigInt' several times since coming on board, but I don't know what that means."

"Signal Intelligence, Dr. Driver," Harper explained. "It means our capability to intercept, analyze, and report on enemy communications."

Will nodded. "Ah, I see."

"As far as I'm concerned," Harper continued, "you can wander the boat freely when you're not doing your work. But only under two conditions: First, do not distract my crew from their duties. On a boat like this, attention to detail isn't a luxury, it can mean the difference between success and failure, even life and death."

Will nodded again. "I understand."

"Second," Harper went on, "when this crew is called to battle stations or facing an emergency situation, you are to remain out of the way. You can be in your cabin, the mission compartment, even the conn, but not traipsing through the passageways or otherwise interfering with operations.

"Follow those rules, and together we will succeed in our mission."

Will took a quick sip of water, and then asked, "So what exactly *is* our mission?"

Harper replaced his sandwich on the plate in front of him and took a long pull of hot coffee from his mug. "Our mission, Dr. Driver, is to transit the North Atlantic and station ourselves in the Barents Sea, inside the Arctic Circle but outside Russian territorial waters. There's a large Russian naval base in a town called Polyarnyy, near the city of Murmansk on the Kola Peninsula. Once we're on station, we are to monitor traffic going into and out of Polyarnyy, especially outgoing.

"We'll be waiting for a Russian submarine to leave the base," Harper continued, clearing his throat. "And when we find one, our orders are to follow it, preferably by placing our boat between theirs and the new transmission tower in Tsypnavolok. Then, assuming they receive one of your musical signals, we break off pursuit, analyze the message, and move to a safe distance to call home for further instructions."

"I'm sorry," Will said, leaning forward over the table, "but did you say we're going to put ourselves *between* the Russian sub and their tower?"

"That's what the skipper said," Worth replied, taking another bite of his sandwich.

"Isn't that a little bit dangerous?" Will asked.

"The men on this boat can handle—" the COB began, but he was quickly cut off with a look from his skipper.

"Dr. Driver, this is a nuclear attack submarine in the United States Navy. Dangerous is what we do."

17

In Transit

It took the USS Royal Oak six days to cross the Atlantic Ocean, round the top of Scandinavia, and enter the Barents Sea en route to the spot on the map where they'd stop and wait for a Russian submarine. During the transit, Will split his time between the mission compartment and observations of and conversations with various members of the Royal Oak's crew. And he took dinners every night in the wardroom with the officers.

It turns out the mission compartment was really just a glorified closet. Inside the cramped space, Will found a desk, chair, and computer, as well as a phone that presumably connected the room with other parts of the boat. It all seemed pretty generic.

There were a few hints of forethought, though. On the walls, he noticed some rectangular panels made of soft foam and covered in cloth: acoustic paneling. It would help absorb sound and avoid echoes from sound waves bouncing off the hard, flat, steel surface that comprised most of the bulkheads on the boat. As a result, he'd be able to listen more closely to whatever signals the sub picked up.

Of course, it seemed like every time Will sat down at the computer and began preparing for what he expected to be a brief but intense analysis, some sort of alarm or announcement would come booming over the boat's speaker system, which they called the "1MC," for "number one main circuit." At first, these loud interruptions were quite annoying. However, there wasn't much Will could do in terms of preparation in the mission space, so on the third day of the crossing he decided he'd stop and see what all the fuss was about the next time such an announcement was made.

It didn't take long. An hour or so after breakfast, the XO's voice came over the 1MC: "Fire! Fire! Class B fire in the aft bilge bay! Fire control parties to the aft bilge bay! This is a drill!" Will could swear the XO's voice sounded just like Denzel Washington's in *Crimson Tide*, a thought that put a wide smile on his face. He opened the door to the mission compartment and poked his head out to see six sailors running down the corridor in what looked like HazMat suits. Just another morning on the Royal Oak.

"A fire is the most dangerous thing that can happen on a submarine," West explained during lunch that day. "Depending on the type of fire, there are different ways to fight them. But it can be very difficult when you're cruising at depth, with no access to clean air, and the air on the boat has been contaminated and, in some cases, turned so black you can't see more than an inch in front of you. So we train and practice firefighting constantly."

Another drill that same afternoon had a different purpose. "General quarters! General quarters!" The COB's voice echoed throughout the submarine's compartments. "All hands man your battle stations! Set condition one throughout the boat, man battle stations torpedo. This is a drill!"

Again, Will watched as men ran about in all directions. To the casual observer, it might appear chaotic. But by the third combat drill, he could start to see patterns to their movements, a method to the madness. Each sailor had a place to be and a job to do. And if it were a real emergency, they'd have to rely on each other, trust that each man would do his part, and follow the skipper's orders for the safety of all souls aboard. And they had to trust that the skipper had the knowledge and experience needed to issue the right orders at the right time.

DINNER IN THE wardroom was a slightly more formal affair than lunch. Harper was always there, as was Worth. A small assortment of other officers attended as well, including the chief engineer, the chief communications officer, the chief weapons officer, and the navigator, although there was always at least one officer missing because he was in the conn, in charge of the boat. Harper clearly ran the show, moderating and guiding many of the conversations. But he didn't monopolize them. Rather, it was evident to Will that Harper was a shepherd who really listened to his flock. A man who genuinely enjoyed imparting his knowledge to others, guiding them. A bit like his own father.

There was so much to learn. On the second evening at sea, Will asked the boat's navigator, Mr. Hargraves, "How do you know where you are and where you're going if you're underwater? It's not like you can just whip out your sexton, right?"

Hargraves chuckled as he scooped up a forkful of

spaghetti. "That's true. But dead reckoning—that's what we call figuring out our position without reference points—has come a long way. The ECDIS, or Electronic Chart Display and Information System, has some super-fancy gyros inside. Plus, all the helm and navigation info is automatically fed into the ECDIS computer." He paused to chew his pasta.

"Huh," Will responded. "I never knew that that's what 'dead reckoning' actually means. Fascinating. Is the ECDIS really that good?"

Hargraves swallowed his food. "It's pretty good, but we still check in with GPS satellites every so often to confirm our position. So we're never too far off track."

ONE AFTERNOON ON the fourth day of the transit, Will ambled through the lower level of the boat, observing how every minute space in every compartment, including the passageways, was used. There were pipes, wires, and all sorts of mechanical things he couldn't identify. Wandering forward, he found himself in the torpedo room; he could tell by the green twenty-foot-long cylinders stacked up on either side of the room.

"Professor," Warren Davis said when he saw Will looking around. "Anything I can do for you?"

Will noticed that Davis and the three other crewmen he had been working with were dripping with sweat. "What's going on here?"

Davis mopped his brow with a rag. "The Mk 48, Advanced Capability, or 'ADCAP' torpedo is a lethal fish, but when she's not swimming, she's a heavy-ass bitch!"

Looking up again, Will could see the hooks, chains, and tracks that made up the torpedo room's gantry system. Even as it shouldered the bulk of a torpedo's 3700-pound weight, clearly the men still worked hard to move the weapons around.

"Where are you from, Davis?" Will asked as the other crewmen came off watch and began filing out of the compartment.

"Camden County, Georgia," Davis replied proudly.

"And what led you to serve on a nuclear submarine?"

Davis looked at Will for a moment, then said with a smile, "You've never been to Camden County, have you, professor?"

Will looked to the floor for a moment. "No, I haven't."

"That's alright, prof. Nobody's perfect!" Davis knocked Will on the shoulder. "Kings Bay Submarine Base is there. I grew up watching these boats sail in and out. I knew from before I could talk that I'd spend my life at sea."

Will grinned. "That's as good a reason as any, I suppose."

"What about you, big-shot professor? How'd you get involved in musico-ethnolo..." his voice trailed off as he gave up trying to pronounce the word.

"Ethnomusicology."

"Yeah, that's the one."

"Like you, I knew pretty young I'd end up doing something with music. I just didn't realize until college exactly what that would look like. I got a chance to write a paper about Russian music and I was hooked. And then, when I found the Ket, I just fell in love. The music is beautiful, the culture is beautiful...aside from my wife and kids, it's the most precious thing on this Earth to me."

Davis nodded. "Well, then. I'm glad we both found our way." Then he patted Will on the back and exited the compartment, leaving Will with one sweaty rag and twenty-four torpedoes.

"WITH ALL DUE respect to the admiralty, and to you, Dr.

Driver," Hargraves said one evening over a plate of meatloaf and roasted potatoes, "I don't understand something about this mission. We know the Russians have come up with this newfangled musical comms system, and we know it's severely limited because it basically requires line-of-sight positioning. So, why use it at all?"

Harper raised an eyebrow, acknowledging the question and looking around the table to see if anyone present cared to take a stab at answering.

The engineer took the bait. "Maybe they know that we know all their other codes, their older comms systems. This one is simple, right? Just play a song on a high-powered but narrow beam and aim it in the direction of a ship."

"That part is certainly simple," the comms officer, Lieutenant Katashi, responded. "Which makes it less likely to fail. The more complicated part is deciphering the code that's stored inside the song." He turned and gestured toward Will. "That's why our guest is here."

Will nodded. "Indeed, yes, that's my role. Although I'd dare to say that even the songs themselves are not really 'simple.' They're a rather clever mix of multilingual lyrics mated to dominant and subaltern scalar patterns which, when analyzed serially, reveal numerical values of, apparently, some significance."

There was silence around the table as the officers looked at each other, hoping to see some sign that one of them understood what Will had just said. Nobody dared to move. The only sound was Harper's knife and fork as he moved them through a large piece of potato.

"Right..." Hargraves said slowly, with a smirk. "I guess now there are *two* things I don't understand!"

The men laughed.

Harper began speaking and the rest of the men immediately quieted down. "Back in the days of the Soviet Navy, Russian subs routinely left port with their orders sealed in envelopes, locked away in a safe in the commanding officer's quarters. They wouldn't open the orders until they were at sea."

"Why is that, skipper? Why all the cloak and dagger?" Katashi asked.

The engineer gave the comms officer a gentle punch in the shoulder. "Haven't you seen *Red October*? Sean Connery opens the orders, kills the political officer, burns the orders, and then pulls *another* set of orders out of his pocket. Great movie."

The officers around the table grunted their agreement. Will nodded, glad he wasn't the only one who knew that film so well.

"While I don't think that happened very often," Harper continued, "there is a kernel of truth to the practice. By keeping the orders literally under lock and key until they were underway, the Soviet admirals helped to reduce the opportunities for a dissident—whether in the navy or not—to alter or replace the orders. And, since they were already at sea, the details of the orders could not be leaked."

"Kind of a clever procedure," Katashi said.

"Sure," Worth put in, clearing his throat and reaching for a roll, "but what does it say about the faith the Soviet leadership had in their rank-and-file? If you must open your orders in secret because you're afraid of someone altering them or leaking them, that doesn't indicate a whole lot of trust, does it?"

"Good point, XO," Harper said with a smile. "And as far as we know, that procedure is still in use in today's Russian navy. Only we think they've grown even more paranoid, and the orders aren't even stored in a safe anymore. Instead, they're transmitted using this new code. That gives us an opening, a chance to get a sense of their orders at the same time the Russian ships are reading them."

"Okay, I get all that," Hargraves said, grabbing the last

roll from the basket. "But isn't it *riskier* to transmit orders over the open sea instead of writing them down and locking them away somewhere inside the boat? I mean, they're opening themselves up to someone—say, us!—listening in on the broadcast. Why would they risk it?"

Harper looked to his XO, who answered the navigator's question. "Because they think they've invented the enigma code two-point-oh. They think their new code is unbreakable. Probably because they don't know something about our side."

"Oh yeah? What's that?" The navigator asked.

The XO smiled and pointed his fork at Will. "We have *him*."

"I'M SORRY, WHO is this?" Jackie Fletcher said into the receiver of the phone on the desk in her office. It was rare that anyone used that phone number these days. Most matters were handled by virtual meeting, email, or sometimes just text messages. So she was especially curious when the phone rang, interrupting her reading of an email from a student, complaining that Professor Driver hadn't shown up to class that day.

"Professor Fletcher, this is Admiral Jack Carter, United States Navy, calling from the Pentagon. I'd like to discuss a mutual acquaintance of ours, one William Driver." The voice on the other end of the line had just a hint of a southern drawl to it. But that wasn't what caught Jackie's attention. The mention of Will's name did.

"A navy admiral? Geez, Will's got some friends in high places," Jackie responded, trying humor but unaware of the seriousness with which the admiral approached his work.

"Now I wouldn't exactly call Professor Driver a friend," Carter replied. "But you may have noticed that he hasn't been on campus lately, and I can shed some light on the reason why."

"Actually yes, he hasn't been here lately. I was going to call him at home to make sure everything is okay—"

"That won't be necessary. He is just fine and in very capable hands."

Jackie narrowed her eyes, trying to decipher the admiral's words. "Capable hands?"

"He's going to be out of the office for the next two weeks, maybe more."

With a preemptive chuckle, Jackie said, "What did Will do this time? Did he get himself drafted?"

"I'm afraid this is neither a laughing matter nor one I am at liberty to disclose, Professor Fletcher. However, the navy is prepared to cover the cost of a temporary replacement for Professor Driver, provided you can find one." Carter paused for a moment, letting that part of the message sink in before delivering the next part. "And, upon Professor Driver's return, we will be happy to make a modest contribution to your department's scholarship fund. For your trouble."

"Well!" Jackie said with a smile. The muscles in her shoulders began to relax a little. "That would be…most appreciated, admiral."

"I'm pleased to hear you say so, Professor."

"It will take me a little time to line up an adjunct instructor to cover Will's teaching load. This semester he's got a graduate seminar in ethnomusicology and, I believe, a general education music appreciation class." She began talking more quickly as her thoughts gained speed. "Usually, we wouldn't have the same person do both courses, and we wouldn't ask an adjunct to teach a graduate seminar, but these circumstances are atypical enough that I think I can convince Stan—that is, the Dean—to make an exception. In fact, I think I have someone in mind already. I'll just have to find her phone number. I'm sure it's on this computer somewhere…"

"Excellent." Carter's voice betrayed his smile. "I will have one of my aides, Lieutenant Anderson, get in touch with your university's business office and make the financial arrangements. Thank you for understanding, Professor Fletcher."

"Oh, thank *you*!" Jack responded quickly. "By the way, where *is* Will Driver?"

Carter paused before answering. "Professor, that information is on a need-to-know basis. Suffice it to say, he is *deeply* invested in a project that's of great importance to our nation. Good day to you, Professor."

WILL LEANED BACK on the aft wall of the control room with his arms crossed as he watched the routine movements of personnel around and through the space. It was late afternoon (not that he could really tell, he hadn't seen the sun since they submerged somewhere off Block Island) and they expected to arrive on station sometime early the next morning. Harper and Worth were standing with Hargraves, discussing their course and speed as they steamed through the cold waters off the Scandinavian coast.

Harper then moved to the center of the conn and pushed the button on the intercom mounted overhead. "Sonar, conn. Report all contacts."

The voice of Greg Findlay, the sonar officer, came back through the speaker. "Conn, sonar. My board is clear except for the occasional biologic. I hold no contacts, friend or foe, on the spherical or TB-29 towed sonar array."

"Sonar, conn. Very well." Harper cleared his throat and took a step forward. "Diving officer, let's come up to three hundred feet. The Barents Sea isn't as deep as the Atlantic."

"Coming up to three hundred feet, aye," the diving officer

repeated. He stood by the planesman, who sat and held onto a yoke-shaped control not unlike the "stick" found in an aircraft cockpit. The diving officer repeated the orders to the planesman, who slowly pulled back on the yoke. Somewhere outside on the hull, the hydroplanes rotated, gently driving the boat up from six hundred feet to the new target depth.

With a quick push on the intercom button, Harper activated the 1MC and addressed the entire boat. "Crew of the Royal Oak, this is the captain. We are approaching our station and will commence our mission forthwith. We've trained for this, men, and I have the utmost confidence in the ability of each and every one of you to carry out your duties and orders with exceptional professionalism. Trust each other and trust in your superior officers. That'll be all."

Harper then looked over his shoulder at Will. "Hungry, Dr. Driver?"

"Yes, sir!" Will answered with a smile.

Turning to the navigator, Harper announced, "Mr. Hargraves, you have the conn," as he started for the exit. "Be sure to clear the baffles. Mr. Findlay is the best at what he does, but they call them blind spots for a reason. We don't want any tail out behind us but our own."

"Aye, sir," Hargraves replied with a quick nod.

When Harper and Worth arrived at the wardroom, with Will in tow, most of the other officers were already there. It was chicken casserole night. Not Will's favorite menu of the trip so far. He'd been told that the submarines had the best food in the navy. And he had to admit, for the most part, the meals were pretty good. This one just didn't seem to appeal. Still, Will took a seat at the table as a sailor put a plate in front of him and he poured himself a tall glass of red "bug juice," a sweet concoction somewhat like fruit punch that vaguely reminded him of summer camp.

"Did I hear we'll be on station some time in the next eight hours or so?" The engineering officer asked the group as he scooped some casserole onto his plate.

"You heard right," Worth replied. "It'll be nice to actually do what we've been sent out here to do, you know?"

"I'll drink to that," Katashi said, raising his glass of bug juice.

Will put down his glass and leaned forward to ask a question. "So, you gentlemen have a lot more experience sneaking around enemy coastlines than I do." The officers chuckled, smiled, and nodded. "Exactly what can we expect to encounter up there?"

"Good question, professor," the XO said. "Weps?" He looked to the chief weapons officer, Lieutenant Warren Davis, whom they usually just called "Weps."

Davis took a long sip of water before he answered. "From where we'll be positioned, just beyond the twelve-mile territorial limit, we're going to encounter shipping heading in and out of Murmansk, as that's the only sizable city nearby. But we'll also, hopefully, catch sight of some naval activity going in and out of Polyarnyy. And while there will probably be some surface ships there, that's homeport for the entire submarine force of the Northern Fleet."

"So we'll see another sub. Or two," Will said.

"I'd expect to," Katashi added. "The more interesting question is *which* submarines we'll encounter."

Will popped a bite of casserole in his mouth and asked, "What do you mean?"

"Well, just like our own navy, the Russians have several different classes of submarine warships." Katashi looked to the skipper, who was listening to his officers talk shop and educate the newcomer. Harding nodded, encouraging them to continue.

The chief engineer picked up where the comms officer left off. "Let's see, there's the Oscars. That is, Oscar-class SSGNs, nuclear guided missile subs. They were mostly built back in the 1970s, but they still have a few in service. They're not too difficult to track or evade, if we have to.

"I read recently that the Northern Fleet has two Borei-class nuclear missile subs. You remember *Red October*, of course," he said with a smile. "Well Sean Connery's boat, that was a Typhoon-class ballistic missile boat. They called them 'boomers.' They were huge. Really innovative for their time. They were replaced with Delta IIIs and Delta IVs. The Deltas, in turn, were replaced by the Boreis, which are much smaller but also much stealthier."

"I've heard the Boreis are twice as quiet as the Virginia-class boats. Twice as quiet as the Royal Oak!" Davis said, his voice filled with concern.

Harper chose that moment to speak up, not wanting one young officer's emotion—fear—to infect the others. "The Borei-class boats are certainly dangerous. But remember, as SSBNs, their goal is to hide. It's unlikely they'd be hunting for us, although it's possible. It's just more likely the other way 'round."

"True," Worth chimed in. "The ones we should be concerned about are the Akulas and the Yasens. The Aklulas, those are hunter-killers. SSNs just like the Royal Oak. They're built on older attack-submarine technology, but the later ones have been extensively modernized and several are thought to be active in the Northern Fleet.

"The Yasen-class SSGNs are the ones I'd be worried about. They're the newest and quietest of the Russian subs, with big advances in sonar tech that make them much better than all the other Russian boats when it comes to hearing other subs. Including us."

Will swore he could hear the other officers around the table groan.

PART FOUR

ON STATION

18

WAITING

Will could feel the USS Royal Oak begin to slow as he lay in his bunk, unable to sleep. A week earlier, he'd never even set foot on a submarine. Now he was using submarine shorthand like "COB," "Weps," and "SSGN." He was friendly with the crew and friendlier still with the officers. And he was attuned to very vibration of the boat's hull.

He wondered if any other ethnomusicologist had ever worked on a submarine. With a chuckle, he shook his head at the absurdity of the idea. If another ethnomusicologist *had* ever worked on a submarine, they probably wouldn't be able to talk or write about it, so no one would ever know. And that's probably going to be his fate, too, Will thought. So much for getting a new book publication from this experience.

Slowing down meant they were getting very close to the location from which they'd search for Russian subs leaving Polyarnyy. It seemed as good a reason as any for Will to give up on sleep, grab a quick shower, and hop into a clean set of coveralls (from a seemingly endless supply on board). A week earlier, a "quick shower" would have taken at least thirty minutes between the shower itself, a leisurely shave, and carefully sculpting the brown hair on his head. (His hair had been one of his fixations since middle school, when the class bully accused him of having a cowlick.) Now, a "quick shower" meant no more than three minutes of water, no shave, and a speedy rake of his hair with a classic comb (a gift from the boat's supply officer).

As he entered the control room, Will could see that the first-stringers were on watch. Both the skipper and the XO were present, as were all the senior staff. The lights had been switched to a dark red color, which, Will admitted only to himself, reminded him of a "red alert" on the Enterprise from *Star Trek*. He had to admit, the low lighting helped to keep the sailors focused even amidst what he could clearly tell were rising tensions.

"Approaching designated operational area," Hargraves announced.

"Alright, folks," Harper said loudly, getting everyone's attention. "Seems like we got where we were going. Let's head up for a quick call home to mama, let her know we got here safe and sound. Diving officer, bring us up to periscope depth, make your speed five knots, five degrees up bubble. Comms, float the buoy."

The XO and diving officer repeated the commands in sequence. The planesman set the Royal Oak on a gentle ascent while the boat's propeller slowed yet again.

"Communications buoy is afloat," Worth reported a moment later.

Harper nodded as he pushed a button on the intercom

overhead. "Radio, conn. Prepare for burst transmission: arrival in op area, commencing search. Download the latest traffic and send receipts. Make this a quick one."

"Conn, radio," Katashi replied through the speaker, "preparing to send and receive on the double, aye."

"Very well," Harper responded, pushing the overhead button to close the circuit. "Prepare to raise the photonics mast. Navigation, stand by for GPS fix."

"Photonics mast standing by, sir!" A sailor responded from the corner of the control room, not far from Will's customary observation position along the aft bulkhead.

"Coming up on one hundred feet, on the way to six-two feet," the diving officer reported.

"Ready for GPS location fix," Hargraves said.

Harper looked to Worth while they waited for the boat to complete the ascent, comms exchange, a quick check of their location against the GPS satellite network, and a stealthy scan of the surface. Quietly, the skipper asked the XO, "Think we'll get any exciting news from home in this batch?"

"Holding steady at six-two feet. Now at periscope depth."

"Photonics mast coming up."

Worth rubbed his chin and, taking a step toward the skipper, replied quietly. "I dunno. We've only been sailing a week. How much could possibly go wrong inside of a week?"

"GPS location fix complete. Updating ECDIS system now," Hargraves reported.

"Comms exchange underway."

Harper looked at his XO and raised an eyebrow. "Have you met my kids? No matter how adult they may appear, they're just overgrown children, Rob."

"Well," Worth replied with a smirk, "have you met my boss?"

"Comms exchange complete. Surface scan complete."

"Lower the mast, reel in the buoy," Harper ordered. Small talk was finished. "Take us back down to three hundred feet, five degrees down angle on the planes. I'll be the comms center." He took a step toward the aft passageway. As he passed by Worth, he put a hand on the XO's shoulder. "I hear the boss is a really great guy." Then, more loudly: "XO has the conn."

"I have the conn, aye," Worth said in acknowledgment, shaking his head with a smile.

As he walked by Will at the back of the control room, Harper looked at him and said, "Why don't you come with me, Dr. Driver? Let's see if there's any news you might be interested in." He didn't wait for Will to respond.

LIEUTENANT NANCY DASH had just poured herself her third cup of coffee and returned to her station in NORAD's large control room when her computer alerted her to some new imagery and analysis. Looking at her watch, she nodded. Right on time.

She opened the series of photos to have a look. It always amazed her how good the pictures could be from so far away. Even as she zoomed in, she could almost see what those poor, cold Russians were having for lunch. The detail was that clear. In this particular case, she recognized the Poluostrov Ribachiy right away because of its shape, which she always imagined was similar to that of a sea lion (a thought that routinely made her smile). Moving the image around on her computer, she focused on Kola Bay, where the Tuulomajoki River emptied to the Barents Sea in the northwestern corner of Russia.

Taking a sip from her steaming cup, Dash adjusted her seat and zoomed in even closer until she found the naval base at Polyarnyy. Then she spotted something that caused her mug-bearing arm to pause midway through its descent toward the desktop. A line of tractor-trailers snaked along the road from one of the covered piers that usually housed nuclear submarines. Some were flatbeds filled with ordinance, while others were carrying cargo containers, presumably with other supplies and provisions.

"Well, *that's* interesting..." Dash whispered to herself as she inspected the image further. Then she noticed something sticking out just a little bit from one end of the covered pier: a propeller. "Oops," she said with a smile. "Someone didn't pull all the way into their parking spot..."

After making a copy of the image and marking it up, circling the propeller and the lineup of trucks, she attached it to an email addressed to her supervisor, Major Peter Berry, as well as Lieutenant Albert Donovan in the Office of Naval Intelligence. Maybe one of the ONI analysts could make something of that propellor. Maybe they could even tell what kind of submarine it belonged to.

WILL FOLLOWED THE skipper out of the control room. Their destination wasn't far; the comms suite was in the next compartment, although exiting the conn did require ducking down to fit through the doorway, which was one of the oval-shaped hatches that could be closed to seal off one compartment from another in case of emergency or during combat. They found the door cracked open a few inches, so Harper slid it aside, revealing a space analogous to Will's mission space, just across the hall. It had the same work table, two chairs, and acoustic paneling. But it also had a lot more equipment, including multiple screens, computers, audio and radio equipment, and a pair of printers. Katashi and one of the ensigns in his division sat at the table.

"What have you got for me, gentlemen?" Harper asked.

Katashi reached over to the printer, pulled out a few pages that had just finished printing, clipped them into a clipboard, and handed it over to the skipper.

"Oh, the usual," he said. "There's a weather report, but I'll save you to trouble: it'll be pretty cold up there."

"Mmm," Harper said, quickly scanning the message traffic. On the second page, he slowed down to read more closely. "Satellite imagery shows increased activity at Polyarnyy, Dr. Driver. The Russian Navy, like our own, shelters their newest subs from prying eyes in the sky. So we aren't going to be able to tell exactly what they're doing, or which boat they're doing it to—although the ONI suspects it's either a Borei or a Yasen. Either way, the analysts tell us they're seeing increased numbers of trucks and equipment going in and out of the shelter at the pier. So maybe we'll have some luck on this little fishing expedition of ours."

Will's eyes grew a bit wider and he nodded slowly. "I'll make sure I'm ready."

19

THE KAZAN

"COMMANDER HARDING TO the conn! Commander Harding to the conn!" The announcement echoed through the compartments and passageways of the Royal Oak. Worth's voice was tense.

It took less than thirty seconds for Harding to make it out of his bunk and into the control room.

"What have we got, XO?" Harding asked as he strode into the conn.

Worth turned to face him. "Sir, sonar reports new submerged contact bearing two-six-one. Designate contact Sierra two-three."

Harding nodded and punched the overhead intercom button. "Sonar, conn. Tell me what you're hearing, Findlay."

The response was immediate. "Conn, sonar. I'm holding Sierra two-three on the TB-29 towed sonar array, bearing two-six-one at about fifteen thousand yards. She's somewhere around a hundred feet, give or take, and making turns for ten knots, heading...three-five-zero. Tonals equate to Russian Navy, Yasen-class submarine. The computer is chewing on a more precise—hang on—here it is. Seventy-five percent match for the Kazan, K-561. She's coming on out of the barn, sir."

"Any sign they've detected us?" Harding asked, looking down at the deck as he took in the report.

"No indication of detection, sir. Her depth, course, and speed have remained constant since I first got a whiff of her."

"Good work, Findlay," Harding replied. "Start a track on our new friend. And let me know if anything changes."

"Aye, skipper."

Harding looked up at the XO. "Think we just got lucky?"

Worth nodded his head. "Maybe, sir. Let's take a look."

The two men moved over to the ECDIS chart table. "Based on the info from sonar," Worth began, "the Kazan is here." He placed a mark on the nautical chart displayed on the tabletop. "And we're over here. She's coming more or less directly toward our position."

"Mmm-hmm," Harding said, rubbing his chin as he looked at the marks on the display. The room was quiet as the other officers on watch listened. "Recommendations, XO? Thoughts, anyone?"

"Sir," Hargraves started. He was the closest officer to the ECDIS aside from the skipper and the XO. "We definitely want to track her, sir. We could stop all engines, rig for silent, let her pass overhead, and then rise back up and pursue."

Worth shook his head. "I see two problems with that plan, lieutenant. One has to do with an assumption you're making about our new friend here. The other has to do with the all-stop."

"Let's work the problem, folks," Harding announced. Then he added, "Expeditiously, please."

"Ah! I think I know," Hargraves said excitedly. "I was assuming the Kazan would stay at a constant depth. But if I were the skipper on that boat, I'd probably dive deeper as we made our way farther from shore. That could create a possible collision situation." He smiled as if he'd just placed the last piece of a difficult puzzle. "Sir."

"True," Harding said. "An undersea collision is *not* in anyone's orders, ours or the Russians'. I can promise you that. Now, what about the other problem?"

"I think I got this one," the diving officer spoke up. "It has to do with our tail, right? The TB-29?"

Harding nodded. "Indeed, it does. Go on."

"Well, sir, the whole point is that we tow it. So we have to keep moving. If we stop our boat, the thing is going to start to sink down. And without it all stretched out, in a nice and pretty line, it doesn't work so good. We want it working real good right now, so Findlay can keep his track."

"Right on," Worth said, patting the diving officer on the shoulder.

"Then, if we can't just slide under the Kazan and we don't want to stop moving, what's the plan?" Harding asked the room.

Warren Davis had it. "Maybe Hargraves here can plot us a little circular course. We can take it real slow, getting out of the Kazan's way, keeping the tail kinda straight but definitely not sinking, and setting us up to pull in behind the Russian boat once she passes us by." He nodded conclusively, but with a sneaky smile. "Da?"

"I like it," the XO said, smiling back. "Da."

"Mr. Hargraves? Can you plot us a little meander?" Harding asked.

"With pleasure, sir."

It took several hours, but between the course Hargraves plotted and some careful maneuvering by other crew members, the Royal Oak was exactly where she wanted to be: directly behind the Kazan, in her baffles, matching her course, depth, and speed. Harper was pleased.

"Believe it or not, folks, that was the easy part," the skipper said to everyone working in the control room. "Now we have to shadow our Russian friend and see if he comes up to receive one of those new signals Dr. Driver is here for. What's our distance from the Kola Bay barrier marker?"

Worth looked down at the ECDIS and made a quick measurement. "About twenty-five nautical miles, sir."

"Very well. I expect it will be a little bit before the Kazan comes up for a breath. Let's settle in and keep sharp. Stay rigged for silent."

"HE DID *WHAT*?" Jane Komer shouted into the phone.

"You heard me, big sis," Ashley said, "I got one phone call, in which he didn't tell me anything I didn't already know." She slowed her car as she approached a red light near Marz's middle school. "That was a week ago. Since then, nothing."

"Jeez, little sis. That's awful! Has Will ever pulled a stunt like this before?" Jane's voice was a little calmer, but not exactly calm.

"Nope," Ashley answered with an audible *p* to emphasize the point. "I mean, he can get lost in his work sometimes, but that hasn't really happened in a while. He is forgetful at baseline, but he's taking things to a whole new level this time."

"How are you coping?" Jane's voice was softer, more concerned as they focused on her younger sister. "Do you need anything? Andrew's in the middle of a big project over at TARDEC so I can probably grab a flight out of Detroit and be there tomorrow or the next day if you need me."

"I'm alright, Jane. Wait, isn't Andrew *always* in the middle of a big project at that Army research place?"

"Yeah, I guess. But at least he comes home at night."

Ashley was quiet for a moment.

"Ashley?"

"Yeah, I'm here. I'm just thinking of the last time I saw Will. I basically told him not to come home."

"Oh," Jane said quietly.

"And he hasn't." The light turned green, but Ashley was lost in thought, her mind churning through the possibility that the current state of her marriage might somehow be her own fault. The car behind her honked its horn, bringing her back.

"Little sis, I'm sure he knew you didn't mean it."

Ashley was quiet again.

"You...didn't mean it, did you?"

"I don't know, Jane. I don't know. I mean, deep down he's a good man. I married a good man, sis. But he's flawed, you know? I used to think it was the little things, like forgetting the dry cleaning or leaving the freezer door open. But this is next-level, you know?"

"Sounds like it." Jane paused, unsure of whether to ask the question in her mind. Then she pressed ahead. "You said he denied that it was an affair. Do you believe him?"

Ashley bit her lip, considering the question. The middle school was on the next block, and she could see the lineup of cars and yellow buses waiting to pick up students. The crossing guard walked in front of her, holding up a stop sign as some kids crossed the street. "I think I do. I mean, Will loves his kids. He really does. I don't think he'd cheat on me, Jane. He knows that would ruin the family and really mess up our children. So I really don't think that's what's going on. The problem is, I don't know what else it could be." Her voice cracked; she was starting to cry.

"I'm going to book a ticket. Things here in Grosse Pointe will be just fine without me for a little while. It sounds like you could use a little support," Jane announced.

Ashley let out a sniffle. "I can't let the kids see me like

this."

"I'll text you my itinerary. No need to pick me up at the airport, I can find my way to the house."

Now Ashley was whispering. "Thanks, big sis."

"Don't mention it, little sis."

"Conn, sonar, possible depth change on Sierra two-three," Findlay's voice came over the speaker. He sounded tired; they all were. It had been four hours.

"Sonar, conn, understood," the XO answered. The skipper had left two hours earlier in an attempt to get some sleep before things got exciting. "Which way is she going, Findlay?"

"Give me one sec—sir, she's coming shallow! My guess is she's heading up for call home," the sonar chief said excitedly.

"Very well," the XO said. He looked over to West. "COB, could you please—"

"Already on it," West said, heading aft to wake the skipper and their guest.

It took only a minute for Harper to appear in the control room; two for Will. "XO, report," Harper said as he entered.

"Sir, Sierra two-three is coming shallow, and will likely be at periscope depth in the next five minutes. She's also slowing," Worth reported. "I think she's going to call home."

"Alright," Harper said as he settled into his seat in the center of the compartment. "Let's follow our Russian friends up to periscope depth. Standby to raise the Electronic Support Measures mast."

The mood grew even more serious as various officers and enlisted personnel got to work.

Harper looked at Worth. "Any indication we've been detected?"

Worth shook his head.

"Good," Harper said softly. "But just in case..." The skipper cleared his throat and looked to Davis at the weapons console. "Set battle stations torpedo. Load tubes one and two and assign to Sierra two-three. Keep outer doors closed. No need to broadcast our presence."

"Aye, sir!" Davis responded. "Setting battle stations torpedo. Loading tubes one and two, assigned to Sierra two-three. Starting on a firing solution."

Harper nodded to Davis and reached up for the 1MC. "Battle stations! Battle stations! Set condition battle stations torpedo throughout the ship. Damage control teams lay to your posts. Remain rigged for quiet."

Harper replaced the mic. "XO, reel in the towed array. Helm, we need to open the distance so we can stay undetected when we raise our mast. Slow to three knots. Let's crawl up slowly..."

As Will entered the control room, he could sense the tension, anticipation, and excitement. It was by no means chaotic. Rather, men moved purposefully, even if it seemed like bodies were moving in all directions. He assumed his usual spot, leaning against the rear bulkhead near the doorway to the passageway leading aft.

Worth noticed Will come in. "Dr. Driver, it seems you might actually have something useful to do for a change."

Will nodded and smiled. "Always happy to be of service, XO! If only—"

He was interrupted by Findlay's voice on the intercom. "Conn, sonar. Sierra two-three is running at five knots and raising scopes."

"Sonar, conn. Very well," Harper replied. "Raise the ESM mast."

"Sir," Worth said urgently. "We're not yet at periscope depth. The mast won't break the surface."

Harper swung his head around to look at the XO, then he

directed his glare at the Diving Officer. "What the hell is going on over there?"

"Sir," the Diving Officer responded, straightening his posture, "we're still rising. We're a minute or two behind the target. We didn't start our ascent until after we could hear theirs. We won't be at periscope depth for another—" he checked the digital depth readout and did some quick mental calculations, "—sixty seconds, sir!"

Harper was furious. "Sixty seconds?! The whole show could be *over* in sixty seconds!"

20

In Pursuit

"Raise the ESM mast now!" Harper barked at his crew. "I want that mast fully extended by the time we reach periscope depth. We can't intercept anything if we're not ready and listening!"

"Skipper," Worth started quietly. He didn't want the other sailors to hear him question the boat's commanding officer, but someone had to do it. And it was the XO's job, after all.

"Increase speed to ten knots! That'll get us up there faster," Harper continued, ignoring Worth. "I need a range to Sierra two-three—how far behind the Kazan are we right now?"

The XO stepped closer to his captain. "Skipper."

"Range to target, ten thousand yards," called out one of the noncommissioned officers standing watch.

"Jim," Worth said, at this point standing mere inches from Harper. "This is a risky move. At this speed, the ESM is bound to cause some cavitation, putting sound in the water and potentially alerting Sierra two-three to our presence.

They're not moving very fast, but there's still a reasonable chance their baffles are the blind spots they usually are. We should just stay in them, moving slowly and quietly."

Harper looked straight ahead, not at his XO. But he was listening.

"Conn, sonar," Findlay said over the intercom.

Worth continued. "At this speed, we could even damage the ESM mast. That would greatly hinder our ability to carry out this mission."

Harper finally looked up at Worth as if he were about to reply to his XO's concerns. But instead, he reached up and pushed a button on the comms circuit. "Sonar, conn. Go ahead."

"Sir, I'm picking up some cavitation, own-ship. Whatever you're doing up there is making some noise." Findlay sounded concerned.

"Noted," Harper responded, still keeping his eyes on Worth. Finally, he spoke to the XO. "Rob, sometimes you need to take a risk if you want the reward. When you have your own command, you'll understand. I'll take full responsibility for what happens, as the skipper should. That's something you could—"

"Range to target now nine thousand yards and closing."

Then the Diving Officer spoke up. "Reaching periscope depth now, sir!"

Harper immediately punched another button overhead. "Radio, conn. Lieutenant Katashi, are you picking up anything on the ESM yet?"

Half a second passed, as Harper and Worth continued to lock eyes. It felt like hours.

Then Katashi's voice came through the speaker. "Conn, radio. Yes, sir! I'm getting something…cleaning it up now… yes, yes, sir! I'm dancing back here!"

"Very well," Harper responded, a slight smile creeping across his lips. "Record it and log it. Let me know when the transmission ends, then send it to the mission compartment for Dr. Driver."

"Aye, sir!"

SECOND LIEUTENANT ALISHA Merchant rubbed the pad of her left thumb in circles around the other fingers on her hand, something she routinely did when she was trying to figure out a puzzle or solve a problem. Her jet-black hair was pulled into a tight bun on the back of her head. Her Air Force uniform was especially crisp this morning. If only the data she was looking at were that crisp.

She hadn't been posted to NORAD for very long, maybe two months. Colorado Springs was a nice place, with lots of hiking trails, a cute downtown business district, and even a few restaurants she'd consider classy. That was more than she could say for some of her coworkers, who maintained a certain distance from her. Maybe it was because of her rank, the lowest of commissioned officers, or the fact that she was the newest member of the team in the control room. But, as her mother was fond of reminding her, that would change someday.

With a sigh, Merchant returned to her computer screens. There were two, side by side. One showed a table of readings from the MAGSAT-6 and MAGSAT-14 satellites, while the other superimposed those readings on a geographical image to create something akin to a topographical map. Only instead of measuring altitude or distance above and below sea level, Merchant's data measured minute differences in and disturbances of the Earth's magnetic field.

First developed in the 1940s, MAD (magnetic anomaly detection) was tested as a means for locating submarines hidden in the ocean's depths. After all, subs were constructed from ferrous metals that interact with magnetic fields. In theory, a submarine would create a disturbance in the planet's magnetic field that could be detected by a magnetometer if it was sensitive enough. In practice, it wasn't very easy to do, and anti-submarine warfare ("ASW") relied more on sonobuoys (floating buoys equipped with listening devices and transmitters for sending its findings back to a nearby ship or aircraft) than on MAD devices.

But the technology had come a long way since then. These days, the kinks had been worked out, and MAD techniques were used by surface ships and aircraft conducting ASW searches. Even more recently, the Navy and Air Force had coordinated in a joint effort to utilize data from satellites originally launched by NASA and equipped with MAD technology for scientific research, and they had also placed more sophisticated MAD packages on newer spy satellites.

The ultimate result was a network of MAGSATs that fed data to Merchant's station in NORAD. If she found a significant enough anomaly that could potentially be a submarine, she relayed the finding to her counterparts in Naval Intelligence. What they did with the information was, at that point, no longer her concern.

This morning, however, she was very concerned. The readings she was looking at were all over the place. At times, it appeared there were three distinct anomalies, and then at other times, they merged into two or, at one point, even a single anomaly. She was used to the data coming in rather "noisy"—scientific slang for a bunch of readings within which some (or occasionally many) were erroneous, outliers, or could otherwise be ignored. But this morning's MAGSAT readings weren't especially noisy. They just weren't exactly clear.

With a loud exhale, Merchant spotted one of the few officers in her division who was actually nice to her: Lieutenant Nancy Dash. She'd just entered the large control room carrying a steaming cup of coffee in both hands. Merchant stood up at her station and waved her arm, catching Dash's attention. Then she waived the lieutenant over.

"Sorry to snag you with something first thing in the morning," Merchant said as Dash approached. Her station was on the top level of the tiered room, and all the way on the far side. "Especially since you clearly haven't even finished your coffee…"

Dash smiled and shook her head as if clearing away some fog. "No problem, Merchant. What's going on?"

"Well," Merchant began, "I'm just a little confused by this morning's readings from MAGSATs six and fourteen." She pointed first at the screen with the table of numbers, which indicated latitude, longitude, and magnetic force as measured in amperes per meter (represented as H) and in teslas (represented as T). Then she ran her hand over the map, which showed the northernmost shore of Norway, the Kola Peninsula, and part of the Barents Sea. "At first, I thought I was seeing the MAD system picking up a submarine. Then I thought I saw two separate subs. Then— and this is where you'll think I'm really crazy—I swear I saw *three*."

Dash narrowed her eyes, put her mug down on Merchant's desk, and looked closer at the monitors. Her vision flicked back and forth from the data table to the cartographic representation. "I see what you mean, Alisha," she said quietly.

Merchant smiled. "So, what do you think we've got here?"

"Unclear," Dash said slowly, still deep in thought. "But I don't think you're crazy. I think there's a good chance we *are* seeing three separate submarines in close proximity, right outside Kola Bay and the Polyarnyy naval base."

"Really? Wow!" Merchant gushed. "I've never even seen

two before, but three? How often does *that* happen?"

"Not that often…"

After a moment, Dash backed away from the monitors and picked up her mug again. "This is pretty unusual. I'm going to run this up the flagpole. The only reason I can think of for three subs to be that close together in the open ocean is if one, or even two, is hunting another. If any of those are ours, we'd better let the Navy know."

Dash started to walk away quickly. Then she stopped, turned to look over her shoulder at Merchant, and smiled. "Good work, Lieutenant. You might have just saved the lives of a hundred American sailors. Not a bad way to start the morning, eh?"

Merchant smiled and let out a quiet giggle. "Not bad at all."

"Conn, radio. The transmission appears to have ended. Recommend lowering ESM mast," Katashi's voice came through the speaker in the control room.

"Radio, conn. Acknowledged," Harper said. In the three minutes and twenty-six seconds since they'd begun the intercept, he'd managed to calm himself down considerably. "Good work, Katashi."

"Thank you, s—" Harper cut off the comms officer's voice so he could issue new orders. "Lower the ESM mast and slow to match the target's speed. How's our distance?"

"Closed to eight thousand yards, sir," came the reply.

"Conn, sonar," Findlay's voice echoed through the conn. "Sierra two-three is diving and changing course."

"Sonar, conn. Understood. Let us know as soon as you've worked out the details."

"Aye, sir. Should only take a minute."

"XO, please see to it our latest recording is shared with the boys in SigInt and a copy is sent to Dr. Driver's station," Harper said, now having returned to his usual, completely calm state. "Dr. Driver," he turned and looked at Will, still standing in the back of the conn, "time to get to work."

Will smiled. "Aye, sir!"

Harper nodded in reply, then turned back around to face forward as Will headed for the mission space.

"Conn, sonar. Sierra two-three is turning to course two nine five, running at ten knots. Still diving."

"Sonar, conn. Thank you, Mr. Findlay," Harper replied. Then he looked to his XO. "We're going to stay on this guy while our professor does his part."

"Sir," Worth said, a look of concern on his face. "After we copy one of the new Russian codes, our orders are to break off pursuit, put some distance between us and any other boat in this frozen ocean, and call home for further instructions."

Harper nodded. "I know, Mr. Worth. But we don't know yet what we've intercepted. And we won't know until Dr. Driver has finished his analysis. Until that time, I'm going to keep the Kazan in our sights." He reached overhead and pushed a button. "Sonar, conn. Aside from Sierra two-three, any other contacts to report?"

Findlay's voice came back. "Conn, sonar. Not really, sir. For a moment, just before we sped up to follow two-three, I thought I got something on the lateral array, but I wasn't sure, so I wasn't going to report it. Just as quickly as I had it, I lost it, sir. Could have been nothing, or could have been masked by the cavitation from the ESM mast. Either way, I'll let you know if I hear anything else out there."

"Very well." Harper looked at his XO. "As far as we know, it's us and the Kazan. And one intercepted message. We don't know what that message is or says. Until we do, we're going to stay right where we are: in that Russian's baffles."

"Aye, sir," Worth replied.

21

SECOND ANALYSIS

ARRIVING IN THE mission space, Will flicked on the overhead fluorescent light and set to work. This would be his second song analysis, and he was eager to get started. Not only was this the very task he came here to do—and at potentially great cost to his personal life—but, for the first time since he set foot on the USS Royal Oak, he was actually contributing to the mission. That felt good.

He sat at the desk and powered on the computer. Picking up a pair of headphones nearby, he plugged them in and put them on. Not the most comfortable set he'd ever worn, but they'd get the job done. The computer finished booting up.

```
Checking network for updates and new messages…
```

"Okay," Will said quietly. Hearing his voice reverberating in his own head, and slightly muffled by the headphones, he smiled. He knew he was deep in thought when he conversed with himself.

New message received. From: RadioComms-1, USS
Royal Oak. Contents: 1 file. Type: audio.

"Alright!" Will exclaimed, surprising himself with the level
of excitement in his voice. He clicked on the message and
opened the file containing the broadcast they had
intercepted moments earlier. Then he closed his eyes while
the music played and he listened, once again letting the
sounds wash over him.

He remembered the first of these coded songs, the one
he'd analyzed in that hidden office in a nondescript strip
mall outside Philadelphia. He could tell right away that this
song had a few similar traits: the steady, pounding beat in
duple meter; a bass line that was clearly played on a
synthesizer; and the vocals that carried an artificial shimmer,
which he knew could only be produced with generous doses
of auto-tune algorithms. He hadn't spent much time in
professional recording studios, but they weren't totally
anathema to him. Besides, he'd had a few undergraduates
whose final projects involved compositions recorded on their
computers, so he'd seen students work with synthesized
bass lines and auto-tuned vocal tracks.

"Lyrics first. Let's take it from the top."

Will picked up the pen that had been resting on the
yellow, college-ruled pad on the desk and began transcribing
the words as he played the song a second time. "Similar
double couplets," he remarked. "Probably insignificant, but
grounding the composition in the current pop milieu."

Linguistically, he heard mostly standard Russian. This
song's narrative was nominally about a boy with a crush on
the local mayor's daughter. Of course, the love was
completely unrequited until the song's middle section, the
bridge, when he thinks she smiled at him. There was a clever
key change at that moment, a modulation from the song's
minor key to its parallel major. The device betrayed a hint of

musical sophistication and depth behind an otherwise simple and shallow veneer. In other words, whoever composed this piece wasn't a total hack. They knew something about pop songwriting.

Importantly, Will could immediately identify a handful of phrases outside of the standard Russian dialect and syntax. "Gotcha," he said, smiling, as he began notating the Ket phrases:

Carrying twigs for a new nest
Unseen by the sun and moon, unheard by the creatures below them
Building today for the future tomorrow
All prey turns to carrion

On the one hand, Will wasn't surprised by the natural basis for these phrases, since the Ket metaphors from the first sample song had a similar foundation in the natural world. Indeed, as he had described in his dissertation, much of the Ket cosmology, their system of beliefs, was deeply rooted in nature. In a traditional Ket way of life, it was the preferred way to signify.

On the other hand, however, Will was a little surprised by the last phrase. So much so that he spent a few extra minutes on it, considering all of the possible translations for the Ket words, the etymological possibilities, and how the translation might relate to the other three Ket lines he found in this song. In the end, it was the word *carrion* that gave him the most trouble. But he was confident in the way his translation captured the meaning of the phrases, their intent if not their literal equivalents.

As with the first song, the question remained: what did the phrases mean?

"Hello?" Jackie Fletcher said as she picked up the phone on her desk, again surprised that it rang. That navy admiral was the last person to actually call her.

"Um, hello," the voice on the other end said meekly. "This is Ashley Driver, may I please speak with Professor Jackie Fletcher?"

Jackie furrowed her brow; this was unusual. "Yes, Mrs. Driver, this is Jackie. How are you?"

"Well," Ashley sighed, "I've been better, to be honest. I'm...I'm sorry to bother you—"

"Oh, it's no bother at all! How can I help?"

"It's Will," Ashley explained. "I know he's, well, out of town. But it's been a week now and I haven't heard from him, which is pretty unusual. The kids haven't either. Not even a single text message, and that's downright strange. I mean, he adores our kids and—"

Jackie interrupted again. She didn't like to make a habit of it, but she knew that Ashley could go on for a while and she had a meeting with the dean and other department chairs in fifteen minutes.

She didn't know Ashley all that well; they'd met a few times at university functions, but Will mostly kept family matters separate from work. Nonetheless, Jackie felt a kindred spirit with Ashley, even though they were mere acquaintances at best and Jackie was, she guessed, about ten years older. Certainly, Ashley sounded like she could use a friend right now.

"Have you spoken with the admiral?" Jackie asked.

"—it would be—I'm sorry, what? Who?" Ashley sputtered.

"The admiral," Jackie repeated. "Admiral..." she drew out the last consonant in the word while she searched her brain, and the scattered piles of paper on her desk, for his name. "Oh, I was sure I'd remember his...oh yes! Admiral Carter. Have you spoken with him?"

"I'm afraid I...I don't know who that is." Ashley sniffled.

"Oh," Jackie said, a little surprised. Had Will kept her completely in the dark? "Well, I imagine you could find him. There can't be that many admirals in the United States Navy!" She let out a little laugh, hoping it would lighten the mood. It didn't seem to work.

"An admiral," Ashley repeated.

"Look, hang on one second. I think this phone on my desk keeps track of the calls I've received. I might be able to pull up his number," Jackie offered.

"That would be helpful, I suppose..." Ashley said quietly.

Jackie started pushing the various buttons on the phone. Aside from the usual numbers, all the other buttons had symbols on them. But the symbols seemed to bear little resemblance to any function one might want a telephone to have. And the little screen, which showed at most twelve digits, seemed completely disconnected from the results of any of the buttons. Finally, by sheer luck, Jackie landed on the call history. From there, it took mere seconds to find the number from which she'd received the admiral's call a few days earlier.

"Here it is," Jackie said in as light a tone as she could. "Seven-oh-three, five-five-five, one-two-zero-zero. Did you get that?"

"Yes, thank you." Ashley paused for a moment. "Jackie?"

"Yes, Ashley."

"What did the admiral say to you when he called? Did he tell you where Will was? Or when he'd be back?" Ashley was clearly nervous to ask, though Jackie didn't know why she should be.

"He was fairly vague, I'm afraid. His call seemed mostly about university business, that the navy would cover the cost of a substitute for Will's classes, that sort of thing. He didn't really say anything about where Will was headed, what he would be doing there, or when he'd return." Jackie recalled. "I'm sorry I don't know more."

"That's alright," Ashley replied. Her voice seemed a bit steadier now, like gaining the information about the admiral and a means to contact him somehow calmed her. "I appreciate your help, Jackie. Hopefully, next time we talk I won't sound quite so hysterical!"

"Not to worry, Ashley. I'm sure next time we talk you'll have quite the story to tell about Will and his mysterious trip."

"Let's hope so. Thank you again, Jackie. Have a nice day."

"You're quite welcome. You too. Goodbye."

Jackie hung up the phone and, for a moment, simply sat and stared at it. As strange as the out-of-the-blue call from Admiral Carter had been, it struck her as even stranger that Will would leave without even telling his wife where he was going or when he planned to return. What would compel a man to do that? Will didn't seem like the sort who would cheat on his wife, and, today's call notwithstanding, Ashley didn't seem the sort to let herself be hoodwinked like that. What reason could he possibly have to justify his behavior? Why keep his own wife in the dark?

ONCE AGAIN, WILL hoped a closer examination of the musical details would help clarify the meaning of the Ket phrases he'd identified. This time he didn't bother mapping the song's form. He knew it was rather unremarkable—it was put together like a standard pop song. Instead, he skipped right to an examination of the song's melody. "Let's listen for how the particular collection of pitches in this piece match up with both the standard scalar structures of globalized popular music and the particularities of Ket musical traditions," he said to himself.

As with the first sample, Will noticed a few spots where

the melody, sung by the lead vocalist, seemed to stray from the "standard" major scale. Of course, he was listening for this and knew from his earlier analysis that it was likely to happen at the same time as the switch from Russian to Ket lyrics. It did.

Will nodded and smiled to himself. "Well done." Then he looked around to make sure no one had heard him compliment himself. Finding the mission space empty—still —he chuckled and continued his work.

Next step: harmony. This time around he knew what he'd find. Chords and groups of chords that mostly followed established Western patterns. Right up until the moment the Ket lyrics began, at which point they'd include some of those extra-scalar pitches to create chords well outside Western expectations.

Finally, he muttered, "Time to check for serial procedures," and ripped the top page off the pad on the desk revealing a fresh one beneath. Nobody in the Navy had thought to provide him with staff paper, that is, paper with groups of five horizontal lines that he could use to create a line of musical notation, a *staff*. And, he thought to himself, it was doubtful it would be anywhere on the entire boat. So he'd have to improvise. His lines weren't exactly straight, but they would do. He just needed enough space to notate the tone rows.

And he was smart enough not to bother finding the rows in the "conventional" parts of the song. He knew those were not especially interesting from a cryptological point of view. Rather, he listened closely to the specific sets of pitches, simultaneous and sequential, that occurred under and during the phrases of Ket lyrics.

It took several minutes and multiple times through the song, but Will finally got it:

0 1 4 6 9 10

After writing the last number, he dropped the pen on the yellow pad and sat back, stretching his arms over his head, taking in a deep breath, and exhaling loudly. "That's it. That's the row for this song—different from the other one. And if these rows mean what we think they mean, then this one points to a different location on a Russian map. But where?"

At that moment, the phone on the table buzzed, causing Will to jump and nearly fall out of his seat. He hadn't expected to be interrupted. He eyed the receiver cautiously, as if it might sting him. Slowly and carefully, he picked it up. On the other end, he could hear the XO's voice: "Mission, conn. Dr. Driver, any progress?"

Will swallowed hard. It had seemed like only a few minutes since he got started on this analysis, but a glance at the clock on the wall told him he'd been at it for just over twenty.

"Uh, conn, mission?" He said, unsure of the exact protocol as it was the first time he'd used the boat's internal comms. "Um, yes. Yes, sir, XO. I'm making some progress."

"Good," the XO replied quickly. "The skipper would appreciate an update as soon as you have something to report. In the meantime, is there anything you need?"

"Well, actually, there is." Will paused; he was almost afraid to ask.

"Name it."

"Well, sir, I need a map," he said tentatively. Then, to clarify: "A *Russian* map."

There was a moment of silence. "Pardon?"

"Sir, if the tone rows, er, the strings of numbers I'm discovering are, as the cryptologists suspect, coordinates on a Russian map, I'd like to see where this particular set of numbers points to." Will could feel a bead of sweat drip down the back of his neck. He hadn't been this nervous in a long time.

"I see. Yes, good point." Worth cleared his throat. "Go to the SigInt Suite. The boys in there should be able to help you out. They don't get a lot of visitors—not many on the boat cleared to go in there—so I'll let them know you're coming."

"Thank you, sir."

"Report to the conn as soon as you have something."

"Will do," Will said triumphantly. "Over and out!"

"Uh…" Worth said slowly. "We generally don't say…" he let out an audible sigh. "Alright. Over and, er, conn out."

22

FIRST RESULTS

WILL BURST OUT of the SigInt suite and ran the short distance up the passageway to the conn. In his excitement, he nearly bowled over an enlisted sailor—the passageways on the sub were rather narrow—and barely had time to apologize before exploding into the conn. His heart was beating loudly in his ears and his stomach felt like it was tied up in knots.

Harper, Worth, and Hargraves were gathered around the ECDIS chart table. All three looked up as Will careened into the compartment.

"I think I know where he's going," Will said, panting and out of breath.

"Dr. Driver," Worth said by way of greeting, "I take it your analysis was fruitful?"

"It sure was, XO," Will replied as he put his hands on his knees, beginning to catch his breath. His glasses slid down his sweaty nose. Pushing them back up, he stood for his report. "I've got some more work to do on the Ket phrases, working out the kinks in the metaphorical analysis between the cosmologically based domain and the geographic—"

"Dr. Driver," Harper said calmly. "In language the rest of us can understand, please."

"Right," Will nodded. "Sorry. What I mean is, I don't know yet what the Kazan is going to do when it gets to its destination, but I have a sense of where that destination is." Will walked forward and down a step into the center area of the room, approaching the ECDIS. "May I?" he asked, gesturing at the brightly lit tabletop screen.

"Okay," Hargraves said tentatively.

"Thanks," replied Will. "Now, how do I?—Oh, sure, here, I got it." He found some of the buttons along the side of the digital map and was able to move and scale the image. It took a few moments as he made adjustments and recentered the map. When he finished, it no longer showed the USS Royal Oak's current location in the Barents Sea. Instead, he had shifted it west and south. He had also zoomed out, so the display showed a large portion of the Atlantic, from about 5° to 20° north latitude and 45° to 75° west longitude. The right half of the map was the empty Atlantic, while the left half showed the eastern Caribbean. Near the top left corner of the map were Haiti and the Dominican Republic; the bottom left showed Colombia and Venezuela.

Hargraves whistled. Worth grunted.

"That's a pretty big swath of the map, Driver," Harper said.

Will nodded. "That's true. I can continue to narrow down the Kazan's destination, and if we can intercept more signals maybe that'll help. But it's clear that, wherever she ultimately ends up, she's headed southwest across the North Atlantic Ocean."

"In *theory*," Worth added. Will's head snapped up to look at the XO. "What I mean is, based on your *interpretation* of the Russian pop song, this is where you *think* Sierra two-three has been ordered to go. It remains to be seen if she actually sails there."

Hargraves took a deep breath. "And what she does when she gets there."

LIEUTENANT DONOVAN LEANED back in his chair and reached up with both arms. The move cracked his back, which had been getting stiff after several hours of work, reading reports on the computer. So many reports.

The afternoon had started with the transmission from one of the SSBNs out in the Pacific. They had picked up a pair of Russian frigates steaming northwest, presumably toward the naval base at Vladivostok. Although always worth reporting whenever the naval assets of an adversary are detected, the pair didn't seem to bear any ill intentions and, most importantly, didn't seem to detect the American submarine.

That was followed by a series of brief reports from naval surveillance planes, reporting on Chinese and Iranian naval movements. Nothing unexpected. Nothing exciting.

Donovan knew full well that this was how the intelligence game was played. You collect a million tiny bits of information, put them all together, and see what patterns emerge. The reports were the collection stage, and he was the poor, unlucky officer who had to sift through them.

After a long yawn, he adjusted himself in the chair and turned his attention back to the computer in front of him.

```
NORAD MAD REPORT
REPORT ID#667NG24Z81
ANALYST: MERCHANT, ALISHA
STATUS: URGENT
MEMO:
Cluster  of  3  possible  submarine  signatures
detected via MADSAT at approx 69°82'N/33°59'E.
ATTACHMENT: 1 IMAGE
```

Well, this was interesting. Donovan narrowed his eyes and leaned forward toward the computer screen. Three submarines within close proximity was highly unusual. Yes, that location was just outside Polyarnyy and just within Russian territorial waters, but still.

Running his tongue over his lips, Donovan wondered to himself whether any of the subs were American. Typically, the locations of American submarines were closely guarded secrets, but he knew enough about the USS Royal Oak's passenger and mission to suspect that one of the signatures could be her. And if he was right, it was likely that another was a Russian sub she was tracking. But that only accounted for two of the three subs the satellites detected. Whose was the third? He reached for a nearby phone and quickly dialed a four-digit extension.

"COMSUBLANT operations, duty officer speaking," the voice on the other end answered after the first ring.

"Hi, this is Donovan in the ONI. Is that Phil?" Donovan asked, hoping he recognized the voice of the duty officer in the office of the submarine commander for the Atlantic.

"Al? Hot damn! I haven't seen you in a while. What's shakin'?" Phil said joyfully.

"Not much doin' over here. How's Francine?"

"Oh, you know. Three kids is no joke, man."

"No, I *don't* know, Phil," Donovan said with a chuckle.

Phil laughed too. "Yeah, that's true! Someday, my friend, someday. Now what are you botherin' me about?"

Donovan's voice returned to its professional, serious tone. "Well, I'm looking at an urgent report from NORAD. MADSATs picked up some sub signatures and I'm trying to figure out if any are ours before I bring it to the admiral. Can you verify an op area for me?"

"Sure. Where?"

Donovan relayed the latitude and longitude coordinates from the NORAD report. It took only a moment for the duty officer to pull up the information.

"Lieutenant, I'm showing one American submarine assigned to an op area that includes those coordinates."

"Only one?"

"Affirmative. SSN-812. That's the…" his voice trailed off as he cross-referenced the hull number with the list of active submarine names. "Royal Oak."

"Shit," Donovan replied quickly. "Phil, I gotta go. Thanks for your help."

"No prob—"

Donovan replaced the phone. If the Royal Oak was the only American boat in that part of the world, and if it could be assumed that one of the two remaining submarine signatures was a Russian sub they were tracking, then the most likely explanation for the third signature was that it was another foreign sub—most likely also Russian—tracking the Royal Oak.

"Shit," Donovan said again, this time to no one in particular. He picked up the phone again. This time he dialed a longer number, to be routed outside the Pentagon. It was a number he'd called many times before, but one he didn't enjoy calling after hours.

"Hello?"

Donavan hung his head. He had hoped to reach the admiral, but his wife had answered instead.

"Good evening, Mrs. Carter, I'm sorry to bother you. This is Lieutenant Donovan calling from the office. Is the admiral available please?"

Mrs. Carter's voice sounded older than she really was, although to be honest Donovan didn't really have any idea how old she was. It was one of those voices that could soothe, like a warm cup of tea. "Oh, hello, Albert. Just one moment. I'll get him."

Donovan rubbed his chin as he waited for the admiral to come on the line.

"Donovan, what's going on?" Admiral Carter said gruffly. "What's so important you need to interrupt game night with my granddaughter?"

"I'm sorry to interrupt, sir, but I've received an analysis of MADSAT data from NORAD showing three submarine signatures in the vicinity of Polyarnyy."

"Three? That's damn peculiar," Carter said, his voice betraying genuine surprise and concern. "Well, one of them is probably Jim Harper's boat. Whose are the other two?"

"That's the thing, sir," Donovan replied. "We can probably assume that the Royal Oak is tracking a Russian boat leaving the naval base. Those were her orders, after all. It's the third signature that worries me."

"Have you checked with COMSUBLANT? Made sure we don't have any other assets tasked to that op area?"

"Already done, sir. The Royal Oak is the only one."

The admiral paused for a moment. "So that third boat is probably tailing Harper. He's a good skipper, one of our best. If there's a boat that can sneak up on him, that's a dangerous thing. Do we know whose it is?"

"No, sir. It's probably also Russian, given the location. But we don't know for sure."

"Hmm," the admiral was thinking now. "If they can stay hidden from Harper, it's probably one of their newer subs, maybe even one of those Borei-class boats. Here's what we're going to do, Donovan. First, tell COMSUBLANT to issue an emergency notice on the ULF. At that distance, it's unlikely the Royal Oak will hear it, but the ultra-low-frequency channels are our best bet until they come shallow for a comms check, which they're unlikely to do if they're in pursuit. So we need to try. And second, get back with the folks at NORAD and see if any of our eyes in the sky has seen any other Russian subs—especially Boreis—lurking around there in the past week or so."

"Yes, sir, I'll take care of it," Donovan said.

"Thank you, lieutenant. You did the right thing, bringing this to my immediate attention," Carter said. "Keep me updated."

"Yes, sir."

"ALRIGHT, THEN," HARPER said, jumping into the conversation before tensions got too high. "Let's do this: We'll keep tracking Sierra two-three, staying on her tail. Let's see where she goes. If Driver is right, we'll know soon enough."

"Sir," Worth said quietly, shaking his head. "Our orders are specific. We should break pursuit and call this in. Let the higher-ups decide what to do with this information. See if the guys at the ONI can crack this code."

Will leaned into the conversation. "I've been to the ONI, remember? They called for *me*."

"I hear you, Rob," the skipper said to his XO. "But we need more information before we make a report. Otherwise, we're reporting theory. I want to report fact."

Hargraves scratched the back of his neck as he thought. "And what about the twelve-mile line?"

"What's a twelve-mile line?" Will asked, looking from the XO to the navigator. At this point, he'd had enough conversations with various members of the crew that he didn't feel bad about asking questions. Of course, this was the most high-pressure situation they'd encountered in their mission so far.

The XO answered. "It denotes the limit of a state's legitimate claims to sovereignty over oceans. Formally established at the UNCLOS III conference, in 1982, although some governments have been known to ignore it."

"If an American warship comes within twelve nautical miles of the Russian shore," Harper added, "Moscow could rightly claim that their sovereign territory was breached in an act of war. Even if no shots were fired."

Hargraves cleared his throat. "So the question remains. Look where we are right now, and where Sierra two-three is heading. Both on the Russian side of the line. How long are we going to operate in Russian sovereign waters?"

"If we're in Russian waters," Will said, looking back to Hargraves, "doesn't that make our presence here problematic? Wouldn't the Russians see our presence here as an act of war, if they knew about it?"

"That's the beautiful thing about a submarine, Dr. Driver," Harper said. "If we do our job right, no one will ever even know we were here."

PART FIVE

DISCOVERY

23

CLARIFICATION

"SIR, BEGGING YOUR pardon, sir," Will whispered as he followed Harper away from the chart table and back toward the skipper's seat in the center of the conn. "But this seems really dangerous. I didn't sign up for—"

"Dr. Driver," Harper interrupted, "this is a United States nuclear attack submarine. We do not flinch at the prospect of danger. Our mission is to pursue this target and that is what I intend to do." His tone was quiet but firm.

Will could hear his heart beating in his ears. Maybe the past week had been fun—well, maybe *fun* wasn't the right word for it, but he hadn't hated the experience—but in the past few minutes, it had become clear just how close he, Harper, and the entire boat stood to the precipice of war. It was a line he didn't want to cross. And he didn't want to be responsible for leading others across it, either.

"Skipper," Worth said.

Harper gave Worth a glare, indicating that the time for discussion and debate was over. Worth didn't need any help translating the withering look from his commanding officer.

Harper reached up to the intercom. "Sonar, conn. Where's Sierra two-three and what's she up to?"

"Conn, sonar. I hold Sierra two-three bearing zero-one-two at a depth of approximately three hundred feet. Speed ten knots," Findlay said matter-of-factly. "No indication she's detected us, sir."

"Very well," Harper replied, turning off the intercom. "Nav, what's our current position?"

Hargraves used his sleeve to wipe the sweat from his forehead, then he reached up to scratch the back of his head. "Sir," he began, "hard to say with pinpoint accuracy. We are just about right on the border of Russian sovereign waters."

The XO, standing over the skipper's right shoulder, leaned in. "As far as the Russians are concerned, we might as well be swimming off Polyarnyy beach. We're close enough that they won't care which side of the line we're on. If they detect us, they'll shoot."

Harper looked back at Worth. "We are a *spy* submarine."

"We are also not at war," Worth replied, raising his eyebrows and tipping his head. "Sir."

NORTH KOREAN JETS CROSS DEMILITARIZED ZONE

By Audrey Jenkins, Washington Advocate

A pair of North Korean fighter jets crossed over the demilitarized zone yesterday and briefly entered South Korean airspace before returning to their side of the border, according to South Korean and American military officials. The MiG-21 jets, originally designed for and produced by the Soviet Union, are among the most popular fighter aircraft in the world. They were widely exported from the USSR and, after its dissolution, the Russian Federation. North Korea is estimated to have between two and three dozen such warplanes.

Under the terms of the 1953 Korean Armistice Agreement, which established the demilitarized zone, no military assets were to be used in or across the two-and-a-half-mile-wide buffer between North and South Korea. There have been numerous violations of the agreement in the decades since its adoption, but current geopolitical tensions make this area, already the most heavily militarized border in the world, particularly fraught.

According to anonymous sources, South Korean radar installations reported acquisition of the North Korean jets at 7:32 AM yesterday morning, local time. When the pair did not appear to alter course as they approached the border, the South Korean Air Force scrambled a pair of aircraft from the force's 10th Fighter Wing, at Suwon Air Base, to intercept. The opposing jets came into contact somewhere over Paju, South Korea, after which the North Korean jets returned to their home country.

"Today's incursion marks a significant escalation in tensions on the Korean Peninsula," US military spokesman Brent Eislen said in Washington. "The United States military, along with our partners in the Republic of Korea, work tirelessly to protect the freedom of South Korean civilians and American service members in South Korea. We hope the North Korean government will reconsider its stance toward its southern neighbor and adopt a position of constructive dialogue rather than provocative action."

North Korean officials at the United Nations declined to comment.

These latest provocations come at a time of rising tensions worldwide between the Russian and North Korean alliance, on one side, and the United States and its allies (including South Korea) on the other. Within the past month, border skirmishes have taken place in Finland and Ukraine. Repeated efforts to pass resolutions calling for de-escalation and dialogue at the United Nations Security Council have been vetoed by China, Russia, and the United States.

"If you put this latest incident into perspective," explained Graham Macintosh, a security expert at the Bain-Robinson Foundation, "you can see a clear trend toward testing the strength and resolve of allied forces, without taking on the United States directly. And while the allies stood their ground in Finland and South Korea, and to a lesser degree in Ukraine, the border areas are so huge that it's nearly impossible to predict where Russia or North Korea — or even, perhaps, their friends in China — will test us next. Let's hope that their next provocation will not be directed at an American warship, base, or territory, as that would raise the stakes even further."

THE KAZAN CONTINUED its northwesterly course, appearing as if it were going to skirt the top of Scandinavia before beginning its southwestern transit across the Atlantic. Based on their current position, Hargraves informed the skipper, it was likely they'd leave Russian waters and enter Norwegian territory within the next thirty minutes.

Tensions in the conn remained high. Harper and Worth had disagreed before, of course. It was the skipper's *modus operandi* to solicit opinions and, as the XO, Worth was not shy about offering them. Today's argument would likely be filed under 'friendly differences of perspective' just like all the rest. Harsh glares would be forgotten as the men enjoyed cups of black coffee and briefings and drills and all the quotidian events that occupied a submariner's time at sea.

But Will didn't know about any of that. He wasn't aware of Harper's longstanding friendship with Worth, or the way their relationship fit into Harper's style of command. To Will, the glares and stern tones signaled a deep fissure. They were the signifiers that signified the fraying fabric of the chain of command on board the USS Royal Oak. And given their literal position on the map and the amount of firepower he imagined the American and Russian submarines carried, he grew increasingly nervous about the developing situation. Certainly, his professional work was on the line. After all, they were out here, near the frozen top of the world and within spitting distance of one of their country's most powerful adversaries, because of the analytical skills *he* brought to the mission. But that wasn't the only thing at risk. As had become increasingly clear, his very life was on the line as well.

"Conn, sonar. New contact bearing one-six-five. Definitely a submarine, sir." Findlay's voice yanked Will out of his thoughts and grabbed the attention of everyone in the control room. "Depth two hundred fifty feet, speed six knots, distance ten thousand yards and closing."

"Sonar, conn. Where in holy hell did he come from?" Harper said urgently.

"Right in our baffles," Worth muttered.

"I don't know, sir, he must've been real quiet," Findlay answered, clearly concerned. "The computer says it's likely a Borei, possibly the Yuri Dolgorukiy. Designate contact Sierra two-four."

"Probability of detection?" Harper asked the sonar officer.

"I'd estimate the probably of detection—I'm getting transients, sir. He's opening torpedo tube doors!" The pitch of Findlay's voice began to creep up.

Harper spun his head around to look at Worth, and then to Davis, at the weapons station. "Load tubes three and four and standby on countermeasures!"

Will could hear Davis repeat the skipper's orders and lift a phone handset to talk with the crewmen in the torpedo room. He imaged the men straining to guide the enormous weapons gently into their launch tubes.

"He's not really going to shoot at us, would he?" Will asked aloud to no one in particular.

The XO looked up at Will from his spot in the center of the room, next to the skipper. "He knows we're here, and he's got to know that we heard him open his doors. He could just be sending us a message: get out of our backyard."

"Could be," Harper added, "but these days, you can't be too—"

"Torpedo in the water! Torpedo in the water!" Findlay shouted through the comms. "Sierra two-four has launched two fish, equate to Russian USET-80 torpedoes. Range nine thousand, five hundred yards, inbound on our position. Speed forty knots."

Harper sprang into action. "Snapshots, tubes three and four, on inbound torpedoes' origin! Left full rudder, ahead flank, make your depth five hundred feet! Dive! Dive! Dive!"

As the Royal Oak leaped to its top speed and the bow tilted down at a dramatic angle, Davis spoke up, over the klaxon: "Sir, it's going to take a moment on those snapshots —our tube doors are still closed!"

"Damnit, Weps!" Harper slammed his hand down on the armrest of his seat. They'd been caught unprepared, embarrassed. As much as he wished he could blame his weapons officer, he knew it was his responsibility. Davis wouldn't have opened their torpedo tube doors until ordered to do so, and he was the one who should've given that order.

The XO completed some quick calculations before

reporting: "Estimated impact of inbound weapons in seven minutes, sir. He took a long shot."

Harper looked to Worth. "Lucky for us, I suppose. I'd still prefer not to have twelve hundred pounds of Moscow's finest explosives hurtling through the water at my boat."

Worth nodded vigorously. "Yes, sir!"

"YES, HELLO. I'M looking for an Admiral Carter, please."

The voice on the other end of the line paused for just a moment. "I'm sorry, ma'am, may I ask who's calling?"

"Of course. This is Ashley Driver. My husband, Will, was recently in touch with Admiral Carter about some business trip and I'd like to find out where they went."

"I see...well, Mrs. Driver, I do see an Admiral Carter in the master personnel list here, but I do not see a direct, public line. So, I'm going to have to transfer you to his aides if that's alright." The voice was calm and friendly, but firm.

Ashley took a deep breath. Why had she thought it would be easy to locate an admiral in the Pentagon and just interrogate him about her husband's whereabouts? At least they didn't deny this admiral's very existence, she supposed. "Alright then, if that's what we have to do."

"Yes, ma'am. One moment, please, while I transfer you."

There was a click, a few seconds of silence, and then an automated voice began spouting the benefits of joining the United States Armed Forces while she waited on hold. It didn't take long.

"ONI officer on duty." Lieutenant Anderson announced herself the way receptionists so often do, using a tone that sounds more like a question than a statement.

"Yes, hello, may I speak with Admiral Carter please?" Ashley asked.

"And who, may I ask, is calling?" Anderson responded.

"Right," Ashley replied. "This is Ashley Driver. My husband, William, is on some business trip with the admiral, I think. Or so I've been told. I'd like to know where he is, if that's alright."

"I see…" Anderson said, taking a moment to think about how to handle the call. This wasn't the sort of thing she expected when she picked up the OD's phone line. An image of Will's face crossed her mind, with his I-just-woke-up-like-this hairdo and a cute dimple on his left cheek. She shook the thought out of her head and refocused.

There were a few challenges here. First, she had to somehow verify the identity of the caller. Then, there was the question of whether she could actually speak with the admiral. Fortunately, he wasn't in his office at the moment—some meeting somewhere in the massive complex had pulled him away—so it would be easy, and truthful, to say she'd have to take a message. That would buy her time to address the first problem. "I'm sorry, Mrs. Driver, but the admiral is not in right now. May I take a message for him?"

"When will he be back?" Ashley asked, her voice gaining a hint of an edge.

"I'm afraid I'm not at liberty to say, ma'am."

That was not what Ashley wanted to hear. "Does he have a direct line I can try?"

"I'm afraid not, Mrs. Driver. But I can take a message if you wish." Anderson was genuinely trying to be helpful. She hoped the conversation wouldn't devolve. But if it did, she'd stand her ground.

"Well, when will he call me back?" Ashley asked.

"I'm afraid I can't say," Anderson answered. "His schedule is not made public."

Ashley let out a growl. "Do you know how frustrating this is? How frustrated *I* am? Will disappears for a week, and I get one brief, cryptic call from him in which he tells me nothing. Nothing! Then I have to learn from his department chair about some phone call she got from Carter. So he can call Will's *boss* but he can't call Will's *wife*? This is insane!"

Anderson felt for Ashley. She could only imagine what it must be like in her position. To make things worse, she could still picture him, dozing in his seat on that flight from Andrews to New London. The smile on his face when she gently woke him after they'd arrived. Of course, it wasn't her fault; she didn't call the shots at the ONI. But she wished she could help.

At that moment, the front door of the office opened and Carter strode in, dutifully followed by Lieutenant Donovan. "Still no response to the ULF alert, I take it?" he asked over his shoulder, his slightly gravelly voice sounding a bit hoarser than usual.

"No, sir, no response from the Royal Oak," Donovan replied as the two men approached the desk where Anderson sat.

Anderson put her hand over the phone and whispered to the admiral. "Sir, I have a—"

"Not now, lieutenant," Carter said curtly. "We've got a situation." He finished traversing the outer office and marched into his inner sanctum, closing the heavy wood door behind him.

Anderson looked to Donovan, who remained on the outside of the admiral's door, standing near her desk. "Albert, it's Will Driver's wife," she said quietly.

Donovan looked down at Anderson, who was still holding her hand over the phone. "I don't think he's in the mood to talk to her right now." He let out a sigh. "In fact, after that meeting, I don't think he's in the mood to talk to *anyone* right now."

"CONN, SONAR," FINDLAY'S voice echoed in the control room,

"The Kazan is increasing speed, bearing three-four-six. She's turning to port and going deep."

"Very well," Harper responded.

"Right now, the Kazan's skipper probably thinks those torpedoes are aimed at him. In fact, he's probably surprised as hell to discover he's not alone out here," Worth said calmly. "But once we fire our torpedoes and he sees them swimming *away* from him, he'll realize he's dealing with not one, but *two* other subs. And there's no telling who he'll shoot at when he returns fire."

Weps shouted across the room, "doors open on tubes three and four. Solution ready. Torpedoes ready!"

"Do we want to fight one Russian sub or two?" Worth asked.

Another crewman interjected loudly: "Ship ready!"

"I don't see how we can avoid it, XO," Harper said quietly, rubbing the stubble on his chin. "Sierra two-four knows who we are and where we are. The Kazan, Sierra two-three, *they* still don't know we're here. But if we launch torpedoes, we reveal our presence and location to the Kazan. Problem is, I don't think we can get out of this jam without shooting back at Sierra two-four—we must give that Russian skipper *something* to worry about if we're going to make it out alive."

"Conn, sonar. Incoming torpedoes now running at forty-five knots; distance eight thousand yards and closing. Sierra two-four now at fifteen knots; distance nine thousand yards and closing. She's lining up to take another shot at us, sir!"

Harper looked to Worth.

Worth nodded to his skipper and tried to remain calm as he replied. "Fair point, sir. Let's give *him* something to sweat about for a change."

Harper kept his eyes on Worth while he shouted, "Fire tubes three and four at Sierra two-four, guide-by-wire—"

"Shooting tubes three and four, guide-by-wire," Davis

responded.

Will could feel a slight shudder as highly compressed air propelled the two torpedoes from the tubes along the side of the boat.

"—Right full rudder. Course three-five-zero. Ahead two-thirds," Harper ordered. "Make your depth two hundred feet." He stood and reached for a grab bar anchored on the ceiling amidst the knobs, buttons, handles, and gauges.

The diving officer repeated the skipper's orders while the helmsman, pilot, and planesman steered the boat from their stations. Hargraves made a notation on the ECDIS chart.

"Tubes three and four fired electrically," Davis reported. "Own-ship weapons swimming hot, straight, and normal. Estimated time to impact five minutes, twenty seconds."

Will could feel the boat slow, turn, and begin to rise as the skipper once again changed the boat's speed, direction, and depth in an attempt to outfox the incoming torpedoes. For the first time, he realized that his preferred spot for observing the goings on, leaning against the back wall of the conn, was one of the few spots in the entire compartment not within arm's reach of something to grab onto.

24

EVASION

THE PAIRS OF American Mk. 48 ADCAP and Russian USET-80 torpedoes passed each other under the cold waters of the Barents Sea as Davis put down his station's comms handset. "Mr. Findlay reports own-ship torpedoes approaching target location. Range fifteen hundred yards. Impact in approximately sixty seconds." He took a quick breath. "Incoming ordinance now two thousand yards and still closing. Time to impact..." he did some quick calculations, "...approximately one minute, twenty seconds."

"Understood, Weps," Worth replied.

Harper reached for the intercom. "Sonar, conn. Where's Sierra two-three?"

Findlay's voice came back. "Conn, sonar. Hard to tell, sir. There's a lot of noise in the water. Sierra two-four just launched countermeasures. Last known location on Sierra two-three is nine thousand yards, now bearing two-nine-six. She was turning, increasing speed, and diving. Sir, I'm going to need a quieter ocean to get a good read on her again."

"I'll see what I can do about that," Harper replied with a smirk.

Davis spoke up. "Own-ship weapons closing in on last known target location. Slowing and entering search mode."

"Damn," Hargraves cursed under his breath.

Will whispered to the COB, "What does that mean?"

"It means, Dr. Driver, that the submarine we shot at isn't there anymore. We don't know *where* it is, and our torpedoes are going to start searching for it."

Will nodded. "They'll find it, right?"

The COB shrugged. "Depends on a lot of factors. How well can the enemy sub hide? What other sounds might distract the torpedoes? And how much fuel do they have left?"

"Hmm," Will responded.

The COB smiled. "We'll make a sailor out of you yet, Dr. Driver."

"SUSPENDED?!" ASHLEY YELLED at Jake. "How the hell could you get yourself suspended?" She stood in the main office of Jake's school, towering over the ten-year-old, who sat on one of the chairs in the waiting area.

Her volume attracted the attention of the three secretaries, who froze and watched the proceedings. Parents could be so entertaining when they were angry in public places. Would this mother continue to flip out or would she collect herself and calm down? If only they had a bucket of popcorn.

The principal stuck her head out from her private office. A Black woman with a round face and carefully coiffed hair, Aziza Franklin had a reputation as a no-nonsense, but fair, administrator. "Mrs. Driver? Jacob? Why don't you come in now, please."

Jake crossed his arms in front of his chest and walked past

his mother. Ashley let out a huff and followed. The secretaries sighed, disappointed the show didn't last longer, and returned to their work.

"Mrs. Driver, Jacob, please have a seat," Principal Franklin said as she rounded her desk and sat in her high-back leather chair. "I gather you know why you've been invited here, Mrs. Driver?"

"I do now," Ashley responded, trying to keep herself calm. There was no need to take her anger out on the principal, of course. Especially when she had a son who deserved it. "My son has gone and earned himself a suspension."

"He has," Franklin confirmed, nodding slowly. "As you well know, we have a zero-tolerance policy when it comes to violence in this school. Your son punched another student during their lunch period. That is unacceptable. District policy mandates a minimum three-day suspension."

"Three days?" Ashley asked. Sure, Jake didn't have a spotless record. He occasionally made snarky comments that resulted in emails from teachers. But he'd never been violent before. And never earned three days of suspension.

Ashley turned to her son, seated next to her in front of Franklin's desk. "Why? What's come over you, Jake?"

He looked directly at his mother for the first time since she'd arrived in the school office. Ashley could see a tear forming in his right eye. "Mom," he began with a sniffle.

"What happened, sweetie?" Ashley said, her voice now considerably quieter and warmer.

"It was that stupid kid, Kevin. It was none of his business." Jake sniffled again. "I was telling Jeff how weird it was that Dad just disappeared, totally ghosting us, and Kevin was totally eavesdropping."

"That does not justify—" Franklin began.

But Jake ignored the principal and continued, focusing his attention on his mother. "Then Kevin started saying some really nasty things. About Dad, and about me, and you. Like, he was better off without us, or he abandoned us, or didn't love us anymore. Or that he was dead. I know it was stupid, but I just got so angry, Mom. He has no idea, *no idea* what we've been going through since Dad left."

"Oh, sweetie," Ashely said, putting a hand on Jake's shoulder.

"And he didn't even call. It's like, he's so concerned about being prepared for school and soccer, and following the rules, and being kind—I'm so sick of him reminding me to be kind. But he can't even send us a stupid text message! It's not fair!"

By now, Jake was full-on sobbing. Ashley reached over and hugged her son over the arms of the chairs.

"I'm sorry, Mrs. Driver," Franklin said as sensitively as she could. "But the fact remains that Jacob was physically violent toward another student. We can't overlook that, despite whatever circumstances you're dealing with at home."

Still embracing Jake, Ashley turned her head to look at the principal. "I understand your policy, Principal Franklin. I think Jake needs to be home right now, anyway."

Franklin nodded. "I'll ask Jacob's teachers to send you his homework assignments by email. I believe they already have your address?"

"Own-ship weapons continuing to search," Davis said, a hint of concern in his otherwise professional-sounding delivery.

Worth looked up from the stopwatch he was holding. "Incoming torpedo impact in twenty-five seconds."

"Release countermeasures," Harper ordered, unfazed.

"Countermeasures away," Worth responded, pushing a button on a nearby console. A pair of cylindrical canisters ejected from small tubes mounted on the hull. Immediately, the chemicals inside began producing a torrent of bubbles, causing the canisters to twirl in the water. The bubbles and movements would, hopefully, confuse the incoming torpedoes and draw them away from the Royal Oak.

"Left full rudder," Harper said, looking to the officer of the deck, "come to course two-zero-five. Make your speed five knots. Depth four hundred feet."

The crewmen acknowledged the orders and, once again, Will could feel the boat turn and, this time, dive in an effort to escape the closing torpedoes.

"Sonar, conn," Harper said into the intercom, "let me know if the incoming fish take the bait."

"Conn, sonar," Findlay responded through the speaker, "aye, sir. Standby."

Hargraves looked to Worth, then to Harper. "Skipper, the charts say the floor around here is approximately five hundred feet."

"Soundings returning at four-seven-three feet max depth," the COB reported.

"Understood," Harper replied.

They could dive to four hundred feet, as the skipper had ordered, but they were getting awfully close to the bottom of the ocean. The COB's report indicated they simply didn't have much more room beneath the boat to maneuver. If they needed to dodge any more incoming ordinance, the only Z-axis direction they could go is up.

"Weps, what's going on with our torpedoes?" Worth asked.

Davis answered immediately. "Own-ship weapons continue in search mode, sir."

Worth sighed, disappointed. A snap shot isn't the most accurate sort of attack; it's a quick move to send a torpedo toward the location from which a sound has been detected. It lacks the certainty of triangulation and other computations that go into a proper firing solution. Clearly, the Sierra two-four had taken the time to sneak up on the Royal Oak and develop a good solution—the fact that the Russian torpedoes were getting so close was proof of that—but the Royal Oak hadn't had the same opportunity.

"Conn, sonar," Findlay said through the intercom, "one of the Russian torpedoes went for the countermeasures. The other turned and dove to follow us!"

"Very well," Harper said. He looked over to Worth. "Standby on another set of countermeasures. Let's see if we can get that fish to bite this time."

"Standing by," Worth replied.

"Right full rudder. Come to course zero-four-five, speed twelve knots. And make your depth two-twenty-five," Harper ordered.

Will had heard similar orders enough times now to know he needed to hold onto something as the boat turned, sped up, and began to rise toward its new target depth. The COB began calling out the sub's depth as it ascended.

"Torpedo is turning to follow, sir!" Findlay report.

Worth pounded a nearby console in frustration and reached for the intercom. "Range?"

"Eight hundred yards and still closing!"

"Launch countermeasures," Harper said.

Worth responded almost immediately, "Countermeasures away."

"Increase speed: ahead one-third. Make our depth one-one-five feet," Harper continued.

"Ahead one-third. Coming shallow to one-one-five feet, aye sir!" The COB responded.

"Own-ship weapons are bingo fuel," Davis said. "Sinking and deactivating. Cutting the wires now, sir."

They'd officially missed.

"Incoming torpedo is turning to follow. Range now five hundred yards!" Findlay reported.

"Depth one-seven-five feet," the COB reported.

Harper looked to Worth.

"Four hundred yards!"

"One-five-zero feet."

"Three hundred yards!"

"Standby collision. Sound the alarm," Harper said calmly. Worth pushed a nearby button, activating an alarm throughout the boat. There was no point in worrying about keeping silent now; survival was more important. Everyone in the conn held onto something, most also put their heads down. Will imagined the crew taking the same position throughout the boat.

"Two hundred yards!"

"One-two-five feet."

"Standby…" Findlay's voice trailed off.

"Level at one-one-five feet, sir," the COB reported.

"Haha!" Findlay let out a triumphant laugh. "She's run out of fuel, sir! Incoming torpedo is slowing and sinking!"

Harper inhaled deeply, as if the breath he was taking was a gift.

The COB looked to Will, standing at the back of the compartment, and smiled.

25

GOING DOWN

AT THE START of the encounter, the USS Royal Oak was holding one enemy submarine, the Kazan, Sierra two-three, and pursuing it undetected. At the same time, they were being pursued by another enemy sub, Sierra two-four, which they hadn't detected. When torpedoes were launched, followed by multiple rounds of countermeasures, it became much more difficult for the sonar technicians on each of the boats to keep track of the others. The torpedoes were the highest priority. And the loudest things in the ocean.

Now, however, all the torpedoes had missed, run out of fuel, and dropped harmlessly to the bottom of the Barents Sea. As the acoustic environment became calmer, it also became clearer. And to Findlay, it became clearer that they had no idea where either of the enemy boats were.

"Very well," the skipper said into the intercom after Findlay reported the loss of all contacts. He looked to his XO. "Thoughts, XO? What would you do? If you were the skipper on those boats, where would *you* go?"

Worth exhaled slowly as he thought. "I'm guessing those two boats have different missions. Sierra two-three received her orders using that new code and immediately started heading northwest to get around Scandinavia. The question on the table is, will she then turn southwest to cross the Atlantic as Dr. Driver predicts?"

"Mmm," Harper said, nodding. "And Sierra two-four?"

"We're not really sure what his mission is. But we know the Russian Navy is in a warlike stance, so if I were a betting man, I'd put my money on his mission as a guard dog, watching the traffic going in and out of Polyarnyy and Murmansk. He got a whiff of us, sir, and pounced."

"So, what you're saying is," Hargraves said from the chart table, "Sierra two-three probably resumed course, while Sierra two-four is probably still lurking around, waiting to strike again?"

Worth nodded. "That's exactly what I'm saying. But I've got to caution you," he held up his right index finger as he looked to Hargraves and then to Harper, "I don't have much experience driving Russian boats, and our Navy's standard operating procedures often differ from theirs—sometimes in significant ways."

"Noted," Harper said. "Any other theories?" He looked around the control room.

"With all due respect, sir," Will spoke up, stepping forward from his observation spot with his hands in his pockets, "isn't it equally possible the Kazan doesn't want to leave the area until they're sure we're dead? I mean, it's two-on-one. If I were the captain of the Kazan, I'd feel more confident knowing I've got another ship out there on my side."

"Boat," West said, correcting Will.

Will nodded to the COB, acknowledging the correction. "Boat. Sorry." He would have felt his cheeks flush were his heart not already racing from the battle and his clothing not already soaked in sweat.

"You assume the skipper of the Kazan knows that Sierra two-four is on his team. *We* don't even know whose team that sub is on," Worth said. "I admit," he continued, raising his hands with empty palms facing forward, "I could be wrong. I hope I'm not. But I could be—"

Suddenly, Findlay's voice cut in. "Torpedoes in the water! Torpedoes in the water! Two fish coming in our direction, bearing two-nine-seven. Range four thousand yards, speed forty knots!"

Harper snapped to attention. The time for discussion was over. "Reverse course, all ahead full. Dive for two-seven-five feet," he ordered quickly.

"Sonar, conn," Worth said into the intercom. "Any idea who fired?"

"Conn, sonar. I'm hearing someone's screw picking up speed fast, bearing zero-four-two. It's Sierra two-four, sir. He's racing to dive fast, sir. I think that skipper's trying to get out of the way of those fish, too."

Worth looked to Harper. "That means Sierra two-three fired those torpedoes." Then he looked back to Will. "I guess that answers that question."

Will wasn't about to gloat. Once again, they had high explosives heading in their direction very quickly. As he'd recently learned, it was not a position he enjoyed being in. Now, he could feel the boat turning fast, picking up speed, and diving at a steep angle. At least, by now, he'd figured out where he could grab hold to avoid falling to the deck.

ASHLEY HAD JUST arrived home with Jake when her phone rang. Stepping into the kitchen from the garage, she quickly pushed the button to close the garage door, then reached into her pocket. Her heart began to race, hoping it was Will.

Or at least a number from the Pentagon. But it wasn't.

Instead, the phone's screen showed the number of the main office at Marz's middle school. Quickly checking the time, Ashley thought through her children's schedule of after-school activities. Today should be a rehearsal for the select choir Marz had recently been admitted to. She was supposed to get a ride home from a friend afterward. So what could the school be calling about?

Ashley's heart continued to race, but it was no longer with anticipation. Rather, it was dread. She tapped the screen to answer the call.

"Hello?"

"Hi, this is Gordon French, principal over here at Greenwood Middle School, is this Mr. or Mrs. Driver?"

Mr. French's high-pitched voice had always annoyed Ashley. In a school of about two hundred students spread across three grades, he was familiar with nearly all the kids, though not especially knowledgeable about those who didn't cause much trouble. Marz was one of those students, which made the phone call even more unusual.

"Yes, Mr. French, this is Ashley Driver," Ashley replied, trying to keep her voice friendly.

"Ah, yes, Mrs. Driver," French responded, clearing his throat as if he were nervous, "I'm calling about Margaret."

"Is she alright?" Ashley asked, a rapid succession of imaginary and gruesome injuries and accidents, all involving Marz, suddenly coursing through her mind.

French cleared his throat again. Definitely nervous. "She's fine, yes, she's alright. But we do have a problem, Mrs. Driver."

"And what is that?"

"Margaret left school after first period this morning and did not return until the start of the Belltones choir rehearsal about ten minutes ago."

Ashley was stunned into silence.

"Mrs. Driver? Are you there?" French asked.

Now it was her turn to clear her throat. "Um, yes, I'm here. Are you saying Marz skipped out on school? Are you sure?"

"Quite sure, Mrs. Driver," the principal responded. "We have the attendance records, video footage of Marz leaving through a side door, and two friends of hers who have admitted talking with her about this little…excursion."

"I see," Ashley said, sitting down on one of the kitchen chairs. "And where is she now? The rehearsal, you said?"

"Yes, I just peeked in the room where they were singing, and I saw her there with the rest of the students." French paused for a moment, then continued. "This is a serious offense, Mrs. Driver. Our district takes truancy very seriously."

"I'm sure you do," Ashley replied, rolling her eyes at the second time a principal had quoted district policy to her in as many hours.

"And I must say," French continued, his voice rising as he tried to sound casual but still authoritative, "Marz strikes me as a good student. She has no disciplinary record as far as I can tell. And her grades are excellent. She's clearly enthusiastic about music and drama…"

"What do you intend to do, Mr. French?" Ashley asked, cutting to the chase.

"Since this is the first time we've had this sort of trouble with Marz, I'm inclined to let you and your husband, as the parents, handle the situation. Decide on whatever response you think is appropriate. But I must warn you: next time, the school will have to intervene. As you know, our district—"

"Yes, Mr. French, I understand," Ashley interrupted him before he could quote policy yet again.

"Very good, Mrs. Driver. Now, would you like me to speak with your husband about this? Bring him up to speed, so to speak?"

Ashley let out a guffaw. "If you can find him, Mr. French, please let me know."

"COUNTERMEASURES AWAY," WORTH said loudly, barely a second after the skipper had ordered them deployed.

"Very well," Harper responded. "Now we duck and cover. Right full rudder. Come to course zero-two-five. Reduce speed to ten knots. Make your depth four hundred feet."

Various crewmen acknowledged the orders and once again the submarine twisted and turned as it tried to wriggle its way out of the incoming torpedoes' path.

"Sonar, conn. How far away are those torpedoes?" Harper asked into the intercom.

"Conn, sonar. Torpedoes now at two thousand yards and closing. Estimate impact in one minute, twenty-five seconds," Findlay responded.

"How long until they reach the countermeasures?" Worth asked.

Davis answered. "About fifty seconds to countermeasures, sir."

Worth nodded. "Any news from Sierra two-four?"

Findlay's voice came through the speaker. "There's still a lot of noise in the water, sir. It's hard to hear through the countermeasures and the screws on those torpedoes. Last I heard, she was still diving but also slowing. That's all I've got. I'm sorry, sir."

"That's alright, Findlay," Worth responded. "Let us know when you get her back. I don't want her putting more fish in the water."

"Aye, sir," Findlay said.

"Incoming torpedoes should be approaching countermeasures in fifteen seconds," Davis announced.

For a moment there was silence in the conn. Will could hear his heart beating in his ears. A bead of sweat dripped off his forehead, landing with a splat on the deck at his feet. He couldn't stand the feeling of not having any control over the situation. A deadly situation, at that. How could these sailors stand it?

"Conn, sonar," Findlay spoke up. "Torpedoes have reached the countermeasures...One of the fish has taken the bait and is continuing on its initial course, opening distance from us! The other is in search mode."

"At least that's something," Worth muttered.

Findlay's voice continued, sounding more anxious. "Conn, I'm hearing some really strange sounds from the other fish, like something is—"

The speaker cut out as a loud explosion sounded somewhere outside the boat. Will could feel the whole ship suddenly move, and the entire room tilted violently to the left, throwing him and several other men into consoles, bulkheads, and onto the deck. Everything was shaking and rattling. Alarms were screaming. The overhead lights went out and the glow of the various consoles around the room flickered. Sparks arced through the air like errant fireworks.

Will stumbled forward and then sideways as he tried to regain his balance, swinging his arms wildly. As the boat was convulsing, he could see, out of the corner of his eye, the door of a nearby cabinet swing open. Several thick, heavy three-ring binders were thrown out and sent sailing through the air.

Maybe it was just his vantage point, or maybe it was years of having young children to look after, but in less than a second, Will instinctively projected the binders' path through the air and determined that they would strike a nearby crewman on the side of the head. Without thinking, Will threw himself forward and to the left. With his arms outstretched in front of him, he shoved the crewman aside and down, out of the path of the projectiles.

Falling violently now, Will bounced off the sailor he'd just saved before landing on the floor. His head then smacked against the base of some piece of equipment. He could hear the binders crash against the port-side bulkhead and tumble to the deck.

The lights blinked a few times before coming back on.

"Damage report!" Harper yelled.

Will could hear the skipper's voice through the ringing in his ears. It was the first time he'd heard the man shout. He could also hear several men groaning as they pulled themselves back to their feet, including the man whose head he'd just saved from laceration.

Worth was already standing, holding a sound-powered phone to his ear. "Engineer reports the reactor scrammed per emergency shutdown protocols, but there appears to be no radiation leakage. The drive shaft shows signs of damage, but we won't know the extent until he can make a closer inspection."

"Damn," Harper cursed.

"Damage control teams report negative on hull breaches," Worth continued. "That torpedo didn't hit us, sir, but it was pretty close."

Will breathed a sigh of relief, and he could tell the others around him did too.

Then Worth relayed more news. "We've got flooding in the aft bilge bay and forward torpedo room. We're on battery power until we can get the reactor back up. And there are some reports of injury, but no fatalities, sir."

"Understood, Mr. Worth," Harper said, his voice a bit calmer now.

"Sir," the COB spoke up. "Sir, we're having some trouble maintaining depth. I wonder if the damage includes some of the power lines running to the ballast pumps, because we're having a lot of trouble trimming the tanks." He paused before saying, "We're, well, we're sinking, sir."

Will was feeling the side of his head and looking at the blood on his fingertips when he heard the COB's report. He slowly looked up with concern, his eyes going first to the COB and then to the skipper. The scratch on his scalp didn't seem so serious anymore.

26

Urgency

By comparison, the second underwater explosion wasn't nearly as catastrophic as the first. While Will and the entire crew could hear and feel it, it didn't actually cause any new damage to the boat. But it sure as hell scared everyone on board.

"What the heck was that?!" Will shouted, louder than he had intended to.

As if he'd heard Will's question in the sonar room, Findlay's voice came through the intercom. "Conn, sonar. Explosion in the water, sir, bearing zero-eight-zero. Estimate distance eleven thousand yards."

Hargraves, who had been trying to plot the Royal Oak's exact location on the chart table, lifted his head. "Who? Who exploded?"

Findlay couldn't hear Hargraves, of course. He continued his report. "I'm hearing hull popping sounds. Sir, it's the Borei, Sierra two-four. Direct hit—I think it was the other fish Sierra two-three launched at us, the one that went for the noisemakers—he's going down, sir."

Harper hung his head. The Russians may be the enemy, but the men on that boat were still fellow sailors whose bodies, lives, and spirits were now committed to the deep. Sunk by one of their own. His head still bowed, he reached up for the intercom button.

"Sonar, conn. Acknowledged." He took a breath. "Where's Sierra two-three now?"

"Not entirely confident about this, sir, but I'm pretty sure she's back on her original course now. I'm getting a faint reading to the west-northwest at a distance of somewhere between twenty-four and twenty-eight thousand yards. She's still submerged, I think around a hundred fifty feet, but it's hard to tell right now." Findlay apologized.

"Sir," the XO said calmly to the skipper. He was standing with Hargraves. "Everyone in this corner of the ocean could hear that Borei get hit and go down. But from Sierra two-three's last known position, both the Borei and our boat are at roughly the same bearing. In other words, I think it's likely Sierra two-three thought it was *us* who they hit, *us* who was sunk. The fact that we're slowly sinking makes it seem even more real."

"That would explain why she resumed her original course," Weps added.

"Well, for the moment, maybe having Sierra two-three moving off is a blessing in disguise. We've got enough problems right now; we don't need to prolong this shootout." Harper took another deep breath and turned to look at the COB. "Mr. West, I need an update on our damage and repairs, please."

"Aye, sir," the COB responded quickly, reaching for a nearby intraship phone.

"Thank you," Harper said. Then he looked to Worth. "So, XO, our boat is sinking?"

"Yes, sir," Worth replied, a grim expression on his face.

"Not quickly, but we are definitely sinking as we determine the problem with the ballast pumps. Could be electrical, could be mechanical. We're waiting on engineering division for diagnosis and a plan. In the meantime, we're descending at a rate of about a foot a minute."

"And what's our present depth?"

"Four hundred eighteen feet, sir."

"And the ocean floor at our present location?" Harper asked, moving his gaze from his XO to his navigator.

Hargraves was ready for the question. Indeed, it was one piece of information he had been trained to always keep top of mind. In this case, however, he didn't really like the answer he had to give.

"Sir," the navigator said as calmly as he could, "at present location the floor is five hundred six feet down."

Davis was thinking aloud: "That gives us…"

"Eighty-eight minutes until we bottom out," Worth finished the thought, looking straight at Harper.

Davis gulped. "At least if we do need to land on the ocean floor, we won't be moving very fast when we hit…right?"

Harper turned around so he could see Davis. "That's right, Weps. And, fortunately, this boat can handle five hundred feet. Though it's small consolation."

"Assuming our ballast pumps are functioning properly, sir," Worth pointed out. "At the moment, they're not functioning at all. Even if we stop sinking and rest on the bottom, we're going to continue taking on water. At some point, that's going to be a problem."

Harper didn't turn around to look at his XO, but he nodded in understanding. He kept his eyes on his weapons officer. "Small consolation, indeed."

"THEY'RE PROBABLY JUST acting out. You know that, sis, right?"

"They are *absolutely* acting out, Jane," Ashley said to her sister. They were sitting on the couch, each with a glass of wine in hand. Jake was asleep and Marz was, well, if not asleep at least safely ensconced in her bedroom. The warm yellow light from the table lamp in the corner cast long shadows across the room.

Jane reached over and placed a hand on top of her little sister's knee. "They're good kids, sis. They'll get through this."

Ashley sighed. "I know, but how deep will the scars be?" She could feel herself tearing up again. "That fucker. You know the last thing I asked Will to do? The last time he called?"

Jane shook her head.

"I told him to call his kids. Text them. Do *something* to communicate with them. I didn't care what he'd say, just the fact that he'd reach out to them would have been enough. It would have been enough, Jane. But that fucker couldn't even do that. Maybe he really has stopped caring. Maybe he's really gone for good."

Both women let that last comment hang in the air for a moment, then Ashley shook her head and lifted her glass to her lips.

"Hey, sis?" Jane asked, her voice high and quiet. "Would that be so bad? I mean, have you thought about it, really?"

Ashley lowered the glass and swallowed a mouthful of Riesling. Tipping her head to the side, she asked, "Have I thought about what?"

Jane steeled herself for the next part of the conversation. She'd rehearsed it in her head for a few days now, and for the entire flight from Detroit. Heck, she was never Will's biggest fan to begin with, and now he'd given her a real good reason to question his commitment.

"Maybe you and the kids *are* better off without him," Jane said as warmly as she could, to soften the blow. Clearly,

Ashley had not thought about it yet. That could make the conversation even more difficult.

Ashley drew back, initially repulsed by the idea. Then she narrowed her eyes as she considered it for the first time. She froze, the wine glass halfway between her mouth and her lap.

When they got married, Ashley believed with all her heart that it was forever. She wasn't a particularly religious woman, but she believed there was some spiritual connection between her and Will. Sure, he had his flaws—she'd spent plenty of time reviewing those over the past week—but at the beginning, she figured she could either change his behavior or live with it. In retrospect, had she set herself up for this moment by minimizing (at best) or ignoring (at worst) the parts of Will that would eventually drive a wedge between them?

"Are you," Ashley began, still wrestling with what her sister was proposing. "Are you...saying I should get divorced?" She was whispering now, as if just saying the word out loud would make it come true.

"I don't know, Ash," Jane said. She looked down into the wine glass on her lap, uncrossed and recrossed her legs on the couch, and then slowly began nodding. "I think I am."

"How do I...?" Ashley didn't even know what to say. "Where would I...?" Tears ran down her cheeks.

"I am here for you, little sis," Jane said, once again putting her hand on her sister's knee.

WORTH PUT DOWN the phone and turned to face Harper, who was pacing around the small area in the center of the conn. "Engineer reports visual inspection of the drive shaft complete, sir." He took a deep breath. "He found some moderate damage, which he thinks can be patched up temporarily in about two hours. Then we'll be limited to about twelve knots speed.

"Next, he's located three electrical faults. One is on the circuit with the ballast pumps. Hopefully, once they get those electrical lines fixed up, we'll be able to better control our depth. The other two faults are on circuits powering the water heater for the officers' head and an auxiliary air unit in the forward berthing compartment. With your permission, sir, he'll make those two low-priority repairs."

Harper nodded. It's not like the officers would be showering any time soon, and the crew were certainly not sleeping in their bunks until they could get the boat out of this mess.

"Flooding in the bilge bay is stopped," Worth continued. "Temporary patches applied to the two pipes and fittings that came loose. They'll start pumping out seawater as soon as the power is available."

"What about the reactor?" the skipper asked. Getting the boat's nuclear reactor back up and running would help solve the power problem.

Worth nodded. "That's the last big item, sir. Engineer reports the reactor temperature is low, which is to be expected after a scram. The control rods functioned normally, and everything remains buttoned up tight. No radiation leaks detected. He said he tried a quick restart, but the temperature had dipped too low. Probably on account of us being in the Arctic, I suppose," Worth muttered. "Regardless, he says an expedited restart should be possible, but it'll take another hour at least. In the meantime, we're running on battery with reduced power."

Harper exhaled loudly. "Sounds like damage control teams have it under control. We were lucky, XO. Aside from skirting a direct hit, we didn't lose any people and what damage we sustained seems manageable."

The crewman Will had saved from flying debris stepped

next to Will, who had returned to his spot at the back of the room. "Thanks, Driver. I'll surely have a nice bruise from where we landed on the deck, but at least my head is still in one piece."

Will nodded and smiled. "You're welcome. I'm not sure how I did it, though. It all happened so quickly."

The crewman shrugged his shoulders. "Doesn't matter how you did it, you just did it. You're all right, Driver." He placed a hand on Will's shoulder and gave it a squeeze. Will smiled as the crewman returned to his station.

For the first time in a while, the conn was quiet and almost calm. The skipper stretched his arms out behind him, cracking his back. "Let the engineer work on repairs and that expedited restart. Getting the reactor temp back into optimal range is tricky business. He's got crew who can make the electrical and mechanical repairs in the meantime. We're just damn lucky it wasn't—"

Suddenly, an alarm sounded and a voice came over the 1MC: "Fire! Fire! Fire in forward crew berthing. Class C electrical fire in crew berthing. Fire control parties lay forward!"

"There goes our luck," Harper muttered. Then he spoke louder so he could be heard over the alarm. "COB, see to it that fire's put out before it spreads down the wires to other compartments. If it does, the torpedo room is the first one it'll reach, and we don't want anything in there getting too hot."

"Aye, sir!" the COB said. He grabbed a breathing mask from a nearby storage cabinet and fit it over his head. Attached was a tube that could be plugged into special pipes, located in every compartment and passageway on the boat, which would provide air for breathing as the fire was fought. In an enclosed space, such as a submarine, the air could get toxic very quickly.

Harper pushed the intercom button. "Engineering, conn.

What's your status?"

"Conn, engineering. Petty Officer Woodley here, sir." He was breathing heavily. "The chief's going over plans for the drive shaft with some of the men, sir. Then I think he'll turn his attention back to the reactor."

"Very well, Woodley. You tell the chief we're going to need that reactor—and the drive shaft—on the double. The longer that fire burns in forward berthing, the sooner we're going to need to come to periscope depth and vent the boat. And right now, we're moving in the *opposite* direction. You understand me?"

"Understood, sir," Woodley replied.

Harper turned off the intercom and looked to Worth. "What's our current depth?"

"Current depth is four-seven-four, sir."

"Damn," Harper replied. "That doesn't leave us much time before we bottom out. We could maneuver on batteries, but not without a working drive shaft."

"Or working ballast pumps, sir," Worth reminded him.

"That too," Harper said. He rubbed his right hand over the stubble on his cheeks and then through his greasy hair. "Damn."

"Conn, torpedo room," the COB's voice came through the speaker. Will could hear muffled shouting behind him.

Harper responded eagerly. "Torpedo room, conn. COB, what's your status?"

"Sir, the fire is not yet contained. It's begun burning other combustibles in the berthing area: sheets, blankets, clothing, that sort of stuff. So," he took a breath, coughed, and then resumed, "we're now dealing with both class A and class B. I've got one man down with moderate-to-severe burns on his arms, and another down from smoke inhalation." The COB gasped again for air. "We're fighting it, sir. We'll get it under control."

"Alright, COB," Harper said into the intercom. "Send the

injured to the wardroom. I'll have the corpsman meet them there. I need that fire out right now."

"Aye, sir," the COB said, sounding exhausted.

Worth picked up a phone, notifying the corpsman that the injured would be coming to the wardroom. That space, where the officers usually took their meals, served as the sub's medical bay in situations like this. The dining table would become an operating table, and lights built into the compartment's ceiling would illuminate the patients.

From his spot in the back of the conn, Will had watched the proceedings with awe. He knew enough not to get in the way when the torpedoes were shooting through the water at high speed, or when the crew had to address critical damage to the boat. And he admired the men's professionalism. From the skipper down to the lowliest seaman, for the most part, every man had remained calm and focused on his job. If he was being honest with himself, Will wasn't sure he would have the self-control to behave the way these men did. He would have cracked up at the first hint of trouble, recent heroics notwithstanding.

But in addition to awe, Will felt fear. Fear for the lives of these dedicated American sailors. Fear for his country, whose citizens would pay the price if this incident in the Arctic Circle spun out of control and ignited a broader, perhaps global, conflict. And fear for himself.

It occurred to Will that he hadn't spoken with Ashley, Marz, or Jake in over a week now. That was probably the longest he'd ever gone without at least some communication with his family. Not that he'd been able to communicate while traveling on a submerged submarine. But still, he wondered how his absence had affected his wife and children. And he feared what would happen to them if they couldn't extinguish the fire two decks below, repair the boat, and return to someplace safe.

What would Ashley do if he never came back? How

painfully would her life, and the lives of their children, have to change? Sure, there was his life insurance policy—although he remembered reading somewhere that those policies didn't apply if someone was killed while serving in the military. It would be a challenge for Ashley to argue to the insurance company that Will wasn't actually in the military when he never told her what he was doing.

Would Ashley remain in their house, or would that be too painful? Would she take the kids and move closer to her sister, Jane? He'd heard that metro Detroit was a nice place, and he recalled visiting once, but he couldn't really imagine his family living anywhere but their home in suburban Philadelphia.

A shiver ran through Will's body, and he could feel goosebumps on his arms as he thought of more questions: Would Ashley fall in love again, with someone else? Would they marry? Would that someone replace him as the father to his children?

Harper punched a few buttons on the intercom. His voice brought Will back to the present. "Sonar, conn. Report all contacts."

"Conn, sonar," Findlay said. "I hold no contacts, sir."

"Very well," Harper responded. Then he looked to Worth, who was just putting down the phone. "At least there's no one out there to shoot at us."

A light on a console near Worth blinked, and he picked up the phone receiver. "Yes. Go ahead." He listened for a moment, then added, "Very well. Good work. Carry on."

Replacing the handset, Worth turned to face the skipper. "Sir, engineering reports work continues. But between the reactor, the drive shaft, and the electrical problem, he's running out of men."

Harper gave Worth a quizzical look. "Running out of men? How could he possibly—"

"The fire, sir. He had to send a few men to help with

firefighting duties, and one additional man from the division is among the injured," Worth explained. "He's asking if there's anyone from another division who could help Seaman Burke on the electrical repair. Preferably someone with electrical experience."

"I can try to help."

Will heard the words as they filled the conn, but it took a moment before he realized: *he* had spoken them. Then he noticed that the skipper, the XO, Weps, and the navigator were all looking at him. He gulped.

"Look, I know I'm not really part of this crew. But you've got a lot going on right now and your engineering team needs help," Will took a step forward, sounding more confident. "I've done some electrical work. If I can help, I will. If I don't know how to fix it, I'm smart enough to stop and let somebody else try."

Harper looked to Worth, who shrugged, raised his left eyebrow, and nodded.

"Alright, Driver," Harper said. "Let's see what you can do."

IT TOOK ONLY a few minutes for one of the petty officers to lead Will to a darkened passageway somewhere on the lowest level of the boat, where he met Seaman Alexander Burke. Will was surprised at how young Burke was: probably in his early twenties, he could have easily been one of Will's students. His short-cropped black hair sat atop his face, on which sat glasses in a rather large, black plastic frame. Will could see the sweat stains under Burke's arms and the way the dim overhead lighting made the seaman's dark black skin glisten.

"Hey Dr. Driver, uh, sir," Burke said, sounding almost apologetic.

"No need to call me sir, Burke," Will responded. "I'm not actually navy. I'm just, well, along for the ride." He wasn't sure how much Burke knew about his role in their mission, and he didn't want to reveal anything that the Seaman shouldn't know. "I hear we have an electrical problem?"

"That's right, sir, uh, mister, well, doctor—"

"Why don't you just call me Will, okay? What's your name, Burke?"

"Seaman Alexander Burke, USS Royal Oak," the young man replied stiffly. So stiffly that Will was a little surprised he didn't salute.

Will suppressed a laugh. "Settle down, Alex—can I call you Alex?"

"Um, well, okay."

"Good. Now, show me where the problem is."

Burke nodded and led Will a few feet aft. On the wall of the narrow passageway was a dull gray metal conduit, which ran into a junction box. Burke had already removed the cover from the box and pulled out some of the wires.

"Alright. Alex, tell me what you've been able to figure out about our problem so far," Will said, using a tone that he recognized was once his father's. He knew, somehow, that if he acted calm and in control, it would help Burke feel more confident and focused.

Burke nodded. "We know the lines on this side of the box are still working good, but the lines on the other side are not. So, we think the problem is in here."

"That's a good start," Will said. "Now, I don't want to be presumptuous, but can you confirm that you've shut off the power to the lines on both sides of the box? It'd sure be a shame to survive a Russian torpedo attack only to get zapped to death doing a simple electrical repair."

"Yeah, uh, Will. The power is off. But...how do you know this is, um, simple?"

Will smiled at the young man. "I don't. I'm just hoping for

the best and planning for the worst. Now, what do we know about electrical wiring on board a submarine of this class? Or marine-grade wiring of any kind?"

Burke's cheeks immediately flushed, and he quickly looked down to the deck beneath his feet.

"Not much, I take it?" Will asked.

The seaman shook his head. "Yeah, not much. I've been trying to study and qualify and do good on my exams and all, but I got this learning disability—or at least that's what they told me to call it—and I haven't made it to electrical stuff yet."

Will took a deep breath. "Don't worry about it, Alex. Together, we'll figure this out. I can see you've pulled out what looks like eight, maybe ten-gauge wires. But there's still—what?" Will leaned in closer to the open junction box on the wall. So close that he could smell Burke's sweat. "Well, I'll be…"

"What do you see, Will? Can you fix it?" Burke asked eagerly.

"Yes, Alex. Yes. I believe I can."

AS TALKS BEGIN, VAST DIFFERENCES ARE REVEALED

Leigh Kierfer, Washington Advocate

Representatives from the United States, the United Kingdom, the European Union, South Korea, and Australia met with their counterparts from Russia and North Korea yesterday in what many hoped would be the first of several productive discussions that would calm tensions around the globe and offer a pathway toward a resumption of business-as-usual following the confrontations of the past few months. Those hopes were dashed, however, as the representatives emerged from a four-hour, closed-door meeting in Zurich with neither a plan for de-escalation nor a sense of hope that one could even be agreed upon.

In the press conference following the meeting, the two sides seemed to agree on little. Each painted the other as the aggressor, and neither seemed willing to be the first to retreat from their fortified positions across Eastern Europe or the Korean Peninsula. The gulf between the two parties was so vast, in fact, that they could not even agree upon a date or location for their next meeting.

"It is a shame that the stability of Eastern Europe and Southeast Asia should continue to be threatened by Western greed," Alexei Popilov, the Russian representative said. "We have seen this a thousand times in the past five hundred years. They smile and talk sweetly. And then their imperial motives are revealed, and they conquer and exploit. We will not let this happen again. The time has come to end the threat of Western imperialism once and for all."

"We regret the lack of substantive progress in today's talks," Eric Moseley, the Australian representative told members of the press. "We kindly remind our Russian and North Korean friends that it was the launch of a massive cyber-attack on the American election, coordinated with the launch of multiple intercontinental ballistic missiles, that set off this whole ballyhoo. We welcome the next meeting, whenever and wherever it will be, to continue to try to reach some sort of amicable resolution to our differences."

Analysts were mostly united in their interpretation of the day's talks. "I can't say I'm surprised, although I do find it disappointing," commentator Karl Heislich wrote in an op-ed in the prominent German newspaper, Täglich. "A bloody waste," Nigel Cawthorne remarked in a widely viewed BBC broadcast.

Even as the representatives traded barbs and commentators shouted over one another in contrived outrage, military forces from both sides continued to remain on high alert. The South Korean army announced plans to prepare a round of general conscription. France and the UK announced increased air patrols over Northern Europe, southern Scandinavia, and the Baltic states. And the US Air Force confirmed the deployment of additional anti-aircraft and missile defense batteries to Alaska and Guam.

"SIR!" WORTH SAID excitedly to the skipper as Will strode back into the conn. "Engineer reports the electrical circuits have been repaired and tested successfully on battery power. Waiting on the reactor for full power; Chief estimates another twenty minutes. In the meantime, we can restart the ballast pumps on battery power if you'd like."

"Do it," Harper responded, jabbing the air as he pointed to his XO. "Tell the SigInt suite to power down their supercomputers or whatever they work on in there. That should help balance the electrical load while we're waiting on the reactor."

"Aye, sir," Worth said, already picking up the phone to relay the orders.

Harper turned to look at Will, who was back to leaning on the aft bulkhead. "You and Burke patched things up right quick."

Will smiled. "Well, I may not have served on a submarine before, but I watched my old man do a lot of electrical work as a kid. So, once I saw the problem and recognized it, it was an easy fix. In fact, I made the same repair in my own house just last week."

"Well, then I'm glad we had you on board for this little adventure. You've turned out to be a useful crewman after all," Harper said with a smile.

"Sir," Will said, keeping the skipper's attention. "Burke is a good kid. He just needs guidance and patience. He'll be alright."

Harper nodded in reply.

Then Will could feel a new vibration in the deck as the pumps started up. Under normal conditions, it was probably masked by the engines. But with the engines still out of commission, it was noticeable. Unlike the past few times the Royal Oak changed depth, he couldn't feel the boat rising as water was ejected from the large ballast tanks that occupied the spaces between the boat's inner and outer hulls. Without any forward motion, their ascent was considerably slower. But a look at the digital depth gauge on the forward bulkhead showed the numbers declining as the boat rose, about a foot every thirty or forty seconds.

"Diving officer," Harper said, sitting himself back down in the captain's chair for the first time in a while, "let's see if we can get up to periscope depth, even if it takes a while."

The diving officer nodded. "Target depth six-two feet, aye, sir."

A moment later, the intercom speaker came to life. "Conn, torpedo room," an out-of-breath COB said, "the fire is contained. We should have it fully extinguished within ten minutes. I'll post a reflash watch forthwith."

The skipper responded. "Torpedo, conn. Good work, COB."

"Sir," the COB continued, "I had to send another man to medical. It was Seaman Martin, sir. His first cruise. I'm afraid this one looked pretty bad, sir."

Harper looked to the floor as he inhaled deeply.

"Understood, COB. Hopefully, the corpsman can work a miracle for us."

"Yes, sir. I'll report back once the fire is fully extinguished."

As the COB finished, Worth picked up his phone, nodded, and replaced it. "Engineering reports the drive shaft is as good as it's going to get. Chief recommends we stay below twelve knots, fifteen in an emergency. Any more than that, he says, and we could damage it beyond repair."

"Alright," Harper replied. "Nobody wants to be dragged home by a tow rope. Hopefully, wherever we go next, it won't be quite so eventful."

A few minutes later, the COB reported the fire extinguished. His voice was hoarse and, when he reemerged in the conn, his face, hands, and uniform were covered in black ash.

It was then that Will noticed the odor in the air. It smelled like a combination of motor oil, firewood, and charred flesh. The combination turned his stomach so forcefully that he raced to the aft passageway, through his cabin door, and into the attached head, where he promptly vomited into the sink.

This room smelled marginally better but was poorly lit. The reduced electrical capacity of the boat meant that only a dim emergency light illuminated the room. It was about as powerful as the vanity light in his Subaru. Which is to say, measly and weak.

Looking at the dark outline of his face in the mirror over the sink, he couldn't see the sweat dripping off his chin. But he could feel it. He reached forward to turn on the water to rinse out the sink. It came out of the faucet extremely cold, but Will didn't mind. After cleaning the sink, he splashed some on his face, letting the icy liquid spill down his cheeks and off the tip of his nose.

That was when the lights came back on at full power. It was a signifier, he told himself, that the sub's nuclear reactor had been successfully restarted. And a sign that revealed, in his reflection, just how beat and drained he was. His skin was fading from green to pale, except for the dark circles under his eyes and the hint of a five o'clock shadow that seemed to sparkle with a combination of water and some little gray hairs. It was like he'd aged five years in the past five hours, and the mission wasn't even over yet.

27

SECOND RESULTS

THE USS ROYAL Oak finally made it up to periscope depth. After a quick 360 look-around with the scope and another check with Findlay in sonar, Harper was satisfied that they had this little corner of the Barents Sea to themselves. At least for now.

Mere seconds after he and Worth finished viewing the scope's circular sweep on the large view screen in the control room, Harper ordered the snorkel mast raised and the ventilation procedure began. With the help of some blowers and fans, the stale, smoky air (which by now had permeated the boat) was pushed out while fresh sea air was pulled down. Within minutes, Will and the rest of the crew in the conn could smell and taste the difference. Breathing was easier and vision wasn't hazy anymore. A big improvement.

A moment later, the skipper ordered the communications mast raised. Hargraves could use a good GPS location fix, since, even with the most advanced dead reckoning computers in the world, all the twists, turns, and depth changes during the battle made for a rather large margin of error on the ECDIS. Fortunately, it took only about twenty seconds for the digital handshake between submarine and satellite.

It took the same amount of time for Katashi, in the radio room, to upload a message to Washington, informing the navy brass of the battle they'd just survived, including the damage to the boat and her crew. Simultaneously, he downloaded and acknowledged the latest flash traffic from COMSUBLANT, which included several messages queued up for the Royal Oak. Katashi skimmed them all as they came off the printer and he attached them to a clipboard. One of the messages caught his attention, and he put it on top of the stack. Then he made his way forward to the conn to present them to the skipper.

"You'll really enjoy the first one, sir," Katashi said with a smirk as he handed the clipboard to Harper. By now, the comms mast had been lowered, leaving only the snorkel up, poking just a few inches above the surface so as not to give away their position.

Harper looked over the message traffic and quickly understood why Katashi was smiling like that. "A warning, huh? About a possible second Russian submarine in our vicinity? To borrow a nautical metaphor: that ship sure has sailed, hasn't it?"

"Yes, sir," Katashi responded. He was glad the skipper had a good sense of humor. Other commanders would have called for the comms officer's head for not delivering the message earlier—even if, as was the case today, there was no way to retrieve the message, or even know it was waiting for them, without coming shallow and raising the comms mast or floating the buoy. Clearly not something they could have done in the heat of battle.

Worth looked over Harper's shoulder and quickly read the message. "Aye, sir. I'd say that's water over the dam!"

"Did you send our preliminary report?" Harper asked Katashi.

"Yes, sir. I expect an answer should be ready in about an hour, under normal circumstances."

"Well, today hasn't exactly been normal, but I imagine we will still have to wait for further instructions." Then Harper spoke louder as he addressed the crew in the conn: "We're not going to loiter up here while the admirals ponder our next move from behind their big desks in Washington. Stand down from battle stations. Mr. Hargraves, plot us a course toward the nearest friendly port. Diving officer, take us down to one hundred fifty. Helm, make revolutions for ten knots."

Then he pushed the button on the intercom for the 1MC so he could address the whole boat. "Crew of the Royal Oak, this is the captain. We may be bruised but we are sure as hell not beaten. I'm proud of how each and every one of you performed your duty today. As we make our way to friendlier waters, our thoughts are with our injured crewmen. I'm sorry to say we lost Seaman Martin. He was a good sailor, and his death will not have been in vain. We will repair, recover, and recoup, and then the Royal Oak will get back in the fight. That is all." He replaced the microphone.

"It's been a long night, or day, or whatever," Harper continued, addressing the officers in the room. "I'm going to turn in and get a few hours of shuteye. Weps, you have the conn. Take us back up for a comms check in one hour. Katashi, if our orders are anything other than to get back into friendly waters, have someone wake me. Otherwise, COB, please see to it we get ourselves back on a normal watch rotation. XO, you'd better grab a few hours of rack time too."

Will couldn't hear the chorus of "aye, sir" because he was already asleep on his bunk. But it wasn't restful sleep. Not with the amount of adrenaline that had coursed through his body over the past few hours.

Mildly frustrated, Will stretched and put his feet down on the cold deck. A minute later he was in a clean uniform and headed out the door. After grabbing some coffee from the crew's mess, he made his way back up to the mission space. There, he'd get back to work on the latest song they'd intercepted. If he couldn't sleep, at least he'd do something productive.

"AND, FINALLY, JACK. What's the latest from Naval Intelligence?" asked the Secretary of the Navy from the head of the large conference room table. "Anything worth mentioning to the joint chiefs?"

Admiral Carter cleared his throat, as much to move the phlegm that seemed to permanently reside there as it was to say to his colleagues how bored he'd been, listening to their reports for the past fifty-two minutes. Without actually saying it, of course. These meetings weren't meant to be entertaining to their participants. In fact, the more boring the meeting, the quieter and more peaceful the world probably was. Today's wasn't the worst Carter had attended, but it was certainly not the best, either.

"The ONI is currently tracking fourteen potential threat vectors, including a detachment of Russian destroyers out of St. Petersburg, a pair of frigates outside Vladivostok, four Russian ballistic missile subs, and an incident off Murmansk that my office just received word about this morning." He paused, looking around the table at the faces of his colleagues from other offices and departments in the navy, as well as the Secretary. Most were attentive but not emotive. The Secretary, however, had raised an eyebrow, his interest piqued.

"I assume we have assets tracking the destroyers and the

missile boats?" the Secretary asked.

Carter nodded. "We do, Mister Secretary."

"Then tell me about the incident in the Barents Sea."

"It involves the SSN Royal Oak, Mister Secretary, one of our Virginias modified for intelligence gathering. On her last tour of the Barents, she began picking up a new sort of coded signal coming from transmission stations not far from Polyarnyy. We sent her back out with an additional intelligence asset, an ethnomusicologist named—"

"I'm sorry, Jack, an ethno-what-did-you-say?"

"Ethnomusicologist, Mister Secretary. An expert in music and culture. This particular—"

"Jack, are we starting some sort of band program on our submarines now? You know subs are supposed to be quiet boats, right? Standard operating procedure and all..."

The Secretary's wisecrack was met with laughter from around the table. Except from Carter, who remained stone-faced.

"I'm well aware of the SOPs for submarines, Mister Secretary. I commanded more than one, if you recall."

The Secretary was still laughing but trying to calm himself. "Come on, Jack. Just a little joke." He took a deep breath and a drink from the glass of water on the table in front of him. "Please, go on. Why does the ONI need an ethnomusicologist?"

"Because he is the only American to have spent significant time among the Ket."

"The who?" This time it was the Captain to Carter's left, whose office handled provisioning and resupply missions.

"The Ket," Carter explained. "They are an ethnic group indigenous to west-central Russia, including parts of Siberia. Their language and culture are distinct from Russian, and it seems that the Russian Navy has decided to use that distinctiveness to run a new 'codetalkers' routine." He looked to the young captain on his left, but didn't give the man time to interrupt. "For those who need a little history lesson, it was an intelligence and communications program used during the Second World War, based on the Navajo Diné and other Native American languages. Because the Japanese had no exposure to the Navajo or their culture, it made for a very effective code. Now the Russians are doing it with the Ket language."

"Okay, Jack, you've got our attention now," the Secretary said. "What's been going on in the Barents Sea? And has the Navy's first ethnomusicologist been able to make heads or tails of this Ket stuff?"

Carter nodded. "The short answer is yes. They intercepted a new signal, and, based on the preliminary report we received from the Royal Oak this morning, initial analysis predicted the Russian sub they were tracking, a Yasen-class, would run up over the top of Scandinavia and cross the Atlantic."

"And did she?"

"Yes, our ethnomusicologist was correct in his prediction. But in the process, another Russian boat, a Borei-class sub, engaged the Royal Oak. Ultimately, the Yasen sub sank the Borei, according to the Royal Oak."

This revelation prompted a vigorous reaction from all the men gathered around the table. Each turned to the officer next to them or across the table, raising anxious and hurried questions about how the sinking of a Russian submarine would affect their operations, the Navy, and the unstable geopolitical situation.

"Quiet! Quiet, everyone," the Secretary shouted as he raised his palms over the tabletop. As the men stopped yelling and sat back down, he addressed Carter again. "How much faith do you have in this preliminary report from the Royal Oak, Admiral?"

Carter noticed the way the Secretary had addressed him by rank, an indication of the serious turn the conversation had taken. "Her skipper is Jim Harper, one of our best. I trust him completely. And once we get the sonar logs and tapes, those records will back him up."

"I see," the Secretary rubbed his chin. "Where is Harper now?"

"Still in the Barents, Mister Secretary, but at a distance safe enough to send in the report by satellite uplink. They also took some damage in the skirmish; they weren't hit but had a close call. They've made some repairs at sea, but, with your permission, I'd like to order them to Faslane for a more comprehensive repair, then back to Groton."

The Secretary cleared his throat, signaling the end of the meeting. "Yes, tell them to make best speed for Faslane. I'll tell my counterpart in the Royal Navy to expect them, and then I'll take this to the Joint Chiefs. That is all, gentlemen."

He stood, gathered his papers, and looked down the length of the table to Carter. The two men met eyes, and the Secretary nodded as if to say *good job*. Without actually saying it.

"I KNOW WHERE she's going. I know I said that before, but this time I know *exactly* where the Kazan is going," Will said excitedly as he entered the conn from the aft passageway.

Harper was back in the captain's seat. Several hours had passed, and the XO was still in his cabin. Harper held up a finger, silencing Will as he read the latest reports from around the boat and the latest messages from the Pentagon.

"Dr. Driver," the skipper said, "I have news for you, too. It seems we've been ordered to Faslane, His Majesty's Royal Navy's submarine base in Scotland. There, while we make more substantial repairs and resupply, you will be on your way home."

Will was momentarily stunned. The thought of going

home hadn't crossed his mind in a while. He'd been so focused on his analyses, then the battle against the Russian subs, and then the efforts to save the boat... A flood of emotions washed over him: joy, relief, anxiety. What would Ashley say? And what would he be allowed to tell her?

"Will?" The skipper's voice refocused him. "Was there something you wanted to share?"

"Uh, yes... I just finished some additional analysis on that coded song, and I think I've made a breakthrough. That is to say, I think I may know where the orders are sending the Kazan."

"You *think* you *may* know?" Harper asked, a skeptical tone to his voice.

"I do. I mean, sir, I know where the Russian boat is headed."

Harper's face grew more serious. "Alright, then. Mr. Hargraves, plot us a course to Faslane, best quiet speed. Davis, you have the conn. Come shallow in another three hours for a comms check and GPS fix."

"Aye, sir," the navigator and weapons officer said.

"Driver, let's you and I take this discussion to my cabin."

Will followed Harper out of the control room and into the passageway. It was only a few steps, past the mission space, sonar room, radio room, and the SigInt suite, to his cabin. Harper opened the door for Will, who walked in and found the small folding chair folded against a bulkhead. Opening it, he sat while the skipper walked through the room to the head, splashed some water on his face, and finally returned to the stateroom. He pulled down the desk from the wall and sat behind it.

"Alright, professor. What have you got?"

Will cleared his throat. "I'll spare you all the details—"

"Ah, you're learning!" The XO said as he entered the room through the connected head. He rubbed sleep from his eyes and smoothed out his hair.

Will smiled. "You *can* teach this old dog a few new tricks, it seems. Anyway, bottom line is, the Kazan is heading to Venezuela, most likely somewhere along the western side of the country's Caribbean coast."

"Venezuela?" Worth said.

Harper looked up over his shoulder at his XO. "It makes some sense. Russia and Venezuela have had a rather comfortable relationship for some time, at least since the days of Chávez and Maduro. Both are oil producers but not formally part of OPEC. And both have had rather frosty relationships with Uncle Sam."

"True," Worth replied. "And it wouldn't be the first time Russian assets ended up close to the US. Remember those missiles in Cuba?"

"Mmm," Harper said. Then he turned back to Will. "What else have you found out?"

"You're not going to like this," Will said tentatively. "But some of the Ket lyrics seem to refer to 'tentacles reaching through narrow spaces,' and others speak about 'great destructive power.'"

"Damn right I don't like the sound of *that*," Harper said.

Worth stepped into the room from the doorway. "Let's look at those one at a time. What kind of 'narrow spaces' could they be talking about?"

Harper reached over and pulled his tablet computer out of a pocket mounted on the wall. With a few taps, he had a chart of Central America, the Caribbean, and the mid-Atlantic on the screen. He turned the device around to show Will and Worth. The grimace on his face silently spoke volumes.

"Oh, wow," said Worth.

Will looked between the two officers. "What? What am I missing here?"

Worth put a hand on Will's shoulder. "There's one significant 'narrow space' in that part of the world…"

"The Panama Canal," Harper finished the thought.

"Hmm," Will said, following the logic. "If my analysis is correct, the Kazan's course will take it about here." He pointed to a spot on the screen. "Somewhere near Maracaibo."

"A convenient spot for a naval base," Worth said. "If Russia can threaten shipping through the canal from there, they can do some real economic damage and shift the balance of power in this part of the world—"

"The *entire* world, Rob," Harper said.

Worth nodded. "Right. They can shift the balance of power all over the world. That's not something Uncle Sam can just stand by and allow to happen, no matter how strong the desire for peaceful resolution may be."

"I see," Will said, taking it all in. Had he just uncovered some kind of sinister geopolitical plot?

"And as for 'great destructive power,'" Worth continued, "well, I think we all know what that means: nuclear weapons."

There was a solemn moment of silence as all three men contemplated the severity of the threat.

That's when it dawned on Will, rushing to the forefront of his mind with terrifying speed. "This may be about a naval base. Perhaps missile subs. But I also remember hearing a news story, before joining this crew, about some sort of Russian technology that allows the same missiles to be fired from submarines or from land-based launchers."

"That sort of interoperability…" Worth started.

Harper finished the thought. "…makes this threat serious. Very serious, indeed."

PART SIX

CODA

28

FASLANE

WILL HAD NEVER been to Scotland before. The closest he'd come was a connecting flight in London on his way to Siberia, but that was years ago. It seemed like a different time, then. Everyone seemed to agree that peace and cooperation were worth the effort. Not anymore.

It was early morning when the USS Royal Oak entered the channel that led to HMNV Clyde, the British naval base better known as Faslane. It was home to several of the Royal Navy's nuclear submarines, including both missile and attack boats. There was a layer of fog hugging the surface of the channel, but Will could still see the shore from the corner of the bridge atop the sub's sail where he'd found a place to stand.

The transit from the Barents Sea across the top of Scandinavia was largely uneventful. The COB had seen to it that every sailor received adequate downtime after the tense and exhausting encounter off Murmansk. The return to a normal routine of watch standing was a welcomed development, and conversations in the crew's mess and the wardroom were more animated and lighthearted the closer they got to a safe harbor.

As the Royal Oak quietly passed Gourock and turned to port toward Gare Loch, on which Faslane Bay was situated, Will could see the lights of Helensburgh, the small city just south of the base. Pairs of headlights moved along the coast as men and women made their way to work and school. It was hard to believe that, after all the extraordinary events of the past few days, so many people here and all around the world would continue to go about their daily lives, never knowing how close this new Cold War had come to turning very hot, very quickly.

Will listened to the sound of the water lapping over the Royal Oak's bow as it gently plied its way toward a pier. The air was cool and damp. Aside from a few gulls and the gentle waves, it was quiet.

His mind wandered to Ashley and the kids, which prompted a wave of guilt and sadness. He owed them all a phone call, if not a full explanation. His cell phone was back in his cabin, the battery dead. (In the rush to get from the Pentagon to Groton and aboard the Royal Oak, he didn't have time to grab a charger.) What were they thinking, he wondered. Were they worried about him? Angry with him? He wouldn't blame them if they were.

"We should have you ashore inside thirty minutes, Dr. Driver," Worth said to him while he scanned the water around them with his binoculars. "I imagine you're eager to get home and back to your everyday life. You know, teaching at the university, driving your kids around."

Will considered the XO's words. Sure, he was eager to see his family. But the idea of returning to the old routine? That was considerably less exciting now that he'd spent some time on the navy's finest submarine. His work on board had made a real difference. Yes, the final analysis revealed some rather terrifying new Russian plans. But without him, how long would it have taken for the United States to realize what Russia was up to? How many lives would have been lost in the process? How many lives had he saved?

How could he possibly return to the life he had before?

"Dr. Driver. Will," the COB said as the linesmen finished putting knots into the thick ropes that would hold the sub to the pier. "It's been, well, interesting sailing with you. I think I learned a thing or two."

The two men smiled at each other. "Thanks, COB. I appreciate it. I think I learned a lot."

Worth held out his hand; Will grabbed it and shook. "Safe travels, professor." Will nodded before looking to the skipper.

"Dr. Driver," Harper said as he shook Will's hand. "You were crucial to this mission, in more ways than one. Not only did you crack the code on those Russian signals, I'm told you also single-handedly saved one of my crew from what could have been a fatal head injury, and you managed to repair the boat's electrical systems when we needed them most. You, sir, are welcome on my boat any time."

Will was overcome with pride as he shook the skipper's hand vigorously. "Thank you, sir. It's been an honor."

THERE HADN'T BEEN time, after leaving the boat, to make any calls. A cordial but firm Scottish petty officer insisted Will go directly to the nearby airfield where a chopper whisked him off, southeast toward London. In what felt like only minutes, he was stepping off the helicopter onto the tarmac at Heathrow International Airport. Another petty officer led him into the terminal building and pressed a boarding pass into his hand for the next British Airways flight to Washington.

Finally, Will had some time to himself—a funny thought considering Heathrow was one of the busiest airports in the world. But he knew exactly what he needed to do. Walking briskly past the duty-free shops, Costa Coffee bars, and W.H. Smith bookstores, he found a bank of pay phones (itself an accomplishment considering how few of those remained in an era of pocket-sized cell phones).

With the operator's assistance, Will placed a collect call home. He was feeling nervous after imagining the many different ways Ashley could feel about his recent absence. As he heard a few clicks on the phone line, he decided he would come completely clean: he would tell Ashley everything. With the mission over, he thought to himself, the threat to his family would be behind them, right?

Ashley would certainly appreciate the honesty. And he imagined that his story would sound so preposterous, at least at first, that she'd have little choice but to believe him. After all, who would make up such a crazy tale?

Once she decided to believe him, she'd see that all his actions, from his behavior at dinner at the Tavern to his sudden and complete absence, made sense. She may not *like* what had happened, but at least she would *understand* it. And with Ashley, understanding was the key. He knew his wife: what she couldn't understand frustrated her, and what she could wrap her mind around was somehow less threatening.

Finally, the phone rang. Will could feel his heart speeding up. He hadn't even bothered to figure out what time it would be in Philadelphia. A quick mental calculation told him it would be morning. Not too early, thankfully, but probably around the time Ashley and the kids would be having breakfast and getting ready for the day.

The phone rang a second time. Any moment, now, he'd hear her voice. He could tell so much by its tone. He knew when she was excited, angry, and tired simply by the way she said "hello."

What if Marz answered? A teenager, she was a bit more volatile and a bit less predictable. But in the end, he told himself, she would be happy to hear from him. And if Jake answered, he'd probably just dive into the story of his latest soccer game or something like that.

With a click, the line connected. Will drew in a breath, ready to hear from someone he loved.

Then a robotic voice spoke. "We're sorry, but your call cannot be completed as dialed. The line has been disconnected."

Will could feel his heart sink.

"Sir? It appears that it's not a valid number," the operator came back on, speaking in a sweet British accent. "Perhaps you've mistaken one of the digits? Would you like me to try again?"

She read the number back to him, but it was correct. Disconnected? What happened? Was Ashley cutting him off? Or had the ONI agents been right all along, and his wife and children had been kidnapped—or worse—by the Russians? How would the Russians have even known?

And with that, any hope for a happy, joyful reunion vanished.

29

REDIRECTED

WILL STOOD AT the pay phone in disbelief. No, shock. The way he saw it, there were two possibilities: either she didn't *want* to hear from him, or she was *unable* to hear from him (likely because she was kidnapped—or worse). Either scenario scared him. He wasn't sure which one scared him more.

Yet, as he continued to think about it, the more likely scenario was that she didn't *want* to hear from him. After all, if someone like the Russians had kidnapped her (and possibly Marz and Jake), then why would they go to the trouble of contacting the phone company and disconnecting the line? No, this was intentional, and the intent was Ashley's.

The realization made Will's knees weak. He knew he hadn't been the perfect husband, especially recently, but he never thought it would come to this. Would he come home to find the locks changed? Or would he come home to find the house empty? Who could he call to find out what was really going on?

Jane.

Ugh. He knew she had never liked him. Going to Jane Komer would be like groveling. Not something he'd enjoy, but given the situation, he didn't see any other option. He'd have to do it.

But what was her phone number? Without a working cell phone, he had no access to his contacts. Of course, he had a few phone numbers memorized: Ashley's, Marz's, his parents'. But not his sneering sister-in-law's.

Will tried to calm himself, to slow his breathing while his life was yanked out from under his feet. He heard the announcement on the PA that his flight would be boarding shortly. With a sigh, he hung up the phone and moved away, heading for the boarding gates.

During the ten-minute walk through the airport, his surroundings barely registered. There were luggage shops, luxury clothing stores, and newsstands, but he just sort of floated down the wide corridors, through the anonymous crowds of travelers. None of them mattered when the world was closing in around him. Why pay attention to those details?

That's probably why, as he absentmindedly handed the boarding pass to the perpetually smiling gate agent, Will didn't initially notice the two black-suited men emerge from the jetway and make a direct line for him. On any other day he would have seen them coming, but today he was surprised to find them suddenly standing in front of him, blocking his way through the gate. Toward whatever uncertain future was on the other side.

"Dr. Driver?" the one on the left said in a deep voice and a British accent. Will suddenly looked up, noticing the man's sunglasses covering his eyes.

"Um, yeah?" was the best Will could manage.

"I'm afraid we're going to have to ask you not to board

this aircraft."

"I'm sorry, what?" Will was thoroughly confused.

Now the other one spoke. "Dr. Driver, you need to come with us now."

Will sighed. All he wanted was to go home. Or to whatever was left of it. "Thanks for the invitation, but—"

"Admiral Carter asked us to impress upon you the urgency of the situation," the first one said, a bit more forcefully. "It is, in the eyes of the American Office of Naval Intelligence and His Majesty's Defence Intelligence, a matter of the *utmost* importance."

Will looked from one to the other and back. Could this really be happening?

Again?

"Dr. Driver, your services are once again required."

Ethnomusicology

Yes, ethnomusicology is a real thing!

Ethnomusicologists study music in its cultural context. With roots in the related fields of historical musicology, anthropology, folklore, and music theory, today's ethnomusicologists draw on additional neighboring fields such as linguistics, cultural studies, sociology, and performance studies to enhance their work. While the first scholars who might call themselves ethnomusicologists, and those who came before them, typically studied non-Western musical traditions using ethnographic methods—living among a group of people for an extended period of time, conducting participant-observations and interviews, taking field notes and reflecting on them, etc.—more recent generations of ethnomusicologists have embraced the study of all musics, including Western and popular traditions. And while, at one time, ethnomusicologists were somewhat united in their use of *in situ* fieldwork as a research method, these days fieldwork can be conducted in one's own culture or even virtually, through internet message boards, chat rooms, and videoconferencing.

If you're interested in learning more about ethnomusicology, here are a few resources to get your started:

- The Society for Ethnomusicology, https://www.ethnomusicology.org
- *Ethnomusicology: A Very Short Introduction*, by Timothy Rice (Oxford University Press, 2013). ISBN 9780199794379
- *The Study of Ethnomusicology: Thirty-Three Discussions*, by Bruno Nettl (University of Illinois Press, 2015). ISBN 9780252080821

Semiotics

Broadly speaking, semiotics is the study of anything that communicates meaning, intentionally or unintentionally. Most semiotic theories include processes by which meaning is ultimately made, beginning with the *sign*, a thing that can stand for something else (or, put more simply, *mean* something). Unlike linguistics, semiotics involves signs that are not based on language, per se, such as music.

In the chapter where Will Driver is teaching a seminar at the University of Philadelphia, he mentions two versions of semiotics that are, in fact, part of its intellectual history. Swiss linguist Ferdinand de Saussure (1857–1913) theorized "semiosis" to mean a way of analyzing language as a formal system, which includes a *signifier* and a *signified*, the thing that stands for the meaning and the meaning itself, respectively. Meanwhile, American philosopher Charles Sander Peirce (1839–1914) devised a three-part system comprised of a *sign*, an *object*, and an *interpretant*. Moreover, Peirce subdivides each part of his system into three subparts to classify the widest possible variety of meaning-making processes.

To learn more about semiotics, I recommend:

- *Semiotics: The Basics*, 4th edition, by Daniel Chandler (Routledge, 2022). ISBN 9780367726539.
- Ferdinand de Saussure's *Course in General Linguistics*, edited by Charles Bally and Albert Sechehaye, translated by Wade Baskin, and subsequently edited by Perry Meisel and Haun Saussy (Columbia University Press, 2011). ISBN 9780231157278.
- *Peirce on Signs: Writings on Semiotic*, by Charles S. Peirce, edited by James Hoopes (University of North Carolina Press, 1991). ISBN 9780807843420.

The Ket

The Ket are an ethnic group indigenous to the Yenisei River basin in Siberia. Although none of the characters in this book are of Ket descent, and little is said about their culture, their language (once known as Yenisei Ostyak) plays a crucial role in the story.

After enduring "collectivization"—forced modernization and assimilation into Russian culture, especially but not exclusively during the twentieth century—there are relatively few Ket alive today and fewer still who speak the language. While this fact makes for a compelling plot point, it is also intended to draw attention to languages and cultures on the verge of extinction more broadly. As our world grows increasingly interconnected, let us not forget to honor all peoples for their distinctiveness, which adds to the diverse tapestry of human culture.

Most of the scholarship on the Ket examines their language or their genetics, looking for connections with other peoples of North and Northeast Asia as well as Northwest North America. Few sources look at Ket culture directly, although the Ket are mentioned in several books and articles surveying various aspects of Arctic cultures (especially religion). For more information about the Ket, you may consult:

- *Sámánok nyomában Szibéria földjén. Egy néprajzi kutatóút története*, by Vilmos Diószegi. Terebess Ázsia E-Tár (in Hungarian). Budapest: Magvető Könyvkiadó, 1960. The book has been translated to English: Vilmost Diószegi, *Tracing shamans in Siberia: The story of an ethnographical research expedition*, translated from Hungarian by Anita Rajkay Babó (Oosterhout: Anthropological Publications; New York: Humanities Press, 1968). [One of the few book-length treatments of the Ket, this one focusing on their religious practices.]

- "The Origin of the Na-Dene," by Merritt Ruhlen, in *Proceedings of the National Academy of Sciences* 95, no. 23 (1998): 13994-13996. [A theory, with which some experts have disagreed, linking Ket and indigenous North American languages.]

- "The Formation of the Modern Peoples of the Soviet North," by B.O. Dolgikh, translated by Chester S. Chard, in *Arctic Anthropology* 9, no. 1 (1972): 17-26. [An overview of indigenous groups, written during the Soviet period.]

About the Author

Joshua S. Duchan, Ph.D., is an ethnomusicologist and lifelong submarine enthusiast. As an academic, his research focuses on American popular music. He has published three books and a variety of articles in scholarly journals and chapters in edited collections. His favorite submarine film is *The Hunt for Red October*. This is his first novel.

Mailing List

My sincerest thanks for reading this book. I hope you had as much fun getting to know Will, Ashley, Harper, Worth, and the rest of the crew, and following their adventures, as I had writing about them.

To learn about new works in the Code Song series, gain author insights, and hear about special offers, simply send an email to joshuasduchan@gmail.com and I'll put you on my mailing list right away.

-JSD